C000134924

Confessions of an Invisible Man

Graham Hey

Dedication

H.F. Saint for inspiring me,

my fantastic daughters Georgia and Madison,

and Julie Hopper for just being fabulous!

Thanks to: Alwyn Simpson, Michael Griffin, and all my
friends who have to put up with me!

CHAPTER ONE:

When one door closes...

'I can't see you!'

'What?'

'I can't see you anymore!'

'What? What do you mean you can't see me anymore?' I shouted from beneath the steamy mist of my hot shower.

I heard a door slam shut and then she was gone. A six-month relationship had expired, obviously without the need for her to tell me to my face. Sarah Jemson had dramatically walked out of my life - and to make matters worse she had taken my Meat Loaf albums with her.

The two of us had become friends after meeting in the A&E department of my local hospital. We'd sat there for hours waiting to be seen for minor injuries after I'd tripped over a rug in my lounge (more about that later) and Sarah had fallen off her bicycle after a dog ran into her path. The two of us bonded over the NHS's ability to make four hours seems like an eternity. We gelled immediately, dated within twenty-four hours and were living together within three days. It was a relationship which began too quickly, with two people making the wrong decisions, so deep down I knew it wasn't going to last. That still didn't make it any easier for me and I felt all alone.

My name is Cooper McRae and as I made my girlfriend-less way to work on the morning of the 18th of December 2019, I wasn't positive about who I was or where I was going, to work or in life to be honest.

It was a Wednesday morning, nothing special about it, a grey but surprisingly mild day, heading towards the "most wonderful time of the year". I wasn't feeling it. The tube was a complete nightmare, packed to the brim. After standing all the way I arrived at work ten minutes late. It was par-for-the-course.

It was difficult to get excited about my workplace or my insignificant job at JC Cosmetic Developments, an apparently unimportant company, located behind Spitalfields Market in the heart of London, where Jack the Ripper used to ply his grisly trade in the 1880's. From the outside it looked like any other small company. It had a shiny brass sign beside the front door and frosted windows on the ground floor. If you'd clambered up onto the windowsill to peep inside, you would have seen two people sat at a large IKEA reception desk on which stood two computers, two telephones, some papers and a receptacle containing pens and pencils. Just a normal, boring reception area. Every other area of the company looked normal and boring too.

But it wasn't.

I was not a cosmetic development scientist or any other kind of scientist, although I did get to observe some pretty interesting mould specimens – I worked in the canteen, doing a variety of kitchen duties and generally cleaned up after the development boffins. They may have had brains much bigger than most people's, but they were fucking messy eaters. On December 18th at 9.10am I headed straight for the canteen to fulfil my imaginatively titled role of 'Kitchen Technician Operative'. What a load of shit.

By 9.20am I had no reason to think that December 18th was going to be anything other than the mundane day I was expecting. When I was on the tube my mind had wandered and I fantasised about a career which would give me satisfaction and a purpose. Little did I know that everything was about to change – forever.

What I thought was going to be just another day of collecting tea and coffee mugs from around the building and washing up people's empties was going to be the most amazing, dumbfounding, unfathomable, wondrous day I could ever imagine.

I was going to be completely invisible for exactly 7 days.

This is how it happened and is my honest confession of how I spent my unbelievable week.

CHAPTER TWO:

Ledley & Love

The kitchen and canteen area of JC Cosmetic Developments was managed by my friend Ledley, who hailed from Birmingham via Trinidad. He had a huge afro, a huge smile and a capacity to look beyond the mundane working environment we shared daily. Ledley, my friend and boss wore very short trousers, which bothered me somewhat. He told me that they were fashionable, I often told him that they were an inch away from being 'Rainman'.

'Hey Ledley!' How was your weekend?' I asked, while attempting to put on my white over-sized catering smock.

'Fabulous! In fact, it was double-double-fabulous!' he replied, actually singing his answer in the style of Bob Marley. He then nodded in my direction, waiting for me to ask why.

'OK, why was it double-fabulous then Ledley?'

'It was double-double fabulous...' replied Ledley.

'Yes, I've got that, but *why* was it double-double fabulous then?'

'Because I met a new lady, aye. I went to Camden and met the deliriously delightful Deborah!'

'Great. Is she a looker?'

'She is a goddess. She looks amazing. I'm thinking of asking her to marry me…'

Ledley was a true romantic, he loved the notion of being in love, almost as much as being in love. He was impetuous, dreamy and usually scared-off girls within twenty-four hours of proclaiming his love for them.

'Ledley!! For god's sake, you've only just met her. Leave the poor girl alone. Take it easy and see what develops over a period of time!'

'OK, I'll wait until Thursday to ask her…'

'You will NOT ask her to marry you on Thursday. You will try and be NORMAL, like a normal person, if that's possible.' I said in a raised voice, to make sure my point hit home.

Ledley was twenty-four years old and had been engaged six times already. Three times in the past twelve months. That's why I sometimes called him 'Mr. Love!' he wasn't one of those guys that wanted to sleep around. He just wanted to get married. He bought all the wedding magazines and perused them over a coffee at break times. Despite spooking newly-met girls, the ironic thing was that he would have made a brilliant husband. He was also my boss, but had never adapted to being in a position of authority. He never asked or told me to do anything, I had to suggest things to him and then he would agree. I suppose from that point of view, he was the perfect boss.

'What time is it?' I asked, 'Have we got time for a cuppa before we crack on?'

'Yes, I'll tell you the time on my new watch!'

5

I looked closely at Ledley's new timepiece. 'Wow, that's a lovely watch…' I said, examining it more closely, 'but I've never seen Rolex spelt like that!'

'I got it from a friend of mine for twenty quid. Is it an original Coop?'

'Let me have a think about that Ledley. You say it cost twenty quid?'

'Yeah.'

'I'm going to go out on a limb and say it's probably not a new Rolex then…'

By 11.30 am, it was time for me to do my rounds and collect the tea and coffee cups from the various departments. The company was quite traditional in the sense that it possessed a tea-trolley. And I was the trolley dolly.

'Ledley, shall I go and do my rounds?'

'That's not a bad idea,' he agreed. 'Very good idea, if that's what you want to do.' Replied my boss, still examining his fake watch, which now appeared to be malfunctioning. He shook it against his ear.

'OK, but do not get engaged to anyone while I'm away!' I said as I left the kitchen.

The four-story building was a rabbit warren of offices with the ground floor devoted to the kitchen, canteen and administration areas, with the second and third floors specifically for the development of special cosmetics used in the treatment of burn victims. I referred to these floors as 'Boffin-Land'. The fourth floor was the management level with a boardroom and lots of other meeting areas. This floor was out-of-bounds to me and anyone else who was not classed as 'senior management.'

I always looked forward to collecting the used cups, saucers and plates, as it gave me the possible opportunity to catch a glimpse of Lucy Pendleton in admin.

For the past eight months I had secretly been in love with Miss Pendleton, ever since she apologised for spilling tea over her computer keyboard. She was genuinely sorry and grateful for my help, even though all I had done was wipe up the tea with my cloth. There were not many staff at the company who respected the ancillary or kitchen staff. There had only been three occasions when I had even spoken to her, but when she was nice to me, I felt elated – how I imagine Elephant Man John Merrick must have felt when someone showed him a little kindness.

Lucy Pendleton. Whenever I thought about her, the image always faded into soft-focus with violin music playing. Lucy Pendleton with her curly dark hair, beautiful deep blue eyes and perfect lips. She was petite, slim and dressed in a cool 1960's style reminiscent of the singer Dusty Springfield. Lucy Pendleton!

Sadly, no great romance flourished between us, in fact, like I said, we hardly ever spoke to each other – and I'm confident that she wouldn't even have recognised me if they put me in the middle of six over-sized Sumo wrestlers in a police line-up. I was completely invisible to her.

My trolley rumbled through the first-floor admin area where I paused for a moment to look at the empty chair where Miss Pendleton's lovely bottom would normally perch. Maybe she had the day off, or maybe she was busy in the photocopying room? I lingered for a minute or two, just in case she returned, but she didn't.

As I moved along between the desks, I picked up miscellaneous crockery and biscuit wrappers and nodded at anyone who cared to acknowledge me.

I entered the lift at the very far end of the first floor. Even though the building had been renovated just a few years earlier, the lift was like something you'd see in Paris in the 1920's. It clanked, scraped and shuddered each time it moved, and I always felt like I'd achieved something special arriving at my destination in one piece. Three sides of the lift were mirrored, so I took the opportunity to examine myself. I looked crap. I had bags under my eyes, needed a shave and my hair was a mess – although some might consider it to be fashionable. I was a 25-year-old Kitchen Technician Operative. And sadly, I looked like one.

When the lift came to a standstill, I noticed that I was actually on the fourth floor – a place where I was strictly forbidden to go. However, as the doors automatically opened, I could see some china which needed collecting, so I ventured into the secret, wood-panelling lair of 'senior management'.

I knew it was wrong – especially as there were signs saying 'Strictly No Unauthorised Personnel' everywhere. There didn't seem to be anyone around, so I pushed my trolley out of the lift and began doing my job. After all, I wasn't a spy from a competing cosmetics company, I was a girlfriend-less washer-upper. There was a subtle difference.

As I poked my head into empty offices looking for more items, I heard the lift doors and the sound of voices in the distance, so quickly pushed my trolley into an alcove and dashed into the nearest office out of the way. The last thing I needed was to be sacked with rent day looming.

Just when I thought I was safe, I heard the voices getting nearer, so I jumped inside an empty stationery cupboard and tried to be as quiet as possible. A window in the office itself was open, so there was some exterior noise which helped me feel a little more comfortable. At least whoever it was, wouldn't be able to hear the sound of me breathing.

The cupboard was actually more like a wardrobe and smelled of wax crayons. It contained a selection of box files, paper trays and miscellaneous office equipment, but there was ample room for a five-foot eleven kitchen operative to stand inside. Conscious of making a sound from moving my feet, I quickly established a comfortable position and then tried my best to stay completely still.

Two people entered the very office I was hiding in and one of them could hardly contain their excitement. I heard the door close behind them.

'I've done it! Honestly – this is going to change the world!! I've achieved what I thought was going to be impossible, yet I, Christopher Wyngard have gone and done it! Make sure no one is outside the door...'

No-one was outside the door, but unfortunately for them, someone was inside the cupboard. Me.

A second, much more measured voice – the voice of a woman replied, 'Calm down Wyngard. Tell me slowly what you've done...'

There was a pause, and I could hear him take a deep breath, just a few feet away from me.

'I have invented a special oil that makes things invisible!'

There was another pause before the woman started laughing. It wasn't a laugh of ridicule, but a laugh which to me, sounded more of nervousness.

'I knew you wouldn't believe me!' said Wyngard. 'I've been close to perfecting this oil for months. Every hypothesis has been examined with all the key variables exhaustively tested... And now it's PERFECT! Samantha, this is going to make BILLIONS. We have to keep this breakthrough ultra-top secret...'

I guessed that the Samantha he was talking to was Samantha Penhaligan, the glamorous company MD. I had never met her, but I knew from clearing-up after board meetings that she never finished drinking her coffee and she only ever ate one finger of KitKat. What sort of person would only half eat a chocolate treat? But that was irrelevant – was I hearing correctly, or was this some sort of practical joke? A type of oil that could make things invisible? It sounded like an idea from a crap 1950's B Movie. But the sort of movie I LOVED!

CHAPTER THREE:

"It really works!"

'Show me!' said Samantha, excitedly. 'I really want to believe it's true. C'mon show me, show me!' she added, clapping her hands together. She'd suddenly changed from being a poker-faced corporate high-flier into an excited child.

'I have to wear these specially designed metal-foil gloves, as it's the only substance that the oil cannot penetrate.' Explained Wyngard the scientist, in a slow, methodical manner.

Stereotypically, I pictured him being about 60, balding, with a nervous twitch and BO.

'I'll show you with this mobile phone…' he continued deliberately. 'All I have to do is coat the phone – a very, very thin coat – and in about thirty seconds or so…'

There was silence.

And more silence.

And more silence.

'OH MY GOD! OH MY GOD! OH MY GOD!' whispered Samantha, obviously witnessing the miracle that

I could only imagine from behind my door. The excitement was killing me. I just wanted to jump out and observe the miracle for myself, not feel like I was listening to an audio book.

'This really is going to change the world. The mobile phone really is invisible! It's gone. It's re…ally go…ne…''

'But feel it – it's still there!' said Wyngard. 'it's… it's… still…there… and there is no oily residue left behind – the mobile still feels exactly like a mobile. There is nothing different about it. It's still the tangible object it always was, it still physically exists as before – the only difference is that you now cannot see it…' he continued, tapping the mobile on the table-top to demonstrate his point.

'This is absolutely incredible!'

'I know!' continued the slow-talking boffin. 'We are going to have to make sure we get security in place for this, because if anyone ever finds out about it…'

'No!' said the MD. 'If we suddenly get security all over the place, we'll simply be drawing attention to ourselves. We just have to be careful and don't tell anyone else about this for the moment. Store this with the other development trials and so it won't draw attention. We have to think about this. Let's not rush into anything…'

At this point, Samantha Penhaligan obviously picked up the invisible mobile.

'It's right here in my hand… but it's invisible. Invisible…' her voice tailed off in disbelief. 'it's a solid object… yet I can't see it…'

This was one of, if not *THE* greatest achievement in the history of mankind… and I was only two feet away from it in a cupboard. One to tell the grandkids, I thought!

Finally, I knew I had to witness this for myself and so I very gently eased the door open until a slither of light opened-up. Luckily, I could clearly see Samantha's hand grasping an object that wasn't there, or at least couldn't be seen. She was holding the now invisible mobile phone. It was true. Jesus Christ, it was true.

'The molecular structure of this batch means that whatever it is applied to will be invisible for 168 hours. Or exactly 7 days, to be precise. To the very second. And, like I said, the mobile isn't even covered in oil – the substance has a capacity to melt into the object it covers and as far as I can ascertain, it is completely harmless.'

'Wyngard… the oil works on a solid object like a mobile, but does it work on a living…'

'Human?' said the boffin completing Samantha's phrase. He'd been waiting excitedly for this very question.

'Yes, does it work on humans?' asked Samantha.

'Yes, it does,' replied Wyngard taking a deep breath. 'You may not recall, but in August and September I was off sick for quite a few weeks, and everyone thought I had some terrible illness. When really, I was at home because my hands were invisible! I was busy developing the special foil gloves. Yes, my hands were invisible, exactly like the mobile is…

'Let's say you wanted to make someone completely invisible…'

'Yes, let's!'

'The clever thing is it is quite a simple process. If you wanted to be completely invisible, all you have to do is put a single phial of EH320 into your bath water and lie in it. Then get rid of the bathwater as normal and the evidence literally goes down the plug-hole. The only thing is, it will not work on liquids and certain metallic substances, but I'm working on that…'

'And what about the formula?'

'That is only in my head, so it is not at risk of being stolen, so don't worry about that.'

'This is mind-blowing. Imagine the applications for this… forget about the cosmetics industry, governments of the world would kill for this!' gasped Penhaligan. 'Wyngard, I need to think about the implications, everything. We keep this quiet for now. We have to have a plan, do you understand?'

The scientist agreed.

As the two made their plans where to store the oil, I knew that I had to have it. I wanted to be invisible. I mean, who wouldn't? It was a once in a lifetime opportunity.

In a considered voice, the MD then made a statement like she was announcing it to the world, rather than to an audience of the one person who created it.

'For mankind, this is the next generation of science. We have a unique responsibility to ensure that the human race embraces this landmark achievement in a way which benefits everyone in society. Necessity is, indeed, the mother of invention – and the irrefutable truth is that we are the new torchbearers of a golden future. The vision is ours!'

I had my own vision. I wanted to see Lucy Pendleton in her underwear. Science was fucking ace!

CHAPTER FOUR:

The plot thickens

As soon as the coast was clear, I collected my trolley and made my way euphorically back to the kitchen. My mind was buzzing with the unbelievable scene I had just witnessed. I decided that I had to keep it to myself until I had time to think about things. If I told Ledley, he would no doubt think it was a huge practical joke and just take the piss out of me. No, it was *my* secret and nobody else's.

Ledley was flicking through a wedding magazine when I enthusiastically pushed my trolley through the swing doors, like it was time to knock off on a Friday.

"Hey!' said Ledley, looking up from a feature on wedding bouquets, 'I've got some news for you…'

'What?' I asked, trying to clear my head.

'Your Lucy Pendleton is not in today, she's ill!'

'Oh, how do you know?' I asked.

'Because I was talking to Jane who sits opposite her, and she told me. She said that Lucy is apparently a real party girl and goes clubbing all the time. Over the weekend, she was out socialisin' for about 48 hours – and now she has a dreadful hangover!'

I was a little surprised by this, as I always thought she was quite shy and reserved. I couldn't visualise her in one of those trendy clubs, but then again, I didn't really know her at all, so I never gave it any more thought after my initial surprise. I had other things on my mind. And it had to be something extra special to relegate Lucy into second place.

The end of my working day couldn't come fast enough. I needed some time on my own to think about what I had experienced and what I planned to do about the secrets I'd stumbled upon, from within the confines of the fourth-floor cupboard.

My flat was on the second floor of number 56 Eversholt Street, in Camden Town. Immediately below me lived a trendy couple called Tim and Tina, who worked in the 'media', whatever that meant. They were nice enough, but they made a lot of noise when they had sex, several times a week. No wonder they were always late for work. Above me lived a gentleman who I suspected was a serial killer. He lived alone, never had any visitors and in my opinion unnecessarily moved his furniture around. He seemed to leave his flat at all hours of the day and night. I passed him briefly on the stairs once and he smelled of popcorn. I just called him 'Big Guy'.

My own flat was quite basic, with lots of flat-pack furniture combined with pieces picked up at local flea markets. The wallpaper was definitely 1960's, so I was going retro with the "look" well at least that's what I told myself, I'd placed my record player and Meat Loaf-free record collection under the bay-window, which over-looked the busy street below. I lived just a few hundred yards from "The Stables", which was a huge indoor market and food court where you could buy anything from full-size red telephone boxes, to drugs paraphernalia. On a Saturday morning I loved to hang out there and have a Chinese for breakfast.

My lounge and kitchen areas were open-plan and the walls were covered with vintage movie posters – pride of place going to "The Great Escape" starring Steve McQueen.

On the floor was a rug which I always managed to trip over. It featured a grinning Rylan Clark-Neal and was an ill-judged Christmas present from Ledley. It remained in my lounge as Ledley had the habit of turning up unannounced, I didn't have the heart to tell him that it didn't actually fit in with my interior design aesthetic.

As soon as I got in, I put the kettle on and grabbed a packet of chocolate biscuits from the fridge. They were placed on to the table along with my notebook and pen.

I was going to be totally invisible for a whole seven days. Unless I was party to some sort of elaborate hoax. Exactly seven days, right down to the second – that's what Professor Wyngard said.

The first thing I realised was that it was absolutely perfect timing. December 21st was the day the company closed until January 2nd, so if I swiped the oil on the very last day before the Christmas holidays, no one would know that anything was missing. I couldn't have planned it any better myself. The only possible downside to this was that it was already the 18th, so it didn't leave me long to formulate a plan.

The first thing that came into my mind was the voyeuristic nature of mankind. I wanted to see ladies in different stages of undress – specifically Lucy Pendleton. However, even though seeing Lucy in her nether-garments was a joy I was keen to behold, ideally, I wanted her to fall in love with me. I wanted her to be my girlfriend. Without knowing her, I wanted to marry her. I was beginning to think like Ledley! Anyhow, I wasn't sure how I could achieve that goal when I'd be invisible, but as Lucy acted like I was already invisible most of the time anyway, it seemed like the best chance I would have. Young and foolish I was, yet I also had a much deeper, intellectual side to me which I kept pretty well hidden – under my bed. I was inspired by Oscar Wilde, Erica Jong, Günter Grass and more. Their books piled up under my mattress and I regularly looked forward to an early night to devour their wisdom and wit. Wilde's views on love, and everything else, were always entertaining and eloquent and I vowed to use his ingenuity to help me in my seven-day romantic quest.

I wrote: Number 1. Win the heart of Lucy Pendleton.

CHAPTER FIVE:

The plan comes together

Yes… that's an obvious thing to do from a male's point of view: Get the girl! I imagined that most men who had the opportunity to be invisible for a week would probably have wanked themselves to death within forty-eight hours. However, I was going to let romance take precedence over naughty lust. At least that was what the angel sitting on one of my shoulders was saying. The devil on the other shoulder had ideas of his own. And they involved several boxes of Kleenex.

But what else was I going to do? Well, the thought of making a ton of money was also very appealing. It had to be an impressive amount as this was my golden opportunity to make more money in one week than I could realistically hope to make in a lifetime of scrubbing pans at work. I decided to set myself a target of one million pounds. That was a nice, round figure which would mean I could pack in my job and do something I was actually interested in.

I wrote: Number 2. Accumulate one million pounds.

Was asking for a million pounds being too greedy? I mean let's face it, that was only enough to buy three-week's worth of shopping in Waitrose. No, I decided to be sensible and not set the bar too high. One million pounds would suffice.

What else could I do when I was invisible? Obviously, I could get in free to watch gigs, sporting events, the cinema – but that's nothing special – when I had a million pounds, I could do those things all the time anyway *and* pay for the privilege. Surely with an opportunity like this, it had to be something big and bold. I could do absolutely anything, I'd be invisible... I sipped my tea and devoured a couple of milk chocolate digestives. I wet my finger, dabbed at the crumbs on my plastic tablecloth and ate them whilst I stared into space.

As I pondered the incredible power I would soon to have, I thought perhaps I should do something dramatic such as kill someone? While I was invisible would be the perfect opportunity. It wouldn't matter if there were CCTV cameras there or not! But who would or should I kill? 'Dixon' the bully from when I was at school? No, he was a twat, but probably didn't deserve to die for squishing his thumb into my lemon meringue pie seventeen years earlier. But then again... it still upset me, so... he was definitely a candidate.

No, if I was going to kill someone it would have to be someone who deserved it. A cold-blooded murderer or a rapist would be perfect. Yes, they certainly deserved to die for all the misery and devastation they'd caused innocent people. Or perhaps I should 'take out' a despot? Hmm, I liked the idea of helping the oppressed – but that would probably mean flying to somewhere in Africa or Eastern Europe.

However, the thought of killing someone was merely a Quentin Taratino-esque fantasy-thought in my head. I was scared of spiders in the bath, so how would I ever be able to kill anyone? My morals were quite high, so I could never ever do anything like that no matter how much someone deserved it. No, I would have to use my power for a much more pleasurable and positive experience.

Then suddenly I got it. The answer was right there in front of me as I looked at my vinyl record collection. Part three of my plan would be to visit one of the all-time music greats and see what he was really like away from the glitz and glamour of superstardom.

I wrote: 3. Visit Elton John.

CHAPTER SIX:

The plan is complete

I was ecstatic! I had a plan of sorts. Get the girl, get the money, meet Elton. That would be a very productive week indeed. OK, it wasn't earth-shattering stuff. Was it fate that I was offered this unbelievable opportunity? And if so, would I be scolded for squandering the power on something as inconsequential as meeting Elton?

But, what could I do with the power of invisibility that would be more meaningful and vital? It was a question which would irritate me for days.

Throwing myself dramatically on to the settee, I contemplated the first draft of my audacious plan. I was going to be invisible in approximately five days, so I had a lot of detail to add. The most difficult aspect was how would I be able to keep the whole invisible thing a secret as it was so outrageous? But then again, if I went around telling everyone I was going to be invisible, you could be sure I would soon have my own room at an establishment for the mentally deranged. It would be an en-suite containing a straitjacket, some crayons and some jump leads.

Stretched out on the settee, my mobile rang. I glanced at the screen to see it was my best friend Michael.

Michael was quirky and gullible. He also had OCD and was addicted to keeping things clean. Everyone loved him as he always had time for them and took a genuine interest in what they were doing. Imagine the perfect vicar from a quiet, English country village and you'd be looking at Michael. He was tall, slim and wore little round glasses. He could walk straight into any Agatha Christie drama and you'd find him consoling villagers after a body had been found in the library.

Michael had a very innocent manner – and people felt so comfortable with him, that they willingly divulged their inner-most secrets. But, I wouldn't be telling him mine. Not yet anyway. It would be great to do a big reveal all after my seven-day adventure was over and when I was sitting comfortably on a million pounds! Yes, I'd tell Michael and his girlfriend Rebecca, when the time was right, but the excitement was killing me already.

Rebecca was a lovely girl and perfectly suited to Michael. Some would say they were chalk and cheese, but they complemented each other's personalities. Whereas Michael was a very positive person, always looking to the future, Rebecca sometimes had days when she found it difficult to cope with her day-to-day existence.

Every now and again, the stresses and anxieties of everyday life seemed to take over and she would withdraw into her own world for a while. Michael knew exactly how to handle the situation and his endless patience was admirable. When she was not down, which to be fair was quite often, she was hilarious, sharp and knowledgeable.

I picked up my mobile. I didn't have a ringtone; I just had a repetitive message which announced: "Wanker Alert! Wanker Alert!"

'Hi Michael!'

'Hey, Coop! What's going on?'

'Nothing!' I said, hiding the greatest thing to happen in the world, ever. Jesus, I was already bursting to tell someone what had happened. How on earth would I keep it a secret for a whole week and more?

'What have you been up to lately?'

'Well, at the weekend me and Sarah got up early and by 9am had already had sex in the lounge area, then we followed that up with a session in the bedrooms and bathroom. Finally, we had sex on the rugs. That's the good news. The bad news is that we've been banned from IKEA.'

'Have you really?

'No, I'm joking, of course we haven't been banned - we just got a ticking off! I'M JOKING MICHAEL. Oh, you're so easy to wind up…'

'Oh, yes, right. A joke. Well, I was just checking to see if you and Sarah are still coming over for Xmas dinner?'

'Well, I'll be coming on my own as Sarah has just dumped me.'

'Great!' said Michael. 'Rebecca has already bought the turkey and all the trimmings.'

'I said Sarah has just dumped me.' It had gone straight over his head.

Suddenly, with my exciting new plans for Christmas week, I wouldn't be able to make it for the turkey dinner anyway, I'd have to think of a good excuse to get out of it.

Michael was sympathetic to my relationship woes and seemed to be genuinely more upset than I myself was. Sarah, I found out later, had met someone else.

CHAPTER SEVEN:

The money issue

The next few days were a haze. I had to go into work and do my duty with the Marigolds, but it was difficult to keep my mind on the mundane, when a real-life science-fiction plot was waiting for me.

In the evenings I began to pencil in more details about how I would achieve my goals. Firstly, Lucy Pendleton. I wanted to charm her into my open arms, but after hours of thought, I couldn't come up with anything worthwhile. I decided that I would just go around to where she lived and play-it-by-ear.

The one million pounds conundrum was slightly easier to plot, even if not to execute. I didn't want to rob ordinary people on the street, that would be immoral. Plus, I envisaged that even though I myself would be invisible – the money would not, so I would have to do something in the dead of night where I could move cash in relative secrecy. But, where would I actually get the money from? Shops? They probably had a decent amount of cash, but again, they didn't deserve to suffer, so I knocked that idea on the head.

Who really deserves to pay? Bankers! Yes, bankers – the whole lot of them were crooks in suits! They'd been responsible for a whole host of illegal financial dealings in recent years and I was confident there were new revelations in the pipeline. Yet how many of them had actually ended up in court to answer for their miss-deeds?

The big question was, how could I get actual cash from the crooked banks? It would probably be unrealistic to get one million pounds from a cashpoint machine – especially with a two hundred quid limit. No, it would have to be from a different outlet... and it had to be as legal as possible.

I moved on to the possibility of meeting my hero Elton John. It would be easy enough to find out where he lived, but would he be at home in his elf costume, ready to celebrate Christmas with David, or would he be away doing shows? My mum loved Elton and his outrageous outfits. One of my fondest memories of my mum was us all laughing and singing along to 'Crocodile Rock' whenever my dad put it on the record player. It was the only time my mum ever sang, so it always stuck in my memory. We played the record at mum's funeral. I wore some Elton John glasses too. She would've loved that.

CHAPTER EIGHT:

My last day at work

December 21st. The last day before JC Cosmetics closed for the Christmas holidays and there was still no sign of Lucy Pendleton.

I abused my position as Kitchen Technician to linger in the HR department at break time and managed to make a note of Miss Pendleton's home address. That would be my first port of call once I was see-through.

Ledley's friend Norman was the onsite security officer. Standing at about four-foot ten tall and addicted to online gambling, he spent much of his day glued to his mobile phone and was not difficult to manipulate, so I would have no trouble smuggling out the special invisibility oils in my bag. There were no real security measures in place and the only time I ever remember Norman being called into action was when a pigeon got into the building and caused a kerfuffle in the reception area.

When the workforce left at 2pm for Christmas drinks at the King George pub around the corner on Brick Lane, the place was deserted apart from Ledley, Norman and I.

Norman was busy placing bets on up-coming horse races, and whilst he studied their form, I took the opportunity to go to the third floor and into the refrigeration area. Samantha Penhaligan's ruse to leave the batch of invisibility oil in plain sight was quite a reasonable thing to do – unless there happened to be someone hiding in a nearby cupboard to over-hear everything. I had been in the right place at the right time for once in my life and it would be up to me to make the most of the unique circumstances.

I opened the refrigerator to find a selection of coded phials and quickly located batch EH302 – the breakthrough oils that Wyngard had placed there. There they stood, between other batches of miscellaneous concoctions, just waiting to offer the experience of a lifetime to a willing participant.

A note said: 'Trial batch EH302. Please do not remove. CW'. That was the stuff! That simple message hid the most incredible scientific breakthrough of our time. Looking at the small containers, it was difficult to comprehend what was positioned there in the high-tech fridge. Amusingly, someone had left their sandwiches on the same shelf, which made the whole thing quite surreal and unbelievable.

There were twenty-four special phials which looked like miniature milk bottles clasped with metallic collars and alongside them was another container marked 'FOIL GLOVES'.

I tucked three of the bottles into my bag along with a pile of gloves and hid my bag in the bottom of my trolley where they were lost beneath my lunchbox, a pile of tea towels and a couple of issues of Wedding Monthly magazine, which Ledley had recommended for bedtime reading.

When I arrived back at the kitchen, the security guard Norman had changed into his going-out clothes. He wore an orange shirt with extra-large lapels, flared black trousers and white shoes.

'I'm not sure if that's a fashion statement or a mental issue!' I said, without a hint of sarcasm.

Ledley laughed, while Norman looked up from his mobile, mildly offended.

'Some girl's gunna be lucky tonight!' said Norman, adjusting his collar.

'Why, are you staying in?' replied Ledley, who then burst out laughing.

'Go on, fuck off and have a great Christmas,' said Norman removing a small mirror from his back pocket and admiring himself from different angles.

I bid both of them farewell with a group Christmas-hug and promised to catch up with Ledley for a drink over the festive period. Mine would be a *very* festive period once I ended up with a million quid, I thought. But just as I was about to disappear out of the building, Norman the security guard unexpectedly called me back.

'Cooper, do you mind if I have a look at your bag?' He asked, but it wasn't really a question. Suddenly I had the urge to bolt and keep running until Norman lost interest. He'd never been interested in matters of security before, despite his job title, and so it immediately made me anxious and break out in a sweat. Had I been rumbled before my audacious plan had even started?

Turning back and taking a deep breath, I handed over my bag. Almost resigned to the fact I had been caught mid-crime, I was ready to admit to being culpable when Norman said something I hadn't expected.

'That's a Tumi messenger bag isn't it?'

'Yes…'

'These are brilliant, I'm going to get myself one for Christmas!'

Norman handled my bag as if it was a precious artefact. Holding it at different angles, he nodded his head admiringly and tried the clasp and took a peek inside. I was just about to snatch it away from him in haste when he offered it back to me. Had he seen anything inside? Obviously not. And that was it. All he'd wanted to do was to take a look at my desirable fashion accessory. It was a stressful moment, even though the security guard was *only* Norman. I breathed a huge sigh of relief, threw the strap over my shoulder and I was out of the building like a shot.

Making my joyous way to the tube station with my full invisibility-kit tucked in my bag, I felt like I'd been given a super-power by the Gods, even though I hadn't even tried it yet. I looked around the tube train with an air of excitement - and what made it even better was that I knew that for a whole week, I wouldn't have to buy a ticket.

CHAPTER NINE:

I'm so excited. And I just can't hide it.

Once I got to my flat, I tripped over my Rylan rug, as usual and then unpacked my golden future. I stared at the insignificant phials of oil before me. God knows how much I could get for these on Ebay, I thought. No, some twat would offer me a fiver. I was annoyed by the thought of someone insulting me with a low offer, even though I would obviously never put them on Ebay.

Maybe the Russians would give me ten million quid for them? I knew where the Russian Embassy was, perhaps I should pop round there and see if Putin was interested? I bet he had a bin-liner full of Rubles lying around in his stationery cupboard. My thoughts were all just fantasy – no one but me was going to sample the delights of invisibility.

I stared at the magic potion for what seemed like ages. This seemingly innocent oil was going to make the rest of my life a complete joy. Never again would I have to try and get on a tube train at rush hour, crammed against people with suspect body-hygiene, and never again would I have to scrape un-eaten lasagne from the rustic-style plates of JC Cosmetic Developments. This golden-tinted nectar was going to shape my future... I was conscious that my thoughts were beginning to sound like a shite TV advert, so took a final look before placing the magic oils carefully into my own fridge.

Putting on the kettle, I opened the Terry's Chocolate Orange I'd been saving for a special occasion. This was *that* occasion.

With all the ingredients to change the world – or at least my bit of it, I couldn't wait to get started – but I had a couple of things to do first.

After much deliberation, I had decided to tell my friends I was going away for a week's holiday. It seemed to make complete sense and wasn't anything that would automatically raise suspicion. Lots of people went on holiday over Christmas. I called Michael, but he was asleep in front of the TV, so Rebecca answered his mobile.

'Oh, hi Rebecca. Is Michael around?'

'No!' she laughed, he's spark-out. Can you make this a quick call, Cooper, 'cos I'm hoping to shag the next-door neighbour before Michael wakes up!'

Rebecca often liked to shock me, just to see my reaction. She liked to see the funny side of things and never took herself too seriously. She was blonde and always looked like she was about to laugh. Her eyes had a certain sparkle, like there was going to be mischief.

'No problem Rebecca, I'll keep this quick then. Don't hate me, but I'm going to have to miss our Christmas dinner together because a friend at work has asked me to go on holiday with her... I hope you don't mind? Please don't be angry…' I put on my 'sorry' face, even though it wouldn't be seen over the phone.

'What, you're going with another girl, already?'

'Yes!" I then realised that it had only been five days since Sarah Jemson walked out of my life, so it looked a bit quick to be hooking up with someone. Anyway, it was all a lie – I just needed an excuse to go missing for seven days.

'Yes, with a girl, but only a friend from work. There is definitely nothing going on at all.'

'Going with a girl?' said Rebecca again. 'What's her name?'

I had to think quickly.

'Samantha I said off the top of my head. I'd once worked with a girl called Samantha and for some reason the name just popped out.

'Ooooh, Samantha!' said Rebecca, 'And where are you two love-birds going for Christmas then?'

'We're definitely NOT lovebirds,' I said firmly. 'And we're going to er… Venice.' I have no idea where Venice came from. And then I wittily added. 'It was a good deal and they threw in a free hire car.'

Rebecca didn't get the joke about hiring a car in Venice but I moved swiftly on with my clever plot. I was starting to feel like an International spy. It was all very exciting, and I continued to embellish my fake-holiday – even adding a couple of excursions to our 'package-deal.' I was actually starting to look forward to the non-existent trip. It sounded fantastic!

It was now time to instigate part of the plan I'd devised whilst stuffing my face with chocolate biscuits over the previous few nights.

I explained to Rebecca that I had drawn out my life savings of two-thousand one-hundred and eighty-nine pounds in cash and left it in an envelope in the fruit bowl on my kitchen table. Michael and Rebecca had a spare key and I gave them strict instructions: 'If I ring you during the next seven days and ask you to do something with the money, I want you to do it without question,' I stated dramatically. 'Do you promise?'

'I solemnly do promise!' said Rebecca.

'This is serious,' I replied. 'Whatever I want you to do with it, please just do it – no matter how bizarre it might seem, OK?'

Rebecca promised once more, and we said goodbye.

Following this, I then made a call to my dad Geoff, who lived in a 1950's ex-council house in East Ham. My dad worked as a school caretaker at Brandesburton Primary school. It was a bit of a shit job really. The kids weren't the nicest, and several of the teachers looked down on him. That pissed me off. They didn't know anything about my dad yet were quick to judge him. He'd written several plays, two of which had been produced professionally, and from eighteen-to-twenty, he was an apprentice professional footballer with West Ham United. He never mentioned any of that to anyone. That was typical of my dad. When my mum died, he lost much more than the love of his life, he lost his confidence and pretty much all the drive he'd previously had. However, on top of all that, we didn't get on very well.

'Hi Dad, it's Cooper…'

'Oh, let me just turn the TV down will you, I'm just watching that Derek Achora looking for some ghosts…'

'I thought he was dead?'

'Yes, he is, but it's one he made *before* he died.'

'You mean rather than one he made *AFTER* he died?' I remarked sarcastically.

'Anyway, are you still doing that terrible job?' asked my dad. He was in one of his confrontational moods again.

'Well, it might be shit, but at least it's a job. And it pays my rent' I replied, slightly annoyed.

No, I didn't want to be a kitchen operative forever, but I was looking for other things. I didn't have a bucketful of GCSE's or a university education, so my opportunities were a little limited.

'So, your own job is amazingly fantastic then is it?'

'Well, if you're happy to continue being a skivvy, that's fine! Your mother always said…'

Here we go, I thought!

'She said you were better than that, but…'

I had to quickly change the subject before I slammed the phone down and the only way to do that was to talk about either ghosts or conspiracy theories.

He didn't believe for a second that they landed on the moon: "Are you telling me they could put a man on the moon almost sixty years ago, but I can't get a decent internet signal to watch BBC iPlayer for an hour without it cutting out?"

My dad also believed that aliens landed on earth years ago and at one point said that he suspected many of the staff in Asda were from another planet. I remember visiting the supermarket one day and watching them struggle with simple human tasks. Maybe he was right.

Dad was forever engrossed in all that psychic shite. My mum, who had passed away five years before, was well-used to having to put up with my dad's quirky beliefs.

'Dad, I won't be around over Christmas as I'm taking a last-minute break in Venice,' I announced with more confidence this time. 'I'm going with a friend from work. We've booked a nice hotel and it even has a jacuzzi!'

'Those motorbikes are dangerous.'

'No that's a Suzuki' I said, despairing of my dad's inability to join the real world.

It was always hard work phoning my dad, but at least he provided me with some interesting anecdotes to tell my friends.

Dad's favourite conspiracy theory involved The Illuminati. He said they were a shadowy underworld organisation which had actually been running the world without anyone realising it. My dad said the owners of big business secretly ran the world, and that's why Google, Starbucks and Amazon never pay any tax. 'No Dad,' I said, 'the reason Google, Starbucks and Amazon never pay any tax is because they're crooks,'

I was of the opinion that he needed to get out more and socialise. Informing my dad that I had to urgently to confirm my holiday travel arrangements, I said I'd call him later.

When my mum was diagnosed with cancer, I thought that everything was going to be alright. Everyone told me that. She wasn't alright, and she died without me ever really getting the chance to say a proper goodbye. I was eleven years old. In a way, I suppose I held my dad accountable as he kept promising me my mum would get better. Of course, I was too young to know any different, but when she died, she was removed from my life and barely spoken of again. To me, it was like people never acknowledged she existed. My mum was almost like a conspiracy theory herself, yet I

37

had a photograph forever in my wallet which proved she was real. Mum was holding my hand on Brighton beach, and I was eating an ice cream. It was the happiest day of my life - even though I couldn't remember a single detail of it. But the photograph proved it and I carried it with me everywhere.

After my frustrating phone call, I finished off the evening watching H G Wells' Invisible Man on DVD. I thought it might have given me some ideas of what to do with the special skills I was about to receive, but it was a much darker movie than I had bargained for.

That night I could hardly sleep. My mind was in a whirl. Was this just too incredible to be true? I wondered if I'd had some sort of stroke and was imagining the whole thing. I was like a kid trying to sleep on Christmas Eve. It was a hopeless task really, but by 3am, I had drifted off. It was probably the longest night of my life. Completely frustrating, it was like watching the Antiques Roadshow waiting for the expert to actually put a price on that piece of crap brought in by Mr. Wilson of Uttoxeter.

CHAPTER TEN:

"Don't count the days – make the days count." *Muhammed Ali*

As I ran my nice, relaxing bath first thing the following morning, it felt like a religious experience. I had decided to film the experience on my mobile as a record of my remarkable change from solid, real person, to see-through, invisible man. My experience would be charted on a blog or something like that, but I knew that I couldn't do anything with the footage until after the event, if at all, otherwise I could find myself in big trouble.

The bulb from inside my fridge seemed to light up the room like a biblical vision as I carefully removed a single phial of the special oil on the morning of December 22nd. I'd craftily hidden the invisibility formula behind a pack of low-fat sausages and giant-size tub of Flora margarine, just in case I'd got burgled.

For my week of invisibility, I opted to wear my favourite jacket and jumper, a pair of denim jeans and a pair of sturdy Doc Marten boots – after all, it was winter, so I had to make sure I was going to be warm if I was out and about. I nervously changed into my invisibility outfit. In my wardrobe was a little tin box which contained certain good-luck charms from when I was a kid. Slowly, I placed my lucky blue pebble into my jacket pocket, along with my lucky pen knife. I was all set and prepared for any eventuality.

Then, I slowly and deliberately opened the phial of special liquid lovingly created by Professor Wyngard. Dramatically I removed the metallic screw-top, held the phial high into the air and then watched the golden liquid descend into my hot bath water, like a small-scale Amazonian waterfall.

Would Wyngard's special brew actually work? It seemed so far-fetched that I almost called the whole thing off and pulled the plug out. The whole thing suddenly struck me as quite ridiculous. I started to laugh at the sheer stupidity of it. When I'd over-heard the revelation of invisibility from within the office cupboard it all seemed so real and believable, but standing beside my bath, ready to get in fully clothed I felt pretty stupid and self-conscious. Was my life about to change? Was I about to start the most amazing, magical Chapter of my life... of anyone's life?

It was time to get in and find out.

CHAPTER ELEVEN:

In at the deep end

Taking a deep breath, in one swift movement, I got straight into the bath and scooped water over my head to make sure I was 100% covered. From what I could remember, that would do the trick – unless this was a very extravagant practical joke. For a few moments I even looked around the bathroom to check for hidden cameras. I had no desire to be the next online viral sensation.

I waited, but nothing seemed to be happening. Nothing. After just a few seconds I started to feel humiliated. Oh, I knew it was too good to be true, I never seemed to have any luck with anything. My life was shit, and I now I was realising that it was *always* going to be shit.

Fuck it. I decided to go to the pub, get pissed and have a kebab on the way home. I was just about to reach over to my mobile which I'd propped-up on a chair when something strange started to happen.

Just as I was about to get out of the bath, I placed my hand on to the metal support handle and slowly but surely, my hand seemed to turn into a turquoise crystal colour…

and then it dissolved into thin air. My arm then followed suit. In the bath water I could see my legs beginning to fade away. The realisation that this was becoming real was shocking. Watching myself fade to nothingness was traumatic and I couldn't help but be physically sick.

I sat there in my own fading mess, soaked through. Rapidly becoming invisible, I didn't feel quite as euphoric as I'd imagined. I pulled the plug out of the bath and watched the water level slowly go down. Within a few minutes, the water had all gone. And so had I. There was nothing left of me, I had become 100% transparent. I tried to comprehend what had just happened. It would take a lot of getting used to. My mind was rapidly trying to process what was going on, what had just taken place. I could feel myself, so I still existed, but there was nothing to see.

After jumping out of the bath I headed straight to my bathroom cabinet to look at myself in the mirror. I wasn't there, yet I could feel myself as normal. I placed my hands onto my face and felt my skin, my eyelids, my ears and my hair. I was all there! Of course, I had to thoroughly examine my genitals – that was an important part of any young man's daily ritual, but it was even more important to have a good rummage in that department when it couldn't be seen. It was like a part of my manliness had been taken away. Gratefully, everything was still there, and it seemed to be the same size as before. If anything, it actually seemed a little larger, but perhaps that was wishful thinking. Examining my face and then my body on my full-length wardrobe mirror was a spine-tingling experience. God, this was beyond words.

Even the ring on the middle finger of my left hand was invisible. My ring was an unusual design with a small angel motif on it and had been given to me as a gift by Michael's girlfriend Rebecca for my birthday. She'd told me it would bring me good luck. Normally I wasn't the sort of person to wear a ring like that, but there was something about it which appealed to me. It was made from silver. The only substance the invisibility oil wouldn't penetrate was steel - at least that's what I'd overheard from Wyngard whilst inside the cramped stationery cupboard a few days earlier.

I looked at the time on my mobile. It was exactly 9.15am on December 22nd. That meant that my invisibility would wear off at exactly 9.15am on December 29th. Holding up my mobile I stared at it as it appeared to be floating in the air. I held it up to the mirror so that I could see the miracle for myself. It was incredible. Like something you'd imagine from the bible, only much cooler. Searching in my bathroom tumbler to see what else I could do, I squeezed out some toothpaste onto my toothbrush and watched as the action took place in mid-air. This was better than CGI!

In order to get drier quicker, I removed my clothes and put them into my spin drier. I realised it would take me longer to get dressed as all my clothes were invisible. An hour later, I was dry, warm and fully clothed. I think I put my boxer shorts on the wrong way round, but apart from that I was ready to see some action!

Despite trying to see the positive side of my new power, I was feeling anxious and even though I didn't want to admit it, afraid. Having invisibility suddenly bestowed on me was beyond comprehension. Perhaps I should have let it sink in a little more and contemplated the position I was in, but I was eager to sample the outside world.

Before I left the flat, I picked up a few objects and was captivated by how they looked to be floating in mid-air.

Sunglasses and a bobble hat were donned. It was hilarious! I could've been an incredible contestant on Britain's Got Talent, I thought, but I'd have probably got beaten by a dog that could walk on its hind legs, backwards… Destiny was knocking loudly on my front door… and I was about to answer it, grab it by the scruff of the neck and throw it around like a rag doll!

A final check that every part of my body was still there and still all attached to the right bits and I was ready to rumble. I was scared. But, everything seemed fine. I slowly moved my hands over my face, yes, I was still me. I put my fingers inside my mouth. My teeth were there, so was my tongue. I couldn't see a thing, but what about other people, could they see me? It was just so unbelievable. Could I really just do anything that I wanted? Was there really anybody who could stop me? God bless Wyngard for inventing this. I was definitely the luckiest man in the world!

CHAPTER TWELVE:

Lucy here I come

Lucy Pendleton lived on the 12th floor of Ovett House, an attractive fifteen-story apartment block overlooking a small park. It was a modern structure with lots of additional features and was one of the more expensive places to live on Moore Street, Camden. That was going to be my first port of call. Miss Pendleton, here I come.

As I opened my front door, I knew immediately that the weather was extremely mild for the time of year, which was great, as I had made my jacket invisible but not my winter coat. I was shaking with excitement about what I could and would do on my very first day. For a second, I realised I had forgotten my wallet – but as I patted my trouser pockets, it struck me that for the next seven days I wouldn't have to pay for anything anyway. And, it would be impossible to pay with invisible money, so any financial interactions could be discounted.

Just as I was leaving, the big guy from the flat above bumped right into me. Instinctively, I said, 'For fuck's sake!' Of course, he couldn't see anyone. He stopped and looked around with a bemused look upon his big face. He stood there, with a package under his arm, rubbed his big forehead and then continued his way up the steps and into the building. I'd never really said anything to him before but I had noticed a steady stream of deliveries to his address. I thought that he must buy and sell on Ebay or something, but I'd never actually seen him taking parcels out of the building.

Outside on the street, immediately I had to step out of the way of an old couple making their way to the coffee shop just beyond me. I was now an unseen obstacle in people's path – I hadn't given any thought to the fact that I would have to dodge in and out of people in the street. If someone was walking behind me, only at a faster pace then there was bound to be a collision. I found this out in the first five minutes when I was in the tube station. To the commuters, I represented an open space in which to walk, I was nothing, but an opportunity to speed up and get to where they wanted to be more quickly.

When I was on the tube train, there was a young guy who didn't have any socks on – a fashion which I couldn't get my head around. It was winter, after all! He had his music blasting out, even though he had headphones on and was making the journey of two old ladies most uncomfortable – especially as the music he played was full of expletives. I took great delight in pulling them off his inconsiderate head. And when he put them back on, I pulled them off again. I also whispered to him, 'Turn your music down, or face the consequences!' In reality, I had no idea what those consequences were, but I took satisfaction in making sure he conformed. My actions really freaked him out! As the train moved from station-to-station, I looked at the window to see my reflection. Normally I used it like a mirror to check my hair, but now there was nothing to see. The reality of that was quite hard to take. My journey was uncomfortable as I was constantly aware that someone could come and sit on me at any moment.

Day one was going well. I wasn't part of some elaborate hoax, I really was in the position that most people have probably imagined at some point in their lives. I was beginning to get excited about the prospect of seeing Lucy Pendleton up-close and very personal. She had a lovely figure and a perfect bottom. I wondered whether the fantasy would be much better than the intrusive reality.

I thought about what I was going to do. Was I going to stand there like a lampshade for several hours, watching Lucy read a book or something? It had the potential to be the sexiest moment I'd ever witnessed, or one of the most mundane. Still, just being in the same room as Lucy was a treat I was really looking forward to. At work I could never really get close to her. She wasn't unfriendly, just that I was merely a fleeting presence. That was all going to change. I was looking forwards to finding out more about her, what books she liked to read, what food she liked to eat, what her bedroom looked like…

Despite giving me complete freedom, being invisible also gave me an intense feeling of insecurity. Whatever I did, I was entirely alone with my inner monologue. There was no one to interact with, no one to confide in and no one to protect me. My spine tingled as I realised the last time I had felt so acutely vulnerable was when my mum died. Already, the highs and lows of being unapparent were beginning to impact on me.

Side-stepping through London to avoid collisions, I stared up at the incredible architecture. Impressive columns of stone were everywhere, and they offered me a place to lean on as I made my way to Lucy's place of residence.

There were a lot of stairs at Ovett House and at one point I almost got bulldozed by a group of teenagers who left no space for anyone to get past them. I stood as tightly against the wall as I could and tried to guide them past me. They smelled of cigarettes and Lynx.

When I got to Lucy's apartment, I heard raised voices from within. Gently turning the door handle I quickly moved inside and fortunately, the door led straight into a small hallway, so no-one could see or hear the door open. In the lounge, Lucy was in a state of distress, arguing with a tattooed guy who looked like a thug. Lucy had bruises to her face – and immediately I realised why she hadn't been in work for the past few days – how could she turn up in that state?

'How could you?' said Lucy, wiping her tears. 'Those things were given to me by my grandma. They meant a lot to me…'

'Don't be so pathetic!' replied the bruiser. His head was shaved and intricate tattoos weaved around his neck. He wore a tight white t-shirt, black jeans - which were far too short, and white socks. He bore a small scar on his cheek and paced around in an agitated state.

On the mantlepiece there were photographs of the pair together, obviously in happier times. It was plain to see that this arsehole was her boyfriend.

'My grandma left me that jewellery when she died. I can't believe you sold it!" cried Lucy, who was sitting on the settee with her knees up towards her face in a defensive position. 'Why did you do it, Carl!'

Carl? He had a shit name to go with his shit tattoos.

Carl obviously had a short fuse and looked like he was about to snap. 'I don't give a shit! Drugs are more important than that crap. If you earned more money, I wouldn't have had to sell the stuff...'

'You already take all my wage... I hate you!'

Carl lunged forward and slapped Lucy across her face, as the poor girl desperately tried to hide herself behind her knees, arms and hands.

'You fucking bitch!' he snarled.

I watched the start of the assault in shock, frozen to the spot. This scenario certainly hadn't been in my plans – it had never even crossed my mind for a second. I had to think quickly before Lucy got seriously hurt. Looking around I noticed a baseball bat propped against the wall. In a split-second I'd grabbed it and smashed it into the angry, spiteful face of Carl. The force sent him backwards and he fell on to the floor, stunned and surprised. A baseball bat floating in the air was freaky enough and then to see it smash into his face was a supernatural sight for both him and Lucy. I held it over his head as if I was about to smash the top of a boiled egg. And I would have loved to, but I held back from what could've been a fatal blow. I didn't have it in me.

Carl staggered to his feet, his eyes glued to the baseball bat still hovering in mid-air. Lucy was screaming.

'Get out!' I shouted to him and swung the bat dramatically towards his skull. I knew I had the upper hand, and I was always going to. The thrill of the power and the advantage I had over him gave me an instant boost of confidence.

Carl edged along the wall, desperate to keep out of the way of the possessed baseball bat. I followed him down the hallway where he frantically tried to find the door handle whilst looking over his shoulder.

'And don't come back!' I said, banging the baseball bat on the wall for extra effect. I was shaking - but felt exhilarated by my actions. I was beginning to think I was some sort of marvel superhero! As Carl moved away from the flat as quickly as he could in the circumstances, I shouted out, 'And your tattoos are shit!' It wasn't the best put down, but it drew the fracas to a close.

CHAPTER THIRTEEN:

Who are you?

What now, I thought? I walked back into the lounge where Lucy was now looking more scared than when her druggy boyfriend had assaulted her. I hadn't bargained for something like this and I certainly wasn't ready for someone to be so scared of me. This wasn't how I expected to be introduced to the luscious Lucy Pendleton. She looked far from luscious after being beaten up by Carl. I hated controlling bullies.

'Please do not be frightened!' I said, slowly placing the bat down on to the floor, as if I was standing in front of an armed response unit. I then said the phrase that I could hardly believe I was saying, and I felt a bit of a twat for how I said it: 'Fear not, for I AM THE INVISIBLE MAN!' It was an obvious statement, but one I felt I had to make in the circumstances, as I was scaring the poor girl to death.

Lucy was looking to where she thought I was standing. It was a completely out-of-this-world experience for her, and for me too. I cringed thinking about my self-righteous phrase.

'I am invisible! You have witnessed what I can do, but don't worry – I will not do you any harm. I was just nearby, and I heard raised voices so came in to investigate.' I said, and then I added, like an even bigger twat: 'I AM A FORCE FOR GOOD!'

I blushed with embarrassment as soon as I'd let that corker out of my mouth, but fortunately Lucy couldn't see my cheeks change colour.

'Please don't hurt me,' she begged, clutching a cushion over her face leaving just her eyes in view. She was crying, confused and alarmed.

'No, please… please listen, I'm not here to hurt you or anything. I stopped to help you. I'm a good person… it's just that you can't see me. That's the only difference, honestly….'

Are you real?' cried Lucy, wiping tears from her cheeks.

'Yes, I'm real! I just happen to be invisible.' I was barely two hours into my week of invisibility and I was already blabbing about my situation. I was supposed to be keeping the whole thing top secret.

'Are you human then?' asked Lucy, sniffling and slightly lowering her protective cushion.

'Yes, of course I'm human! Let me show you. Do you mind if I hold your hand, there's nothing to worry about… then you can feel that I'm real – and human. Honestly, I really am human.'

'OK,' she replied, still shaken by the assault and talking to an invisible man.

'I'm slowly moving towards you – if you hold out your hand, I'll gently hold it…'

Lucy tentatively held out her hand, and as I touched it for the first time, she shrieked at my touch and moved backwards, like she was going to touch a snake or frog.

After a few moments, she composed herself and then held out her hand again and I placed mine in hers. Even though this was not a romantic encounter in any way, shape or form, at the very moment I touched her hand and looked at her sweet, bruised face, I fell in love with her. Perhaps it was her vulnerability, I don't know, but whatever it was, I knew right then that I would kill for her. Maybe it wasn't love, but it was definitely something meaningful.

A wave of emotion came over me and I swear I felt my blood tingle. I had never felt so happy and I had never felt so consumed.

'I can really feel you…' said Lucy, slowly trying to take it all in. I knew what she was thinking – it was impossible. She felt the ring on my finger, not looking at my finger, but staring into space, visualising the shape and contours, like I imagined a blind person would.

'You wear an unusual ring…' she whispered.

'Yes, my friend gave it to me… an angel with her….'

'Wings spread...'said Lucy, finishing my sentence.

After the initial fear-factor gradually subsided, Lucy began to feel more comfortable with me, although I made sure that I didn't reveal exactly who I was. My identity had to remain a secret. If I'd blurted, 'It's me, Cooper, who washes the dishes at work…' She wouldn't have believed me. Plus, why would I want to tell the new love of my life that I was a plate-scraper and dishwasher?

'Don't worry about your boyfriend, I don't think he'll be hurting you anymore...' I said, trying to be convincing, like Batman reassuring the Mayor of Gotham City that the Joker was gone for good – which of course, he never was.

'God, I hope I never have to see him again. I've been trapped in this relationship for months and he's made my life absolute hell! I've lost most of my friends and it's just been a nightmare. And yet he was nice to me when we first started seeing each other...'

Lucy went on to explain that Carl was a small-time drugs-dealer and big-time drugs user. As we chatted, I tried to make Lucy laugh by experimenting with my invisibility. I made various objects float around the room like a low-budget Matilda movie and by the time I had to leave, she seemed to be in much better spirits. And so was I.

After an hour with Lucy, she had begun to relax with my invisibility and had been reassured that I was a friend. In the bathroom I helped tend to Lucy's injuries. Both of us standing in front of the mirror, I gently dabbed her bruises whilst she looked on, bewitched by the magical sight of herself and her new, invisible friend.

When I said I had to leave, she invited me to stay.

'I promise I'll come back later to check on you...' I said, 'And I always keep my promises...'

As I left her flat, she stood on the doorstep and waved. I waved back, which was pointless of course.

I left the apartment block feeling happy, if not on top of the world. I was pleased that my spur-of-the-moment morals had taken preference over my initial voyeuristic ambitions. I'd entered her world as a egocentric waster and left it as her principled guardian.

On the way back to my flat I was feeling hungry and took the opportunity to call in at my favourite Chinese restaurant which I'd nicknamed 'Well Hung's'. It was actually called just Hungs, but I could never resist sticking the word 'well' in front of it, for comedy effect.

I wandered into their bustling kitchens to find something to eat - as otherwise, I'd have had to be content with stealing off other people's plates in the dining area when they weren't looking.

Behind the scenes I took the opportunity to help myself to a delicious portion of chicken chow mein, which had been placed in a take-away container for collection by the person on the counter. I craftily floated it away, along with a plastic fork and ate it whilst sitting out of sight in a storeroom, away from the kitchen. As I ate each mouthful, I watched to see if my food remained visible as it was swallowed. It didn't.

Eating in public was going to be an issue. It was something I hadn't bargained for when forming my plan for the week. My mealtimes would have to be a solitary experience if I wanted to remain out of the public eye.

After I'd eaten, I carried my empty container back into the kitchen and said, 'That's was LOVELY, thank you!' The chefs just stood there open-mouthed. They uttered some words in Chinese. I had no idea what they said, but I guessed it translated to: "What the fuck was that?"

After a very productive morning followed by a delicious free lunch, I walked the streets feeling very satisfied. I could easily get used to this lifestyle, I thought to myself. I stopped briefly when I overheard two old men talking at a bus stop. Just two words caught my attention: 'Easy money'. I stopped in my tracks and listened as the two elderly gents discussed an event that was taking place the following night.

Their topic gave me a most brilliant money-making idea. I laughed out loud at how clever it was. It seemed that I had solved the problem of how to make instant cash.

One man looked like he was in his seventies and was dressed like a gentleman from Victorian times, completely out of place in modern London. His friend looked even older and was exactly what my description of what a cockney wide-boy would be. Drain-pipe jeans, leather jacket, medallion, a crew-cut hairdo and earring. They seemed a totally incongruous pair, but were clearly old friends and laughed together as they discussed life and the event that was going to happen the following night...

Excitedly, I rushed home as I needed to call my friend Michael with the details of my get-rich-quick scheme. I couldn't carry a mobile with me as it would be seen floating around – and If I'd placed my device in the magic bath water, I wouldn't have been able to see it, so it would've been unusable. Communication issues were going to cause me quite a few headaches.

So, what was my grand plan? Well, I was going to be a legend of sorts, live on TV. I'd hidden my door key on top of the door frame as I couldn't carry it around with me either, due to invisibility issues. I was excited, jubilant, elated, and lots of other words which escaped me. I felt like I'd already won the lottery.

I walked in to my flat and almost landed face-down on my floor after tripping on my Rylan rug. Two minutes later I'd composed myself and was calling my friend.

'Michael, it's Cooper. How's it going?

'Hi Coop' – where are you calling from?

'I'm in Switzerland!' I said off the top of my head, 'Anyway, I can't talk for long – I want you to do something for me…'

'Switzerland? I thought you were going to Venice?

'Er, that's right, we got on the wrong plane, so ended up here. It's all mountains and Toblerones for miles around…'

'Wow, that's great. Can you bring me a Toblerone back?'

'Er, yeah, 'course I can! Anyway, I want you to do something for me…'

'An Alpine horn and a pair of leather lederhosen, size 32 waist.'

'What the fuck do you want all that for?'

'The New Year's Eve fancy dress party! This year it has a theme…'

'What's the theme – dress like a twat? Look, I want you to follow these instructions, and I'll bring you back whatever you want!'

'Ok, what do you want me to do?' asked Michael. I knew he'd be standing there with a pen and pad.

'Well, I've left my life savings in my flat – in my fruit bowl, strategically placed under a bunch of bananas. Rebecca knows all about it - and I want you to get it and then go into a betting shop and stick the whole lot on the British boxer Maxwell Green who is fighting Dwayne Dixon from the USA tomorrow night.'

'What?'

'You heard me, stick the lot on Maxwell Green at the O2 arena!'

'What's this all about? You've never gambled in your life! Have you gone frikkin' mad my friend?'

After I went through the details a couple more times, Michael reluctantly agreed – and I also suggested he put as much money of his own on the British boxer too, as I mentioned I had some inside information that was one hundred percent reliable.

'Please just do it! Anyway, I have to dash, as… er… there's an avalanche coming. See you!'

The British boxer Maxwell Green was on the way up. He'd had eight fights and won them all, but the standard of his opponents had often been dubious at best. He was a huge underdog against the World Champion Dwayne Dixon who had a record of 47 fights and 47 victories – and he had fought many world-class opponents, including three ex-World Champions along the way. The chances of Maxwell Green going beyond the first few rounds were quite slim according to the experienced boxing pundits.

My inspired idea was to put all my money on the underdog and then get in the ring and help him win the fight! With me being totally invisible, I was in no danger, but the champion was going to be in for a very tough night. Two against one. It was genius.

The fight was the following night at the O2 Arena. I was excited about the thought of getting into the same ring as the World Champion and began practicing my 'Ali Shuffle' right there and then in my lounge. My boxing heroes were the British Middleweight boxer, the fabulous Tony Sibson (also a favourite of my dad and my grandad) and Muhammed Ali. I'd attended a boxing club when I was twelve in an attempt by my dad to toughen me up, but it ended disastrously on the first night when I got a tooth knocked out while trying to put my gloves on. It wasn't the best start to my boxing career. I recovered and did OK. At one point I was making twenty quid a week just from the tooth fairy alone.

As I contemplated my very first professional bout the next night, I realised that I would have to get some boxing gloves and cover them in my special oil, as it would look a little suspicious seeing an extra pair of boxing gloves floating about the ring. I thought I'd get there early and go into the dressing rooms to prepare my mitts. It would be quite a complicated process, but it was easily doable.

My first day of invisibility had been interesting. I'd beaten up Carl with a baseball bat, revealed my invisibility to Lucy Pendleton, had a nice Chinese lunch at Well-Hung's, fucked with a guy's head on the tube and decided to fight Dwayne Dixon at the O2 arena - and it was still only half-past two in the afternoon.

CHAPTER FOURTEEN:

Time to dream

Suddenly I felt very tired. Were the oils having an impact on me? I decided to have a little snooze – something I'd never done before. Perhaps the thousands of thoughts whizzing around my head had taken their toll. I carefully took off my shoes and placed them exactly beside my chest of drawers, so I could find them easily again when I woke up. Laying on top of the duvet I realised that I couldn't actually close my eyes as I could see through my eyelids. This meant that moisture still got to my eyes and I still blinked as normal, but I couldn't force darkness on myself. I cut a strip of material from an old T-shirt and wrapped it around my head before pulling it down over my eyes. A few minutes later I was asleep. I dreamed that my invisibility was actually part of a dream and in my fantasy, I awoke to find that it had all been brought about by drugs and I was actually talking to a psychiatrist in a mental institution. The whole situation was bizarre. And to make it slightly more weird, the psychiatrist was Vinny Jones and his assistant was the porn star Mia Khalifa. Make of that what you will.

When I awoke in the real world, I realised I'd been asleep for just two hours. I removed my makeshift eye mask and looked into the full-length mirror on my wardrobe door which was directly at the foot of my bed. I wasn't there. This was only my first day of invisibility and even though I now had proof that the oils worked, it was still an incredible situation to be in. Maybe I would never get used to it. But at least it wasn't part of a weird dream... it was actually much weirder.

Lucy Pendleton was in my thoughts and I felt the urge to see her again. Even though it had only been a few hours since I had intervened in her domestic dispute, I knew that she was still vulnerable. I put on my shoes, brushed my teeth, splashed water across my face and took a moment to intimately feel my features and genitals again. All my body parts were still there, still reasonably impressive and still invisible to the naked eye.

Before I set off to see Lucy once more, I decided that I should make a quick plan for the rest of day. I poured a glass of milk and made a few notes on my scribble-pad. The pen looked magical as I wrote – like a scene from the Walt Disney movie Fantasia.

Firstly, I'd go and see Lucy, then maybe have a wander around London and see if any ideas sprang to mind for making more money. With the current betting odds for the Maxwell Green fight, I stood to make about forty thousand pounds when he won. My target was one million though, so I needed to come up with a creative idea to get the other £960,000K.

Stealing some hi-value diamonds from one of those swanky shops in Hatton Garden sounded like a reasonable idea, but I didn't want to just go and steal from people who hadn't done anything to warrant it. I was positive that I wasn't going to take advantage of anyone who was just trying to earn an honest living. It was a difficult problem trying to make money whilst keeping my morals firmly intact.

Hardly anyone worked with real cash these days and this was really making my life difficult. Perhaps I could become the world's number one cat burglar - as long as I didn't leave any DNA at the scene, but I wasn't enthusiastic about breaking into anyone's house to take their family silver. It seemed to be dead-end after dead-end.

Would it be possible for me to fix the lottery for myself to win? No, that was a non-starter. A good idea that I came-up with, was what is called a 'confederate' - someone who is secretly working with you. For example, I thought it would be good to go to a casino and have my confederate doing the gambling, with me standing behind the other players and then whispering to my partner what cards everyone held. It was basically a good idea, but I didn't want to go through the rigmarole of involving anyone else. That would just make things too complicated. Plus, it would still be difficult to win very large amounts. I needed about £960,000K and a confederate would probably want half of that for being a part of my audacious scam.

As I left my flat, the big guy from upstairs was just coming up the steps carrying a well-wrapped package in his sausage-like fingers. I weaved past him and jokily pretended to punch him in the face and then kick him up the arse. He never even flinched of course, as he was totally oblivious to my actions. I suddenly had an overwhelming sense of freedom. I could do ANYTHING I wanted – and no one could stop me. Even if I did something bad, the CCTV cameras wouldn't catch a thing. Thinking about it though, I didn't want to become a media sensation, as I thought that Wyngard the boffin and MD Samantha Penhaligan, the big cheeses at work might put two-and-two together... and come up with Cooper McRae. The last thing I wanted was to spend time at Her Majesty's Pleasure for stealing industrial secrets – no matter how friendly the boys inside were.

CHAPTER FIFTEEN:

I'm on my way, Lucy

As I almost skipped along Grosvenor St, I casually plucked a banana from a street seller's cart, peeled it, took a quick bite from it and threw it towards a nearby bin. It hit the target at the first attempt. I was feeling pretty good about things. No-one saw anything, but then again, it wouldn't have mattered if they did. No one would have believed what they had seen. I made a mental to return after my week was over and pay for the delicious fruit treat.

The streets of London were busy with people heading home after work and those embarking on an afternoon of Christmas shopping. It was still unusually mild and the streets were brightly lit with festive lights and shop window displays which were a tourist attraction in themselves. People were laughing and it felt good to be alive. It felt even better to be alive AND invisible.

Stopping in my tracks, I looked in the window of a trendy fashion boutique as they had a large mirror as their centrepiece. Of course, I couldn't see myself, but I studied where my face would have been. I felt my chin and realised

I need a shave. Would my stubble show? And what would happen if I cut myself? Would my blood show? Probably yes. My thoughts then took a turn for the worse as I contemplated what would happen if I got hit by a car. No one would know to save me. My eyes scanned the streets and people around me. Momentarily I felt depressed and alone. Everything was down to me. I was on my own in the world - I might as well have been an astronaut on a faraway planet. From then on, I knew I had to be careful and put self-preservation at the top of my list.

As I climbed the stairs to Lucy's apartment at Ovett House, which was about a twenty-five minute walk from where I lived, I passed a couple of young lovers who were obviously still in the throes of early-relationship excitement. I wished that one day that would be me and Lucy. Or Lucy 'Perfect 10' Pendleton as I sometimes referred to her when talking to Ledley.

My knuckle tapped on her door. Whilst waiting, I used my hands to smarten my hair and even though it was pointless, I still felt the need to do it. I waited and knocked again. Then I noticed the curtain twitch in the window. No response. After a few seconds I knocked again and shouted, 'It's me, the Invisible Man!' That sounded so fucking stupid, but what else was I to call out?

Once again, the curtain twitched and then the door was very slowly opened. There was Lucy and she was holding a cloth to her face.

'Is it really you?' she asked, self-consciously.

'Yes, just checking in on you to see how you are...'

'Come in,' she said, holding open the door and standing well back as if I was carrying a virus.

'I'm in!' I said, as she still waited by the door. 'Has your er…' I didn't want to even say the word boyfriend.

'Yes, Carl's been back. And he hit me again.' Said Lucy removing the cloth from her face to show fresh marks across her cheek and chin. I could feel myself fast-tracking into Incredible Hulk mode and ready to explode with anger. I wanted to kill Carl. And at that very moment I swear I would have done it. And scarily, I think I might have enjoyed it, that's how angry I felt inside.

'Fuck!' I said, pacing around the lounge. I stopped doing so when I realised that Lucy couldn't follow my movements. 'What happened?'

'I was just going to eat, are you hungry?' replied Lucy, ignoring my question.

'Yes, that would be good. Thank you.' It would be nice to have a meal without having to conceal food and cutlery floating into the air. I could properly relax.

Lucy explained that an hour after leaving, Carl had returned to stash his drugs money in the usual place – behind a piece of skirting-board in the bathroom. He was not only a user, but also a supplier to other small-time distributors. Not content with making a ton of cash, he was also determined to steal everything he could from Lucy. He already took her wage, had pawned her most loved possessions and had now even taken her most expensive clothes and shoes. He was systematically destroying her, emotionally and physically - and I wasn't going to let that happen. I was ready to take sweet revenge. Or at least I thought I was.

Ensuring the water was only lukewarm, I helped bathe the new bruises on Lucy's face and whilst I did so, she gently touched my hands – not romantically, but to re-assure

66

herself that I was really there and that this was really happening.

We sat together and ate spaghetti. Or should I say, I ate spaghetti, Lucy just watched me, captivated by the site of pasta strands disappearing into nothingness.

'Have you always been invisible?'

'…To some people I have,' I replied staring at her beautiful, exhausted eyes. 'No, I haven't… I er… I was once quite normal, doing the same as everybody else. Going to work, going to the pub, meeting friends…you know… perfectly normal things.'

'They used to be perfectly normal things for me too, but not anymore…'

'Well things are about to get a lot better for you. I have a good feeling about it. From now on, your life's going to get so much better,' I said, still inwardly furious about her attacker.

'But, how did you become invisible? It's impossible. I keep thinking I'm dead and this is just some bizarre dream or after-life experience. But I can feel you, you feel normal!'

'I like to think that I *AM* normal. Although not everyone who's normal can do this!' I picked up my bowl of spaghetti, got up from my chair and 'floated' it around the room as if it was possessed. I made a spooky noise for extra effect.

Lucy laughed. It was the first time I'd actually seen her smile. Ever.

'What's your name?'

'Er… Just call me H.G.' I said, referencing H.G. Wells. It was the only thing I could think of off the top of my head.

'OK, H.G.'

'Do you mind if I touch your face?'

I hesitated for a moment and then said, 'I don't see why not.'

My hands took hers and guided them to my face. Nervously, I took a gulp as her soft hands slowly stroked my cheeks and followed the contours of my nose.

She didn't say a word.

Lucy stared at me as if looking directly into my eyes. Of course, she couldn't see anything apart from a band poster for the Arctic Monkeys that was hanging on the far wall directly behind me. She kept staring, as if eventually something would come in to focus and she would see my features. I blushed slightly as she continued to gently discover the contours of my face. I wondered if she could picture me in her own mind? It seemed strange, but already I'd almost forgotten what I looked like myself.

'Right, let's have a look at Carl's stash, shall we?' I said, spinning the utensils on the table.

We went into the bathroom where Lucy showed me the loose skirting board, behind which was a large plastic lunchbox, crammed with money. There must have been several thousand pounds inside.

'Don't take it!' said Lucy, as I removed a bundle of twenty-pound notes. 'He'll kill me… and I mean it.'

'Don't worry, don't worry, I won't!'

'You have no idea how violent he can be. This is nothing! She said, pointing to her facial marks. 'He's callous, vicious and cruel! Sadistic, actually… he enjoys it.

'People like him don't deserve to live!' she added. The thought had already crossed my mind.

As I left Lucy's apartment, she called out, 'Hey! You've got a good face…' I looked back and smiled at her comment. 'That's very kind of you,' I shouted as I left. 'I'll be back later… and don't you worry about anything. I've got a plan…'

I walked away in quite an emotional state. The situation was so bizarre that just a touch from Lucy made me want to cry. It wasn't as if I was a tortured soul, locked in a state of invisibility forever. It was just a week where I was going to be a totally free man. For Lucy, in her dire relationship with her druggie boyfriend, she was the tortured soul - but I was soon going to make her a free woman. I sang *"Are You Ready For Love?"* by Elton John as I went down the stairs two at a time.

Outside Ovett House it was like a classic scene from a Christmas card. Shoppers carried their gifts in festive bags, street sellers bagged roasted chestnuts and buskers dressed as Santa played *'I Wish It Could Be Christmas Every Day'* by Slade. There was a smell of coffee from the street cafes and Lucy Pendleton had touched my face. Life was pretty good and I was determined to ensure that I used my seven days wisely. I wanted to change lives. Bloody hell, that morning I was sexual pervert hoping for sexual gratification by peeking at Lucy in her knickers - just few hours later I was turning into the Camden Gandhi!

CHAPTER SIXTEEN:

The Shard

I was just beginning to embrace the feeling of enlightenment, when I noticed Carl. There he was, swaggering between the Christmas shoppers like an egotistical elf. He was walking in the opposite direction to Ovett House, so I followed him through the streets, taking note of everything from the way his shoe heels were worn to the left, to his exaggerated breathing patterns. On his back was a rucksack which no-doubt carried his ill-gotten gains. He made his way to Aldgate East tube station and I followed him down the escalator. He was heading to either Tower Hill or Monument, I guessed.

Carl stood on the edge of platform two in an agitated state – probably down to drugs, I thought. Slipping between two immaculately dressed ladies, I stood immediately behind him and found myself in the perfect position to push him into the path of an oncoming train. God, this was so easy.

Was this meant to be? Was I really considering pushing Carl under a train? I was a little bit concerned about how easily I was taking to the self-appointed role of grim reaper. Did I have something inside of me that was devoid of compassion or feeling?

Admittedly, I had contemplated hitting him over the head or similar, whilst at Lucy's, but just a little shove in the back would be much more convenient. He had even positioned himself at the very edge of the platform – with his feet *definitely* over the yellow danger line, so in my mind, he was contributing to his own demise. Surely the CCTV footage would show his disregard for his own safety. Plus, he was on drugs as well, so the post-mortem would reveal he was delusional or not fully in control of his own actions. He wasn't, of course – I was.

The clock showed that the next train was due in 2 minutes. I waited patiently, continually looking to either side of me to ensure no one was going to get in my way come the moment of truth. I had never seen a dead body before, let alone been the cause of one.

Suddenly I felt a cold rush of air and heard the unmistakable noise of the train approaching in the distance. A deep rumble and a swishing sound became louder as it came into view from the darkness. I placed both my hands up to my chest, ready to push. Was I really capable of giving Carl a gentle shove into the path of the train? Before I could make a decision, someone walked directly into me from behind, my hands pushed Carl and he began to stumble forward. The collision startled me and I instinctively grabbed on Carl's rucksack and pulled him back, away from certain death. It was a natural reaction and I'd done exactly the opposite of what I'd planned. Carl was alive thanks to me. And now he lived to abuse Lucy another day. In my heart, I knew that I couldn't purposely end someone's life, no matter how much I thought they deserved it. However, it did make me realise that some people always seem to get away with things.

Was Carl happy that someone had saved his life? No. In a temper, he assaulted the man directly behind who had unwittingly stumbled into me. In shock, I did nothing. People scurried on to the train and I got on last, still trying to work out what had just happened. Why was I so useless at everything? At least I knew I definitely wasn't cut out to be a cold-hearted killer – even when I was pushed to the limit.

Standing angrily next to Carl for several tube stops I was frustrated and angry at his behaviour and I followed him as he disembarked at Monument. After collecting some money from a contact, he made his way to Tower Bridge and waited shiftily near to London's tallest building, The Shard. The area was busy, with street vendors selling the usual Christmas-related gifts. The visitors were out in force, with a large group of Japanese tourists converging around a guide holding up a Union Jack umbrella. Carl was obviously waiting to meet up with another one of his criminal cronies.

After ten minutes, two guys wearing hoodies slowly sauntered up to him and they did the quadruple handshake-type-thing that boys 'In da hood' do. It looked like they were all trying to do an invisible Rubik's Cube, for fuck's sake. There was some laughing and a lot of posing going on. If they wanted to draw attention to themselves, they were doing a good job of it. The suspicious trio were queueing up to go into The Shard itself. What a glamorous place to do a drugs transaction, I thought.

I had already realised that the best revenge would be to see Carl get justice from the legal system, so I decided I would just do the right thing and grass him up to the local authorities. I didn't want to waste all my evening just watching drug transactions go down, so I was relieved when I noticed two policemen walking along Joiner Road. As I walked silently alongside them, I whispered, 'the guy with the tattoos on his neck in the queue for The Shard is doing a drugs deal!' They both looked around to see where the tip-off had come from.

Spinning on their heels whilst keeping a tight grip on their firearms, they saw nothing. They both heard what I said and when they couldn't see anyone, they stood back-to-back, trying to pick-up on anything or anyone suspicious. As I grew a little impatient at their lack of action, I said it again, only this time much louder and with an edge to it. I said, 'The guy in the queue for The Shard, the one with tattoos on his neck is a drug dealer and he's about to do some dealing. Are you two going to do your frikkin' duty or what?'

Again, the two police officers were completely baffled, but seemed to have finally got the message. They then cautiously headed towards the queue.

By this time. Carl and his two buddies were through and into The Shard, seemingly oblivious to the police officers nearby. Quickly pushing my way through the queue, I just managed to squeeze into the lift to join them and half a dozen slightly inebriated bankers dressed as Santa. They were occupied by taking photographs of each other.

Once the lift reached the top, we made our way to the outside viewing area and what a view it was. And I swear it looked even better because I hadn't paid for it.

As the bankers gathered together for a rowdy team photo, I hovered near Carl and his seedy looking friends, hoping to overhear some drugs talk. Unfortunately, he was talking about Lucy.

'Did Lucy give you that damage to your face, man?' laughed the shorter hooded figure who later I would know as Joe.

'No, the bitch didn't – I got into some bother with a few guys from the next estate. You should've seen the state of them by the time I'd finished!' boasted Carl.

'I've got her exactly where I want her – in fact, her wage has just paid our tickets to get into The Shard!' continued Carl, laughing. 'And I spent her bonus on the white stuff.'

I was almost ready to explode. In a single day I had not only fallen in love with Lucy, but I had become insanely protective towards her. To calm down, I had to walk away from Carl for a few moments.

As the three suspects continued making light of Lucy's situation as Carl's slave, the two police officers I had tipped-off outside The Shard, entered the outside viewing area. It was then that I saw something I hadn't expected. It was my boss Ledley. I recognised the huge afro and his distinctive laugh, even though I couldn't quite see his face from where I was standing. Yes, it was him, and there he was… in the middle of a romantic liaison with a girl.

I quickly went and stood beside the two policemen as they slowly looked around for their suspect. Ignoring Ledley for the moment, I leaned forward and said: 'The guy you want is to the left of the Santa party!'

Once again, the officers looked momentarily confused, but this time acted promptly on my information. Trying to keep a low profile the two cops headed in Carl's direction. At the same time, I forged my own short cut through the group of jolly Santa's and miscellaneous characters in fancy dress.

'Police, stop right where you are!' shouted the senior officer who could hardly be heard over the top of the festive fun. Their calls took me by surprise and after a few seconds, a few people nearby had begun to realise that something serious was happening.

The group of Santa's laughed, but Carl and his cohorts failed to see the funny side when they got a glimpse of the law heading swiftly in their direction - and they scrambled through the crowds to try and make their escape.

While the two hoodied figures instinctively split up and went in opposite directions, Carl became cornered against a seven-foot high glass wall, above which was a small amount of wire mesh. He was caught like a rabbit in the headlights – and he was moving his weight quickly from foot-to-foot – you could almost hear his mind trying to work out an escape route.

'Stop!' called the police again. 'Don't move!' While one police officer had his weapon pointing at Carl, the other was getting out his tazer.

Totally oblivious to the drama unfolding several feet away from him, Ledley was gearing up for a big romantic moment. In a world of his own, as usual, he was about to propose to some girl who didn't know she was on a date with a serial proposer. As Ledley rummaged in his jacket pocket for the ring, he simultaneously went down on one knee. I swear the girl thought he was doing up his shoelace and as he bowed before the young girl, Carl took a short run towards him and used Ledley's back as leverage to jump up onto the mesh above the specially strengthened glass pane.

The junior officer panicked and fired his tazer. It was slightly too late to get Carl, but had no problem attaching itself to Ledley, who let out a horrifying shriek.

Poor Ledley, he fell forwards and the shiny ring between his thumb and forefinger flew through the air, almost in slow-motion. I stood there watching the action like it was on the TV, not knowing what would happen next. What was Carl doing? Was he under the influence of hallucinogenic drugs? Who knows, but he obviously wasn't of sound mind, clambering up The Shard carrying a rucksack full of drugs. Ledley, whom I doubt was of sound mind either, was on the deck, still not disengaged from the tazer. He writhed around like a goldfish on the floor, whilst the crackle of electricity consumed his body. The poor girl meanwhile was frozen to the spot with her hands covering her face. It was almost as if she was peeping out between her fingers.

As the tourists realised the gravity of the situation, most of them began to disperse, whilst the merry bankers and Japanese tourist pointed their mobiles at the ensuing action. Carl was already halfway on to the mesh, with his rucksack loosely swinging behind him. People started to scream as the scene became more dramatic and in the middle of the action, I jumped to try and grab Carl's leg before he got out of reach.

God knows where he thought he was going, but he wasn't heading towards safety. 'Stay away you bastards!' he shouted, whilst pointing in the general direction of the police.

He was perched on top of the mesh with a drop of around 300 metres below him. One of the police officers then began climbing on top of the other to try and reach Carl.

Whilst the policemen struggled to get to him because of their cumbersome uniforms, Ledley became the man of the moment. Now, just about recovered from his tazering, he quickly scrambled over the officers to where he could almost grab a hold of Carl's trouser leg. But, just as he reached out, Carl slipped, sending himself flying off the edge of the building. The crowd gasped as his rucksack snagged on a pointed piece of The Shard's glass, leaving him hanging perilously over the edge with the streets of old London town a long, long way below.

As the onlookers gasped, Ledley, the police and I all froze. I'm not sure what we were waiting for – perhaps a scream, fading away to nothing-ness as he plummeted towards the tarmac. However, there was nothing. We all waited for something… but for the moment there was nothing. Just an eerie silence. Carl had disappeared over the precipice.

Then we heard something which took us all by surprise. A voice called out; 'Aaarrrgghhhh!' And the cry came from over the edge of the Shard.

'I'm still here! Oi, I'm still HERE! Is anybody listening? Any chance of someone fucking helping me?'

Just when we thought Carl had gone to a better place via a freshly-tarmaced pavement, he'd called out. It was quite a sad, lonely cry. Not the cry of a vicious thug, but the cry of someone who knew that he was about to crap himself.

We all moved forward to see what had happened. Carl's rucksack had snagged on a piece of The Shard and he was hanging there, dangling in space, trying to look back over his shoulder for help.

It seemed that no-one knew what to do. The police were busy calling for help on their radios, but that would take quite a few minutes to arrive, whilst Japanese tourists were busy filming the proceedings for social media. After a few moments, the police decided to try and do something about the situation, but as they looked up at the glass partition where Carl hung precariously, they realised that neither of them were the perfect height to get a good grasp of the tattooed drugs dealer. As they tried to come up with a solution between them, Ledley approached them and there was lots of nodding and animated hand movements. It seemed my boss from JC Cosmetics had a plan – and the two officers of the law seemed to like the idea. Time was precious, as it was just a matter of it before Carl's rucksack straps gave way.

CHAPTER SEVENTEEN:

The Bankers

Ledley's idea actually wasn't amazing at all, in fact I thought it was a little bit stupid, but all things considered it was probably the best option and fully utilised the available components. And what I mean by components, is: the group of bankers.

Ledley had come up with idea of building a human pyramid, with himself perched on top. The police looked on, holding their weapons with pained expressions across their faces.

As Ledley worked on his balance, he used his left hand to stabilise himself and his right arm reached over to try and grasp Carl's rucksack. Ledley's body blocked everyone's view as he struggled to get a firm grip. Once he had a strong hold, he began pulling with all his might. There were grunts and groans and nervous chattering from the drunk bankers who continued to talk to each other throughout the tense situation. Several of them held their mobiles at the best angle they could muster to try and get a recording of the drama as it unfolded.

Ledey was not far from Carl's rucksack, in fact he could get both of his hands on it but was struggling to get leverage. His face was grimacing like that of a weightlifter at the Olympics and his perfect white teeth were showing whilst the tendons in his neck stood out unhealthily.

As my amiable boss gave it his all. He grunted - and then announced chirpily: 'I've got him....'

A few moments of eerie silence followed. 'Well, let me re-phrase that...I've actually got a rucksack... There doesn't seem to be anyone attached to it. Oh dear.'

Somewhere in the distance there was a fading scream.

'Oh dear' didn't seem to be the most appropriate phrase to utter as someone was plummeting to their death, but Ledley didn't have time to consider something more meaningful.

For a few moments, everyone seemed to freeze in shock at what had just happened. I remained calm, but my mind was whirring. If Carl was out of the way for good, my life, and that of Lucy's would be so much better. I was secretly hoping that Carl hadn't got snagged anywhere else on his trip downwards. That would be just my luck, I thought. Several of the tourists began to scream while a group of others hugged each other. The police struggled to see if they could see Carl, but the drug-dealing bully was well on his way to terra firma.

Dashing down to the ground floor as fast as I could, I darted to where his body should have been. There was no sign of a bloody mess on the pavement. I'd slightly miscalculated where he'd fallen from and then I noticed something. There was a section of the street which had been cordoned off and I as I looked to see where Carl had fallen from, I realised he would have fallen behind the partition. I quickly ran around and found a gap where I could squeeze through. Carl's body was sprawled out on top of a skip fully-laden with old carpets, next to a sign that read; NO MORE RUBBISH.

Having never seen a dead body before, I wasn't sure what state Carl would be in when I found him. Suffice to say, the tattooed thug wasn't looking his best. The old carpets may have helped to break his fall, but the three hundred metre drop had taken its toll. I had never seen anyone look so bad, although seeing Ledley the night after his twenty-first birthday celebrations came pretty close.

Flat on his back with both arms stretched out over his head, it looked like he was surrendering. His eyes were closed and he had what looked like a faint smile on his bloodied face. The dust was still settling as I surveyed the scene, which showed the power of his fall.

At that very moment I couldn't tell you exactly how I felt. I looked at Carl's body laid there on top of the skip and it looked like a piece of weird modern art. Just the sort of crap that Tracey Emin would have done and had the Radio Four critics having orgasms about. Carl had truly wasted his life, which was the biggest crime of all. But, who was I to judge? Perhaps he'd been the victim of an abused childhood, maybe he didn't even know his parents? As I stood there, slowly becoming coated in dust, a wave of sympathy came over me. It struck me that some people were doomed to be casualties in life before they had actually started it.

Before the police or anyone else arrived at the scene, I took the opportunity to take myself a souvenir, which I hid nearby for collection later.

CHAPTER EIGHTEEN:

Breaking the news

Carl was dead and he was no longer able to bully, intimidate, steal, deal drugs, bring misery, or be anywhere near Lucy. Talking of whom, I needed to check in with her and tell her the news.

The problem was that I didn't have any money to use one of the old red telephone boxes and I definitely wasn't in a position to be able to carry a mobile – it was something I'd overlooked when I was taking my bath in the invisibility shampoo.

I walked along the Thames and came across some street entertainers. There were the usual statues, which I had little time for, including a guy astride a bike with his coat stuck up in the air behind him as if it was a really windy day, a marble statue… and The Invisible Man!

The Invisible Man looked OK, but he basically had his head concealed where the top button of his shirt was, then there was a hat held aloft by a piece of very thin wire. So, his head and hands were missing - supposedly. I'm sure you get the picture. He didn't look anywhere near as good as me.

In front of him was a small box which held about six or seven pounds in small coins. To his side, there was a chair and his bag of personal belongings. I sat myself on the chair and peered into his bag. I could see a mobile phone. It was then I had a bright idea.

At an opportune moment I whispered to him; 'I'm the real invisible man. I'm really invisible – have a look. You can't see me. If you go along with my little idea, you'll make yourself some money. He gawped towards me in complete disbelief and nodded to go along with it, after all, no one wants to be out-earned by a statue. The busker introduced himself as Nigel as he looked me up and down. He was in a state of shock by how good I was at being invisible – and muttered something about my incredible optical illusion!

After a swift briefing, I changed into the fake invisible man's outfit and removed his bowler hat from the wire which held it aloft. The public then witnessed that I really was invisible, no gimmicks, no nothing. And definitely no hands.

Nigel just sat and stared with his mouth open, whilst the passers-by could not believe their eyes. There was a buzz of excitement and incredulity as I dramatically picked up his mobile and made a call to Lucy. She was delighted to hear from me.

'Lucy, it's me… The Invisible Man!' The ever-increasing crowd burst into spontaneous applause. Some of them were already reaching into their pockets for money, while others began filming on their mobiles. I had to keep my voice down as I couldn't afford to be rumbled if anything was posted online.

'Lucy, I've got some news for you... I'm not sure how to tell you this but...'

'What is it?' she replied.

I was very aware that the public were now hanging on my every word, half wondering how I was doing it, half listening to my conversation.

Turning away from the growing crowd, I said, 'He's gone'

'Who's gone?' replied Lucy, although I think she knew who I meant.

'Carl.' I whispered, covering my mouth. I thought it was probably not the done thing to reveal Carl was dead over the phone, but I didn't want Lucy to be alone in her flat worrying about his next visit. I was determined to tell her the whole story face-to-face later that evening.

As I spoke to Lucy, I instinctively removed my bowler hat, which drew another spontaneous round of applause from my audience. They were loving it. I mean *REALLY* loving it.

'What happened?' asked Lucy.

'He had a nasty fall...' I replied, without going into more detail.

On the other end of the phone, I could hear Lucy becoming emotional. Oh no, don't tell me she really loved him? I consoled her and then ended the call, saying that I would be over to visit her later. The promise seemed to make her feel better.

After the call, I got quite into my role as an entertainer, rolling up my trouser legs to show I was totally invisible. The ever-increasing crowd gasped and cheered and took more video footage on their mobiles.

All the while, Nigel the fake invisible man clapped and shook his head in pure disbelief at the scene before him. After a long five minutes, to what seemed like hundreds of people, I took my bow and thanked everyone for watching. Of course, I also asked them to drop a few coins into the hat. The response was amazing, with hundreds of pounds deposited. Once the crowds had dispersed, Nigel congratulated me and was keen to discover more about my invisibility.

'You've got a fantastic act!' He said enthusiastically. Where did you buy it from?'

'You can't *buy* this – I created it myself.' I said, exaggerating somewhat. 'Enjoy your money!'

'I can't keep all this money,' said Nigel, scooping his hand into his collection hat. 'You earned it, so you deserve to keep it!'

'No,' I replied, 'I want you to have it. You might be able to do me a favour sometime.' I added. There was definitely a few hundred pounds in the pot. Not bad for five minutes work.

My performance was witnessed by large numbers of tourists and I knew that I shouldn't have really put myself in the public eye like that, but at least my performance would probably be put down to some sort of magic trick if it got posted online.

'If I'm passing this way again, I'll definitely stop and say hello!' I said, making to leave.

I knew it was time to skulk back into anonymity, but before I returned to Lucy's I had one more thing I wanted to do. The opportunity was just too good to waste…

CHAPTER NINETEEN:

By Royal appointment

Standing outside Buckingham Palace, I felt like any other tourist in awe of its beauty and I just stood there looking at it, illuminated in the December evening. But even though I stood there just like many other visitors enjoying selfies, I knew that I had a power that they couldn't even begin to imagine: The power to walk right in and see the Queen! Fuck, I was so cool!

My mum had been a big fan of the Royals and when she was a teenager, many people said she actually looked like Queen Elizabeth. Numerous times she recounted the story of how the local butcher once confused her with Her Royal Highness and offered her a discount on sausages.

Standing at the gate of Buckingham Palace, I waited for ten minutes until they opened to let out a vehicle and then I briskly walked calmly past the two guards. Stopping briefly, I looked at the soldiers and examined their pristine uniforms as if I were a foreign leader on a state visit. I looked them up and down, just a few inches away from their faces. As moved on I said, 'Not bad'.

Walking slowly across the gravel courtyard of Buckingham Palace I looked to up the top windows where the lights were on. As my face pointed upwards, I saw and then felt the first snowflakes of winter. It didn't seem like it was cold enough to snow but weaving their way slowly down from the heavens were millions of tiny snowflakes. I stretched out my arms and cupped my hands to try and catch the first droplets. I was having a perfect evening. Carl was out of the picture; I'd had the opportunity to perform a few basic invisibility moves in front of a captivated crowd and I was off to see the Queen. As I looked to the floor, I realised that it wouldn't be long before I would be leaving footprints on the ground.

Looking around for a minute or two, I tried to take it all in. I didn't want to end up in a week's time saying: "I don't remember much of it because it flew by!" I was actually just a few feet away from "*The* Buckingham Palace". The stonework was just inches away. The Queen's guards were looking magnificent in their red tunics and bearskins, despite my flippant comment and it was now snowing a little bit heavier. The sky still looked blue, even though it was a winter's evening.

I stood there, thinking how lucky I was. This was my first day of invisibility and I could see the world from a whole new perspective. Yes, I was definitely in a privileged position to see how humanity really behaved behind closed doors - and it was unsettling. How many more Lucy Pendletons were being beaten up by their bullying, controlling boyfriends? I didn't want to think about it as it was too upsetting. At least there was one less problem in the world now that Carl had met his skip-related end. Anyway... I was going to visit the Queen!

I followed the walls of Buckingham Palace looking for a way to get in and when I'd made my way to the back, a door opened with perfect timing as a staff member came out with a bin-liner full of rubbish. I got the feint whiff of fish and chips and wondered if the Queen and Prince Philip had just had themselves a portion. I decided that Prince Philip was a 'mushy pea' man, whilst the Queen would more-likely go for curry sauce on her chips.

Once inside, I walked from room to room, figuring that the higher I went in the palace, the more likely I was to meet the Queen. The palace itself was pretty much how I imagined it. The walls were covered with portraits of privileged men and women from throughout the ages, who all sat posing seriously in front of huge curtains in spacious drawing rooms. For a second, I thought of my own lounge which boasted a poster of Raquel Welsh in her underwear. I know which I'd rather look at, I thought to myself, quickly moving on with scant regard for the historic importance of my surroundings.

The carpets featured amazingly complex patterns and perched beside most doorways were examples of pottery. There were lots of Chinese vases like you see at half-decent car boot sales, although I guessed that the Queen wouldn't accept a tenner for any of hers. Yes, the palace held no surprises for me, there were a lot of gold-coloured things, fancy settees and furniture you wouldn't find in most people's homes. It was all such a world away from my own upbringing and circumstances that I couldn't really comprehend the wonder of it all. To be honest, it reminded me of being in a boring museum.

Soon I heard voices and I walked briskly through a long dining room and entered a huge lounge area to where three people sat at the far end. As I got closer to them, I knew I had hit the jackpot. There before me were the Queen, Prince Philip and Prince Charles. I could see that they were busy doing something, but I couldn't quite make out what. Even though I was completely invisible I still acted as though the Queen could see me and when I got closer, I even bowed, as if I was in the performing line-up at The London Palladium.

I stood beside them and watched in amazement as the three senior members of the Royal Family played scrabble. I had expected the Queen to be polishing her diamonds, Prince Charles to be reading a book on architecture, and Prince Philip to be learning his highway code – but Scrabble? That was a surprise.

Far from being intimidated by being at such close quarters to three of the world's most famous people, I began to look at the letters they'd got on their little scrabble letter holders. It was the Queen's go and she was stuck. Her letters were k-w-i-f-c-u-t and she was struggling to find a word of merit. Charles was getting a little impatient.

'C'mon ma-ma, don't you have anything? Anything at all?'

'Give her another half a minute Chaz,' said Prince Philip, not looking up from his own selection.

I almost laughed aloud when Charles was called Chaz by his dad.

Charles said, 'I knew we should have played Monopoly instead…'

'You'll never win that,' replied Prince Philip. '…Because your mother already owns everything in London!' He laughed at his own joke. 'Even the Old Kent Road.'

As the Queen tutted, I paid special attention to her letters and in a moment of inspiration, I stumbled upon a seven-letter word. I was so excited I was like a small child on Christmas morning. Fearing the Queen was about to miss out on a right-royal opportunity, I broke with invisibility protocol and whispered the word in her ear. It was as if she had got the thought all by herself, she never looked surprised by a voice whispering in her ear and never looked around. Nothing at all. But she definitely heard a voice.

'C'mon Liz, one has had enough time now, surely…' continued Prince Charles who was opening a bag of crisps. Charles prised open the bag and crisps flew everywhere…

'Fuckwit' said Her Majesty.

'Er, that's a bit harsh my love!' said Philip, looking up from his letters. 'Those crisp bags are appalling, honestly. The lad didn't mean to chuck them all over the Axeminster…'

'One is not talking about the crisps, I'm talking about my word. My scrabble word… It's FUCKWIT! Seven letters. And one is the winner!' announced the Queen, dramatically turning her letter holder around to show off her rude seven-letter word…

I couldn't believe it. I had just helped the Queen of England win a game of scrabble with a seven-letter profanity. Falling on to the floor, I did my best to suppress my laughter. It felt liberating to actually enjoy myself in my new guise. The three members of the Royal Family were in their own little world, as I was in mine. I decided to leave

them to it, after all, what could possibly top the royal
'Fuckwit?'

CHAPTER TWENTY:

Pick pockets

It was time to go and see Lucy. I knew she was waiting for me and I had so much to tell her. So much had happened to me in a single day. I felt guilty and slightly ashamed of myself for the rude, yet appealing thoughts that I'd started my day with. Things had changed so quickly it was difficult to take it all in. Could it be possible for someone to age several years in a single day? My experiences had already been an education and I had a feeling there was still a lot to learn.

I jumped over the tube barrier and timed my trip perfectly as a train was just arriving, so I bounded on enthusiastically just behind an old, well-to-do couple. The gentleman struggled to carry a bag of food shopping, so I stooped and helped him carry it without him even realising.

I was the king of the castle, but couldn't tell anyone about it. Elated, uplifted and happier than I had ever been in my life, I casually looked around the carriage as the train made its way from station to station. My positive mood instantly changed when I saw a couple of guys pickpocketing. I watched them steal the phone of a young girl, who was standing on her own by the closed doors. From the look on her face, she knew she'd been robbed but was too terrified to move. It was a desperate picture.

This one moment that could quite possibly change this girl's life forever. I had no idea who she was, but l couldn't stand there doing nothing. And I didn't have to.

In normal circumstances I would have found it hard to tackle two robbers, and I would have probably chickened out - but these weren't normal circumstances. I knew I had to act, and act reasonably fast before the train hit the next station, or the culprits would most likely be away.

The two robbers were about twenty years old. The taller of the two was white, with a black hoodie, skinny jeans and converse trainers. The smaller, black guy was stockier and had a complicated pattern shaved into his hair. He wore a long coat, which was slightly too long to be called fashionable. I couldn't figure out if his coat was too long or his legs were too short.

Quickly pushing the alarm with my left hand, my right hit the taller guy in the stomach. Instantly winded, he fell dramatically to the floor. Before he had chance to cry out, I'd made my move on his accomplice who had no idea what was happening. The young girl ran to other end of the carriage to the safety of other passengers who watched on in amazement. The sight must have been incredible to them. There were screams, shouts and crying from a watching international tube-train audience.

At that moment swiftly grabbed the large baguette from the old couple's shopping bag and smashed it into the knees of the smaller picket-pocket. I think he thought he was being hit by something more substantial than a French-style treat and he crashed to the ground in a flurry of breadcrumbs. The baguette broke in half, with one piece flying dramatically through the air. I don't think that the baguette really had much impact on the thief, but one of my well-aimed kicks had him clutching his family-jewels in agony.

As the two robbers lay on the floor in obvious and well-deserved agony, I went through their pockets and retrieved the girl's mobile. As the Apple iPhone 'floated' through the air and back to her, the onlookers gasped. It was a miracle of biblical proportions.

The train pulled into the station as several police officers arrived to do their duty. The two scumbags were removed from the train and on to the empty platform where I watched as they were both handcuffed.

'Yes,' I thought. 'It's great being invisible!'

However, the reality was that I was uncovering the worst of mankind. I was witnessing crime on a scale I didn't really know existed. In one day alone, I had been affected by domestic violence, drug dealing and robbery. And that's without mentioning the Queen's foul-mouthed scrabble word. The world was much madder and maddening than I had realised. Jesus, The Daily Mail might be right after all, I said to myself.

The baguette was a write-off, but the old gentleman smiled without saying a word as I returned the remnants of his bread. He said, 'Thank you very much.' And then something strange happened. The watching passengers applauded. I don't know if they knew what they were applauding, but it was spontaneous and life-affirming. I acknowledged the reaction by nodding in their general direction and alighted at the next station.

As I stood on the escalator to get me back to street level, I saw a poster on the white-tiled wall promoting the boxing match I was committed to gambling on, the next night. I was so pleased I'd discovered a way to make big money. It was a fool-proof method – a sure fire way to earn a large amount of cash quickly. And the most satisfying aspect of the whole thing was that it was legitimate cash. Yes, I understood that the method of me actually getting the cash was technically not fair or even legal, but that didn't stop me from buzzing with the crazy, yet inspired idea as I got to Lucy Pendleton's door.

There was no real reason to be nervous as I knocked, but I was. Lucy invited me in as if it was perfectly natural to welcome-in someone invisible. In just a few short hours she had become accustomed to perhaps the greatest miracle the world had ever seen, or not seen, in my case. It was a very strange feeling to be accepted so easily.

'Please tell me your name,' she said, with a hand on each side of my face. She was attempting to stare where she thought my eyes would be. It was a bit weird, but I loved her touch.

'You know I can't do that!' I replied.

'Why not?'

'Er… because I can't. Anyway, I have something, or rather some *things* to tell you.' I said, changing the subject.

I had decided not to beat around the bush.

'Carl has had an accident….'

'An accident? What happened?'

'He was trying to escape from the police… and fell and banged his head,' I said, playing down the effect of a severe head trauma. 'I'm afraid he's dead… and just in case you were wondering, I had nothing to do with it!' Obviously, I was more involved than I had let on, but I thought it best to keep the details scant.

'Dead? Carl's dead?' She slumped to her knees with her hands over her mouth. I couldn't tell if she was pleased or not. I just looked at her, waiting for part two of her reaction.

'He was trying to get away from the police...'

'Is he definitely dead?' said Lucy peeking through her fingers.

'Yes, I'm afraid so. How do you feel about that?'

'Relieved. Just so relieved!'

Thank God she was relieved. I was beginning to think she had real feelings for him, despite him being a violent woman-beater, like Stockholm syndrome or something. I approached her, letting Lucy know I was going to hold her in my arms. She reached out like a child who had fallen in the school playground.

I held her tightly and didn't want to let her go. As our faces brushed each other, I felt the wetness of her tears on my own cheek.

After a few minutes, Lucy put the kettle on and watched transfixed as I put my hand into the steam. I appeared like a ghost, until I almost burnt my hand.

'Ooouch!' I cried, shaking my hand in the air, sending condensation droplets scattering.

'Are you OK, baby?' asked Lucy, sticking out her bottom lip. I was fine, but Lucy had just called me 'baby'. Later, I was to find out that this was a pivotal moment in our relationship. As her protector I was also vulnerable myself, which seemed to connect us more somehow.

Lucy laughed at my reaction to the steam, that in turn set me off, then we enjoyed a chocolate biscuit.

Everything was alright.

I asked Lucy about Carl's secret stash of money.

'It's still hidden in the bathroom behind the skirting-board tiles. I don't know how much there is altogether…'

'Well let's have a look, shall we?' I said, rubbing my hands together in anticipation.

I followed Lucy down the hall. To the left, her bedroom door was open, her bed sheets were thrown to one side, and her underwear lay on the floor. I paused for a moment and looked at her peach-coloured knickers. Very nice. And probably the closest I was going to get to them despite my original fantasy.

'Are you there?' asked Lucy, staring straight down the hall. Actually, I was positioned to the left, with my head inside her bedroom. On her wall was a framed album cover of Never Mind the Bollocks, here's the Sex Pistols. She had excellent taste.

'…Yes, I'm right here!' I replied.

Once in the bathroom I gently took Lucy's arm and moved her out of the way in order to kneel down and remove the tile nearest to the floor. As soon as it was removed I could see bundles of notes. I'd expected them to be in a tin or something, but they were just thrown in there. An elastic band held them together and there were five bundles in all.

'Jesus! He's been a busy boy!' I said holding up a wad of notes in the air. Lucy laughed as they magically floated around. 'This is all yours!' I said to her.

'It's like I've won the lottery!'

'I think you have,' I said. 'I expect you've been keeping him for some time, so to me it looks like you've been repaid. Yeay!' I shouted, holding up two bundles of notes.

'Since you passed my door, it's been good luck all the way...' said Lucy, who sniffled and began to cry. I threw the money on to the floor and held her once more in my see-through arms. 'You're my good luck charm,' she continued, nodding her head while searching for a tissue.

'Well, I wouldn't exactly say that....'

'I feel safe when you're around – even though I can't even see you.'

At that moment I was genuinely happy and content. If only I could have frozen that second in time.

We eventually counted the money and there was just over twelve thousand pounds.

'That's not a bad amount,' I announced as I juggled three wads of money in the air. Lucy couldn't stop laughing and I kept thinking about how much I would have earned as a busker if the London shoppers could have seen me at that very moment.

We made coffee and sat in the lounge, which was quite retro, with lots of pastel colours. It was a mish-mash of styles which all seemed to go together, not unlike my own flat. She had excellent sense of interior design, if not in men.

'So how would you sum up your day?' asked Lucy, playing with her chocolate biscuit wrapper.

'That's a very difficult question to answer.' I said thoughtfully. 'I've seen so many things – so many horrible things and so many great things. And I know that the Queen loves a game of scrabble.'

Lucy just shook her head and smiled. 'You haven't???'

'I'm afraid I have...' I replied. Shame she couldn't see my naughty little boy face as I spoke.

What a fucking day. I was exhausted by it, yet still pumped-up with adrenalin. It was time for me to wind down. I had an even bigger day ahead tomorrow. I had my big money-making scheme and a really good night's sleep was a necessity. Lucy invited me to sleep on the couch, which I accepted. I covered my eyes using one of her t-shirts, which was the next-best-thing to being in bed with her. I could smell her scent and I contentedly drifted off to Narnia.

I left at 7am the following morning while she was still asleep. I wrote a note for her. It said: "Lucy, got to go, I'll call in tomorrow to see you. - HG." I didn't know that the next day was going to bring even more challenges.

CHAPTER TWENTY-ONE:

Day 2, December 23rd

The first day of my adventure had been almost more than I could handle psychologically. I'd seemed to take it all in my stride at the time, but my brain was tired of all the information it had had to process in just twenty-four incredible hours. Normally, my thoughts were pretty mundane, just like my job. The most taxing thought was usually 'what am I going to have for tea?' or 'I wonder what's on the TV?'

Contemplating being the first human to ever be completely invisible, a thought hit me. So, I'm the first ever human to be in this position – and how do I use it? For my own selfish needs, that's how. To improve my unfulfilled life. No, things weren't how I'd imagined my life would be, but this opportunity would never be possible again. Surely I had to make it count, maybe even make my mum proud if she was looking down on me - but how could I use this power to make a real, long-lasting difference to people's lives? When I stopped the robbery on the tube-train I felt euphoric, but I couldn't cure cancer or stop a war. That was preposterous. The more I thought about it, the more I realised that my superpower wasn't actually that good, in the sense that I couldn't *really* change anything.

My brain had enough to process without me chastising myself for being selfish. It was like being a real-life Marvel character without an evil nemesis. What I did know was that invisibility was the ultimate confidence boost. It enabled me to step in and defend people knowing that I couldn't be beaten, or at least the chances were very slim – they'd have to be very sharp to catch me. Plus, I could go anywhere and virtually do anything without having to pay.

As a privileged witness I had the potential to change lives for the better, but I wasn't sure how to convert the potential into substance. Maybe the invisibility oil would have been better if it had fallen into the lap of a more intellectual, erudite person? Maybe I didn't possess the mental capacity to achieve anything of merit…

Anyway, I decided that after my big money-making boxing match I would devote my efforts to doing good in the capital for the remaining five days. Instantly I was back to being the Camden Gandhi again. I would be the calming influence, the bringer of hope, the do-gooder with the magic touch. The main difference between myself and Gandhi would be that I wouldn't be wandering around in what looked like a pair of baggy white underpants. Yes, I was definitely getting carried away.

I knew that I had to get a grip with reality – even though none of this seemed real at all. My brain and body needed to get into gear, after all, I was going to be taking part in a world title fight that very night. My forthcoming title fight was kept a secret from Lucy as I didn't want to have extra pressure on me as I was already having doubts about how I would actually go about trying to KO a world champion.

Oxford street was bustling, and I knew I'd made a mistake taking that way home. As shoppers sought out Christmas retail therapy and that elusive gift for Grandma, I looked up and for the first time noticed the stunning architecture displayed above the shop windows. From elegant Edwardian buildings to Debenham's impressive kinetic, shimmering façade. Largely overlooked, these classic examples of building expertise gave London its timeless appeal – even if no one stopped to admire it.

As soon as I got home, I showered and was almost hypnotised by the shape my body made as the water ran off it. I played with the jets of water, making intricate patterns and cupping my hands to form a puddle of water in mid-air, like a scientific experiment.

Laid on my bed, I contemplated the day and night ahead. Even though I was going to be invisible in the boxing ring, it would still be a mighty challenge for me. After all, I wasn't a big tough boxer-type or anything, I was just a normal person with a normal physique. I weighed about eleven stone and wasn't muscly at all. Just normal – not fat, not thin. The thing I had in my favour was that Dwayne Dixon wouldn't see my sidewinders coming. I was excited by the thought of being on live TV, yet also nervous at the thought of being a world champion. OK, I know it wouldn't be me that would be crowned world champion, it would be Maxwell Green, but that wasn't the point. I was already looking forward to doing my 'Muhammed Ali Double-Shuffle' in front of millions of viewers, even if no-one was going to see it.

Filming myself on my mobile, I reached over to the bedside table and picked up a glass of Coca Cola. I raised the glass and then drank it all. The clip looked sensational. The liquid just disappeared into a void.

'Yep, I just drank that.' I burped, by way of commentary.

I'd just about crammed more in to my first twenty-four hours of being invisible, than I had in the first twenty-five years of my life. That sounded like a dramatic thing to say, but it's true. The sensations I'd had must be like the effect of the most amazing drug – not that I knew - I'd never even taken a drug in my life, unless you count paracetamol. The only downside of my remarkable, death-tainted day was that I had no-one to share it with…

CHAPTER TWENTY-TWO:

There may be trouble ahead...

I laid on my bed until lunchtime, removed my home-made eye-mask and then stared at the body shape I'd left on top of my duvet. 'I definitely exist, there's the proof!' I said out loud.

After brushing my teeth for several minutes and then touching them with my fingers to make sure they were all there, I called Lucy Pendleton. She answered almost immediately.

'Hi Lucy.... It's me, HG.'

'Heyyyy!' she replied enthusiastically. Obviously pleased to hear from me.

'How was your night? Did you sleep OK?' I asked.

'Sorry I had to go early,' I continued, before she had to time to answer. I've got a big day ahead of me and I needed to get my head together - I just felt more comfortable in my own place. I'm sure you understand what I mean...'

'Yes, I do know what you mean, you can't beat the feeling of your own bed...' replied Lucy, who sounded quite distant, as if she was distracted. 'I slept alright considering all that's happened'.

Then there was a knock at the door. At her door. It was so loud that I could hear it down the phone. Lucy went silent.

'Are you still there?'

Nothing.

'Lucy, are you still there?'

She eventually replied as the raps on the door continued.

'Are you expecting anyone?'

'No, nobody. I'm not expecting anyone.'

'OK,' I said firmly, 'just answer the door. Don't worry, it'll probably be a neighbour or something.'

It wasn't a neighbour, it was Carl's two drug-buddies who'd been at the top of The Shard with him, but who'd scarpered at the first hint of trouble. They were after the money Carl had hidden in the bathroom. I was determined they weren't going to get their hands on it. After all – and with Lucy's blessing - I had already earmarked it to gamble on the boxing match that night. I'd re-hidden the cash elsewhere in Lucy's flat, so that was pretty safe.

I quickly suggested to Lucy that she should tell them that the police had been around and searched the place. And they were on the phone to her right now...

About to impersonate an officer of the law, I cleared my throat ready to put on a serious and authoritative demeanour. I told Lucy to leave it to me and she played her part to Oscar-winning perfection.

As the thugs entered, I could hear all the conversation.

'We've come for the money?'

'What money?'

'Don't be smart. The money Carl had, you know he's dead, right?

'Yes, the Police told me. They were round here and searched the place and were asking a lot of questions…' Lucy had a new-found confidence – quite possibly connected to the fact that she had her own guardian angel at the other end of the phone. If only I could have been standing right next to her, then there would be no danger of anything happening to her. At the other end of the mobile, I was pretty helpless, but still determined to try and control the situation.

'What did cops say?' said the smaller of the two thugs, in a threatening manner.

'Sssh!'she said, 'they're actually on the phone to me right now!' She held out her mobile which was snatched by the taller one.

'Who's this?' he said.

'This is the police. We know who you are – who *both* of you are and I suggest you come and hand yourselves in at the police station. We have recovered around twelve thousand pounds from the property you are in right now and it is currently in the possession of forensics… I think you two might have some explaining to do!'

My new role in the Metropolitan Police, was quite satisfying, but I was also aware that I didn't want to antagonise the pair too much as there was a chance that they might take out their frustrations on Lucy.

After my short speech, I heard the word 'fuck' and then a noise. The two criminals had left quickly. They weren't worried about the police, but about the retribution from their own drugs boss. The money was their responsibility and they knew that if they didn't get it back, they would have to pay. Probably with a few broken bones.

I felt pleased at how the situation had gone, but I was also concerned about any possible repercussions that might be heading Lucy's way – even though she was completely innocent of everything. I knew I had to act. And I knew the perfect hosts.

'Lucy, please listen', I said seriously, 'I need to get you out of there as soon as possible. Carl's business partners will definitely be back at some point and you can bet they won't be very happy. Anyway, look – a 'friend-of-a-friend' knows a place where you can go, you'll be totally safe. Let me get the details…'

For a few moments I pretended to be looking for details of the 'safe-house'. In reality, I was going to get my friends Michael and Rebecca to look after her for a while.

I stressed to Lucy that I didn't know the people she'd be staying with, but I could guarantee she would be safe and well looked after. To ensure her safety I also emphasised that she had to keep quiet about what had happened and obviously about meeting someone who was invisible. That could make things very awkward for me.

Later I briefed Michael and Rebecca. 'The girl is a friend of a friend,' I said. 'She's been in a destructive relationship and needs somewhere to stay for about a week.' Michael and Rebecca were more than happy to help, as I knew they would be. Not many people would be pleased to take in a total stranger over the Christmas period, but Michael and Rebecca were so kind that I knew they'd say yes. I felt a little guilty, as I didn't want to impose on them, but this really was an emergency and I didn't think it was appropriate for Lucy to move in with me as I still wanted my anonymity.

CHAPTER TWENTY-THREE:

The fly

Out of my lounge window I could see people going about their day. Most of the snow which had fallen the previous night had disappeared, but it was still a cold day and shoppers were well wrapped-up in their coats and scarves. As I turned my head away from the light, I noticed something peculiar in my flat.

Along my windowsill walked a tiny fly. This was most unusual for the time of year. I was instantly absorbed by it and watched for several minutes in a sort of haze. Oblivious to everything around me, I moved my face closer. I wondered why the fly didn't move – and then I realised that it couldn't see me either. I got as close as I could, until I could see the mesh pattern of its eyes. Placing my finger over its back, it still didn't move. Barely a millimetre away, I could've ended its little life right there and then. I didn't though and the little fly began walking along innocently, not knowing how close he came to being squashed into messy pulp.

The tiny fly cast a tiny shadow. It was something I hadn't thought about. I was going to be in a boxing ring that evening, with a whole load of lights – would my shadow give me away? Was my shadow going to be my downfall?

My plan was in place. Lucy was betting all the drugs money on the British boxer Maxwell Green to win. My friend Michael was placing my own life savings of £2189 on to the unfancied fighter and he was also putting his own savings on too.

Maxwell Green *had* to win if I was to begin making the money I needed to improve my life when my invisibility wore off. I wasn't exactly sure how I was going to improve my life, but one million pounds might make it a little bit easier to decide. And rent day wouldn't be so tortuous.

With the intense atmosphere and thousands of people it was going to be a hot night in the O2 Arena, so I'd pre-prepared a pair of aptly named boxer shorts to fight in. I couldn't realistically wear my normal clothes for a World Title fight.

Fight Night.

The boxers dressing rooms at the O2 Arena were not as flashy as I expected. The walls were painted a sort of dirty-mint colour and the door frames were covered in scuff-marks. Each room had been kitted out with keep-fit type equipment, dumb-bells, workout mats and punch bags. I made myself at home and practiced a few of my moves in front of the large wall-mirrors which ran almost the length of the dressing room. It's a shame I couldn't see myself – I was picturing myself in a "Rocky" movie, working my socks off to try and beat the red-hot favourite.

109

My skipping was pretty good, my Ali shuffle improving, and I finished off with some exaggerated shadow boxing. I wasn't a natural athlete. Still, I was going to be live on TV and I was going to make the most of the opportunity. I hit the punch bag as hard as I could. It barely moved.

As the boxers made last-minute preparations in their dressing rooms, there were so many hangers-on standing in the doorways that even I couldn't squeeze in to find out their tactics. After a bit of jostling, I gave up and decided to make my way into the arena. I had my invisible boxing gloves on (don't ask!), my Scooby-Doo boxer shorts and my trainers.

The arena was packed to capacity with 20,000 fans singing and chanting whilst the lights were swirling their coloured beams around the arena. As I approached the ring, a boxer from the undercard was being carried back to the dressing room. I looked at him close-up as he passed me on his stretcher. There was a big bump over his left eye and blood coming from his lower lip. He looked like I did after doing my last-minute shopping in Aldi last Christmas. It was a tough experience for me – but this night was set to be even tougher.

CHAPTER TWENTY-FOUR:

Ready to rumble

Michael had placed all the money at his disposal on the unfancied British boxer and was sitting with Rebecca, both uncomfortably close to their TV set as they tuned in to watch the fight on their SKY TV Box. Lucy was also watching at her apartment. All the drugs money had been safely placed on the underdog and all that was required was for me to help knock out the world champion: Dwayne 'Feel the Pain' Dixon.

I decided to catapult myself into the ring before the two fighters emerged, so that I could soak in the atmosphere. The ring was quite a bit higher than I'd anticipated. I got tangled in the ropes and hit my chin as I flopped ungraciously on to the canvas. I quickly got to my feet and did an 'Ali shuffle' as if to hide my embarrassment. Fortunately, no one could see my misdemeanour.

When the trumpets began to sound, I knew Dwayne and Maxwell were on their way. There was a huge commotion in the distance as two groups of people made their way down separate aisles. I couldn't actually see the boxers themselves as they were totally surrounded. This is it, I thought. This is my moment. I was Sylvester Stallone, I was Rocky, I was Muhammed Ali, I was Sugar Ray Leonard, Tony Sibson, Marvin Hagler, Rocky Mancini… at least in my own mind.

For half a minute I danced around the ring like a demented Michael Flatley on acid. I bowed to the crowd, I postured like Freddie Mercury at Band Aid and I did the John Travolta – Uma Thurman dance from Pulp Fiction. Yes, if people could've seen me, they would have thought I was a total wanker. But being invisible gave me the power to be whatever I wanted to be, only in secret. I was about to find out if I had the ultimate power – the power to give a world champion a damn good hiding! At least he wasn't going to hit me back, so that gave me a little bit of extra confidence.

With the two fighters in the centre of the ring doing the obligatory staring-each-other-out, I was about two minutes away from being part of a world title fight. The British boxer Maxwell Green wasn't looking very confident. The US boxer Dwight Dixon was. And I was just a few inches away from his hard, cold stare. Even though I wasn't officially part of the fight itself, it was at that moment that I realised adrenaline was brown!

The thing which struck me the most was their physiques. Not an ounce of fat on either of them. These two men were at the peak of their powers. Two gladiators ready to do battle in front of thousands. Or, to be more accurate, two gladiators and an out-of-shape kitchen assistant in his Scooby Do underpants. Already, my task seemed like a tall order.

At two addresses in London, Michael and Rebecca, and Lucy were on the edge of their seats.

I was nervous and already sweating excessively under a hundred lights. This was my moment. And as my bravado quickly dissipated in front of twenty thousand boxing fans, I realised that this could be a little more difficult than how it looked in my fanciful head. And then the bell rang.

Round one.

Straight away, Dixon had Green backing away towards the ropes, with a flurry of razor-sharp jabs. I stood there in awe at the speed and ferociousness of the contact. For a few moments I actually forgot that I was there to help Maxwell. And by the look of it, I had to help him pretty quickly or it could be all over before I got started.

I lunged forward and hit Dixon smack bang on the nose and it had an immediate effect. He stopped in his tracks, stunned by the blow. I had nowhere near the power that Maxwell Green could dish out, but I had the surprise factor. The crowd roared, as if Green himself had made the lighting blow. I found out later that the commentators remarked that Green's punch was so fast, that it was faster than the human eye.

As Dixon shook his head at what had just happened, Green seemed to take some confidence from the crowd's roar – even though he had no responsibility for the punch, if that's what it could have been described as. A playground slap might have been a better description. Momentarily, Dixon shook his head. It was almost as if he'd walked into some sort of forcefield around the British fighter.

I knew I had to time my punches better – they had to land pretty much as Green threw a punch. It wasn't going to be easy. And I was sweating like a pig at a BBQ that had a sausage shortage.

As the boxers engaged in the action centre-ring, I ran around the outside and threw a big punch which caught Dixon at the side of his eye. This time Dixon stopped in his tracks and swayed backwards for a second. The crowd noise went up a level, and Green could hardly believe his luck.

At the end of the first round, I was completely knackered. And whilst the boxers sat on stools provided by their corners, I laid flat out on the canvas in a starfish shape, trying to get my breath back. The referee actually tripped over me as he walked across the ring, and just avoided hitting the deck himself. He quickly grabbed a towel and came to wipe the canvas, so I had to move out of the way pretty sharpish.

When the bell rang for round two, I'd hardly got my breath back.

The next three minutes were pretty even, although I'd say that Dixon still edged it. He was a bit more cautious, but then let rip with bursts of aggression. Because I was already exhausted, I threw less punches, but tried to make them count. At one point I decided to let Dixon have my best body-shot, but when my hand connected, it was like I'd hit a concrete wall. His muscles were like steel.

With my help, the British underdog was doing OK. He was still standing after six minutes, but I knew I had to up my game to secure the financial rewards from the bookmakers.

Round three was very encouraging. The crowd were getting behind Green whilst the champion Dixon had no answer to me bopping him out of the blue on a couple of occasions. Even though I didn't have the power to really hurt him, I could hit him at will and when I did, he looked like he'd got a nervous tick, as he kept moving his face sideways. He constantly looked around nervously, but had no inclination of the powers at work.

The fourth round was another good one. Just as Dixon looked to be getting on top, I walloped him. After one punch I actually did a cheeky dance (YMCA by The Village People), despite my depleted energy reserves. At the end of the fourth round, I whispered to him that he was a beaten man, and that he was going to go down in the fifth. Yes, the fifth was going to be when I made a lot of money. I was becoming more confident myself, even though when I actually laid a glove on Dixon, it sent shockwaves through my own body more than his.

Round Five.

Dwight Dixon seemed really fired-up for round five and perhaps maybe it was my fault for goading him. It's easy to get carried away when you're invisible and by teasing him at the end of round four I hadn't done myself or Maxwell Green any favours. In fact, if anything it looked like I'd really pissed him off. He began with a flurry of punches and had Green rocking on the ropes. Green looked to be tiring fast, so I decided to give Dixon my big 'haymaker'. As I stepped forward ready to give him it, Dixon threw a big 'haymaker' of his own - which Green luckily ducked out of the way from. Unfortunately for me, I didn't.

I was flattened. I laid on the canvas staring at the lights dazzling me from above. Luckily it was a blow that was losing power as it hit me, but it was still powerful enough to lift me off my feet. Unlike the boxers in the ring, I didn't have the luxury of a ten count. Perhaps just as well really as

I wouldn't have made it. After crawling on all-fours for a few moments, I used the ropes to rise shakily to my feet.

Green was under sustained pressure and I knew I had to do something pretty dramatic to make a difference in this fight. Even though I was still slightly dazed, I attempted to do my 'Ali shuffle'. There, that showed how serious I was taking it all. Then the bell went. End of round five. Thank the lord.

Round six.

The break between rounds was a godsend. I was boiling – and had no water. I was exhausted, even though I'd only put in a fraction of the work that Dixon and Green had. These guys were so amazingly fit. I had severely underestimated their sheer power. They were like two walls of concrete with steel girders inside.

Dixon was out-punching Green three-to-one and it seemed just a matter of time before the British boxer was going to be decked. I summoned up all the energy I had left and ran towards Dixon as fast as I could. I must have been going at a reasonable speed as I could feel my Scooby Doo boxer shorts flapping against my legs. I aimed my punch towards Dixon's stomach, but my effort glanced off Green's glove as he tried to land a punch of his own and I hit Dixon right in the balls... and he went down faster than a hooker in an oral sex competition. The poor guy collapsed on the floor in agony. I went down on all fours with the sheer exertion. My God... I'd managed to stop Dixon. Thank God for that.

Green meanwhile was slightly bemused but was celebrating nonetheless whilst his corner men scratched their heads at the sudden turnaround in their man's fortunes. For a few minutes, it seemed that I had salvaged a victory from the jaws of defeat. But, as Dixon's corner protested, I quickly realised that I had made a monumental error. Well, it was accidental, as I hadn't purposely aimed for his tackle.

Green was disqualified for an illegally low punch which had poleaxed the American just as he was coasting to victory. Fuck.

As I began thinking of the ramifications of being a twat, I began to feel dizzy. That clobbering from Dixon was having an impact on me. And to be honest, I probably deserved it for thinking that I could smack a world champion hard enough to stop him beating an inferior fighter. I looked up at the lights in the arena and everything began to blur. The sound all around me became distant and I genuinely heard the tweeting of birds flying around my head.

When I came around twenty minutes later, the fighters had left the ring, the post-fight interviews had been done and Green had been guided back to the dressing room in a state of confusion. He was confused due to the power and frequency of the punches which had pummelled his face and also by the fact that he got disqualified for an illegal punch that he wasn't actually responsible for throwing.

The arena was virtually empty and I had a rotten headache. The sort of headache that two Anadins wasn't going to cure.

Dwayne Dixon's earnings for the night: Fifteen million. My earnings: Zero. In fact, I'd made a loss. Twelve grand of drugs money, over two thousand pounds of my own and then my friends had also lost theirs too. I wasn't going to be very popular with Michael and Rebecca. Or with luscious Lucy Pendleton.

CHAPTER TWENTY-FIVE:

The aftermath

I was told later that back at my friend's house, the conversation went something like this:

Michael: What the chuff just happened?

Rebecca: Did we lose?

Michael: Er, like, yeah!

Rebecca: I thought we were supposed to win?

Michael: That was the general idea.

Rebecca: Coop seemed so convinced our man would win, didn't he?

Michael: Yeah. He said it was a dead cert'. He'll be a dead cert when I get hold of him. And I hope he remembers to bring me that Toblerone when he comes back from Switzerland, because I'm going to enjoy sticking it up his arse!

Rebecca: Don't you think he'll be already feeling bad enough? He's just lost his life savings…

Michael paused.

Michael: …Not just his I'm afraid…

Rebecca: Oh no…

Michael: I'm so sorry Becs…
Rebecca: How much?
Michael: …Everything…
Rebecca cried.

The tube ride to Lucy's was awful. As the train carriage jostled, my head ached even more and even though I virtually had a carriage to myself, I felt hemmed in. A prisoner. A prisoner with a damaged face. Thank God I couldn't see myself reflected in the window.

Walking to Lucy's flat, the wind got up and blew a newspaper against my body. It wrapped around me and I didn't even bother to try and remove it. Being invisible was supposed to be an exhilarating, euphoric experience. Actually, at that moment, it was really shit.

CHAPTER TWENTY-SIX:

The blue pebble

When I was a child, I kept a small metal tin underneath my bed. In it I stored items which I'd found, been given, or that I thought were lucky.

One of my favourite items was a pebble. I'm guessing that most kids have a favourite pebble at some point in their young lives. My pebble was slightly blue, worn smooth and was about an inch and a half in length. For reasons which I shall tell you in a minute, my blue pebble had three signatures on it: Professor Chambon, The Commander-in-Chief of the French Navy and the Mayor of Barfleur. These three officials told me personally that the pebble had magical powers and would always bring me luck.

They'd say any old shit to a kid.

My parents and I were on holiday in the small town of Barfleur in the South of France and found this perfect little beach which most tourists were seemingly unaware of. It was perfect for rock-pooling. My dad surprised us by producing a small glass bottle which had a cork in it. He also produced a piece of paper and a pen.

He said we were going to send a message in a bottle. It was all very dramatic and exciting. My dad wrote the note. I can't remember what it said, but at the end, he wrote: Whoever finds this message in a bottle, please contact Cooper McRae, 56 Poplar road, Wimbledon. England.

The note was rolled-up and placed into the bottle. We did a launch ceremony and threw the bottle out to sea - and that was the last time we saw it. We thought nothing more about it until two years later when we received a letter. Our message in a bottle had been found.

The discovery of our message in a bottle had made national newspapers. It was the talk of the area in which it was discovered. One guy had spent two weeks trying to work out its route, taking into consideration the currents, tides and weather patterns. Our message in a bottle had been on a remarkable adventure. Several local schools had even done projects about it.

Where was it discovered? Wedged between two rocks on a secluded beach near the beautiful coastal town of… Barfleur in the South of France!

Yes, we'd given it the launch with royal salute and dramatically thrust it out to sea. What we didn't see was that it simply came back in on the next wave and got stuck between two rocks, which is where it stayed for a couple of years until it was discovered. Professor Chambon discovered it and assumed it had been sent from the address on the message in England. Of course, when we were contacted by the Mayor of Barfleur, we were told of all the fuss and news coverage, but my dad couldn't bring himself to tell them we launched it while we were there on holiday. He said it seemed such a shame to spoil all their excitement and even suggested that if the truth came out it could spoil

French-Anglo relations – but I didn't know what that meant.

However, we were almost celebrities and were invited over for a free holiday to celebrate and cement our bond-of-adventure. I was personally presented with a polished blue stone which first attracted the professor's attention near to where the bottle was found. As a good luck memento, it was ceremoniously signed by the three officials.

The shiny blue pebble had never brought me any luck that I was aware of – unless you count our free holiday - but I still kept hold of it, just in case. The blue pebble would play a pivotal part in my story.

CHAPTER TWENTY-SEVEN:

And my face still hurt

My boxing debut had been a complete disaster. As I waited outside Lucy's door, I was intending to do a walk of shame along her hallway and I was ready for an inquest. How could I have got it so wrong? It was nearly midnight and after two days of invisibility, I had not only accumulated sweet FA, but I had actually lost money. My life savings were no more, the drugs money was now in the pocket of a bookie and my face was hurting badly along with my pride. To think of all the advantages I had and yet was still a loser was quite a sobering thought, yet as soon as I saw Lucy, it no longer mattered so much.

I almost expected Lucy to say, 'What on earth have you done to your face?' but she couldn't see it, so that never happened. I purposely half-turned away when she put her hands out to greet me.

'Thanks for stopping by,' she said, giving me a big smile, even though she was looking in the wrong direction as I had already moved past her and into the lounge.

I didn't say anything. I was too embarrassed.

'Are you OK, is something wrong?'

'Well… I had a bit of bad luck. And all the money I had, we had… er, well, we don't have it now!'

'Yes, I saw the boxing match. You know what? Money is meaningless,' said Lucy waving her arms in the air. 'All it has ever brought me is pain. I'd rather have a pound and be happy than have a million and be unhappy.'

'That's great!' I replied. Inside I was thinking that I still had five days to make amends, so all was not lost.

'So, what have you been doing this evening, anything exciting? Did you actually see the fight itself?' she enquired.

'I didn't do much,' I replied, grimacing in pain as I touched my face. Of course, I hadn't divulged that I would be in the ring myself as I thought it made me look slightly dishonest.

As I looked around, I could see a couple of suitcases were packed and placed to one side of the settee.

'Are you going on holiday?'

'I'm going to stay at the safe house. Remember? You arranged it!'

'Oh yeah, I did.'

Lucy was being picked up the following morning by Michael and was going to stay with them until I had got safely back from Switzerland or wherever it was, I was supposed to be on holiday. I'd come up with the story off the top of my head and I was regularly getting my alibi mixed up. I really should have written it all down and practiced my story.

Lucy just thought that she was going to some random safehouse, she had no idea they were my best friends. It would be best to keep it like that, or things would get too complicated.

'Remember not to tell them anything about me or the fact that I'm invisible.' I reminded her for the last time. The whole idea seemed so implausible that they would laugh anyway. They'd probably think she was doing drugs.

'Don't worry, I'm not going to say anything at all... my lips are sealed.'

'Good.' I replied, focusing on Lucy's beautiful lips and how much I'd like to kiss them. At least I would when I wasn't in pain.

All my exertions had taken their toll on me and I desperately needed a shower, so Lucy got me a towel and I made my way into the bathroom.

'Don't take this the wrong way,' I said, 'but you can watch me if you like!'

'I've taken that the wrong way,' she said laughing.

'No, you'll be amazed what it looks like when water goes over me, it's incredible!'

I placed all my clothes carefully on a chair so that they'd be easy to find. Despite being invisible I still felt surprisingly self-conscious as Lucy stood in the doorway. When the water was hot enough, I stepped into the shower.

'It's OK, you can come over here,' I said. 'Feast your eyes on this!'

'Is that one of your old chat-up lines?' nodded Lucy, who stood there with her arms folded, as if she'd been through similar scenarios before.

As the individual jets of water hit my body, they began to give me form, a shape. Even I could see that the glistening beads were a thing of beauty, running over the contours of my body. In a non-sexual way, I was exposing myself to Lucy for the first time. She could make out my body shape, my height, my broad shoulders... I was like one of those geography maps where they showed you the shape of the land.

'That is amazing,' She gasped.

'Yeah, that's what all the girls say,' I commented nonchalantly.

Lucy didn't say anything else. She was captivated by the sparkling cascade. At that moment, she felt the thrill of voyeurism. She told me later that it was more like a religious awakening than an erotic encounter.

'So, what do you think then?'

'You've got a very sexy outline... and being completely honest, I don't think I've ever said that to anyone before.' Said Lucy shaking her head.

'I'll take that as a compliment,' I replied, turning off the shower. Lucy walked off as I dried myself.

A few minutes later, we were in deep conversation about movies. I loved Groundhog Day, and so did Lucy. I loved Four Weddings and a Funeral, and so did Lucy. I loved The Holiday and oh, you know the rest.

We chatted away into the early hours. In between our surprise at loving the same movies, I entertained Lucy by moving random objects around in the air, like I was her own private spirit. It would've made a fantastic episode for the TV series 'Most Haunted'. My dad would've loved it.

I stayed the night, falling asleep on the couch whilst trying to conjure up a better plan than my boxing fiasco. My ill-advised foray into the fight game had left me shaken and determined to do good with my new power. But, what could I do with it? I'd make a brilliant fairground attraction, but that was just a form of quirky entertainment – it seemed that no matter how hard I tried, I couldn't elevate my status beyond the whimsical.

The next day was December 24th. Christmas Eve.

I was a big fan of Christmas, but things had been so hectic that it had completely slipped my mind.

CHAPTER TWENTY-EIGHT:

Christmas Eve

My third day of invisibility.

At five minutes to ten in the morning, I felt someone gently touching my shoulder. Lifting the blanket which I'd draped over myself, I watched as Lucy placed a coffee on a small table next to the settee.

'It's Christmas Eve!' chirped Lucy, festively, although there was not a single Christmas decoration or tree to be seen anywhere around her flat. Still, in less than an hour my friends Michael and Rebecca were going to be there to collect her and take her to the safety of their own place. In the kitchen, Lucy had turned on the radio and Bruce Springsteen was singing Santa Claus is coming to town. We both merrily sang along without actually knowing the words, as we had a cup of tea.

I briefed Lucy again about her stay at the "safe house" even though I knew she wouldn't say anything to anyone. She couldn't know who I was, it would only complicate matters and would probably diminish the chances of her falling in love with me – as if *that* was going to happen!

Michael arrived without Rebecca, who he said wasn't feeling well. I secretly watched their first meeting after telling Lucy that I had to leave to sort something out. They were chatting away as they left. Lucy was going to be a guest at 49 Pembridge Crescent, Knightsbridge. It was a delightful place to live - a row of three-story town houses all with fronts painted in different pastel shades. Normally, the rents on such a property would've been way out of Michael and Rebecca's reach, but Michael's grandparents owned several properties and so they got 'family rates' – which Michael said was 'outstanding!'

As expected on Christmas Eve the streets of London were heaving with last-minute shoppers and I'd ventured out without a concrete plan. I was angry with myself for not being better prepared. I knew I had to cash in on my uniqueness as soon as possible. At that moment I was actually worse off than before I had jumped into my magic bath.

The cafés were especially busy, and I would have loved to have stopped for a giant mocha and slice of lemon drizzle cake, but the thing about being invisible – secretly invisible – is that your social life is pretty much restricted. Pandemonium would break out if I sat there and had a coffee as my invisible self. I'd be a freak, a novelty, something to stare at. So, I had to do without. But that didn't stop me looking over the shoulder of a gentleman reading a newspaper as he sat outside Costa. He was wearing a black winter coat and had a furry hat perched awkwardly on his head. He looked like a well-to-do gent, but was surprisingly reading The Daily Star, a tabloid newspaper.

As I scanned the stories, one in particular jumped out to me. The headline read: Serial sex-offender released on technicality. A blunder in procedure had led to the prime suspect in several cases walking free from court. The reporter revealed that the suspect 'smirked' when the judge halted proceedings and ended the trial. I'm pretty sure that the suspect in every case who gets off despite being guilty 'smirks' – or that's what the newspapers would have you believe. But I believed it anyway. The story gave me a purpose. If I couldn't find a method to make money, then it was time I moved into Gandhi – or 'Dexter' mode.

I was a huge fan of the series 'Dexter', the serial killer who worked for the Miami police as a blood splatter expert. He specialised in disposing of criminals who had beaten the system and he dispatched them in a particular way. He abducted them and then wrapped them in cling-film before dismembering them. In my mind I had already put myself in his shoes – and I vowed to visit Poundland and get a role of cling-film as soon as possible! OK, I wasn't suddenly going to turn in to a killer, but at that moment I knew that I wanted to do something of merit and significance. At least it was a way in which I could actually help people using my own uniqueness.

I decided to head for the police station to find out the facts. As I weaved between the shoppers, I decided that without a money-making option, my best option was to do something useful until I did. I wasn't exactly sure what I would do, but I intended to find out who the suspect was, where he lived, and take it from there. Before I had fully finished reading the story, the gentleman turned over the page. Cheekily, I kept turning it back. It looked like a breeze was in control, but I did it several times, much to the amusement of people sitting nearby.

The Police station was located on Grosvenor road and it was simplicity itself to gain entrance to the secure environment. Once inside, I decided to have a wander around to see what was going on in the building. I was about to have my first stroke of luck.

Two men were in custody and were busy having their details taken. It was Carl's two drug-dealing buddies. They stood handcuffed at a desk and were giving their details to the custody sergeant whilst flanked by two sturdy police officers. I followed their progress, made a mental note of their address and proceeded into the office sections of the huge 1970's building. The whole place was carpeted – which I thought must be a nightmare to keep clean – and I eventually arrived in a big, open-plan office space where each officer was cordoned off by Perspex. It was like stepping back into a retro cop TV series. Even the computers had an outdated look to them. However, I wasn't there to pass comment on the unfashionable furnishings, I was there to find out about the serial sex-offender let loose on a technicality. God, I hated technicalities and administrative blunders. Why weren't people held to account for their incompetence? We were talking about people's lives. Did that mean anything to anyone?

Two officers stood discussing the boxing match from the night before. It was hard to hear about it - especially as my face carried the still-painful scars of defeat. In a far corner of the office, a group of police personnel were gathered, and a woman in her fifties was talking. I went over and realised it was a discussion of the previous days court verdict on the sex offender.

'We have to continue, be patient, be methodical, and be diligent,' said the senior officer who wore her hair up in a precarious bun. Her make-up was faultless and whilst she spoke, she rubbed the thumb and forefinger of her left-hand together. I got the impression she was furious, but was trying to suppress it and let her professionalism win the day. At the end of her speech, she lapsed and let her own feelings be known. 'We'll get this bastard!' said Detective Inspector Jane Turner. The group of officers nodded silently. They may have lost the court case through no fault of their own, but they were about to have some additional help. I stood right next to DI Turner, as if I was her newly elected second-in-command.

On a screen to my left showed the case details. The suspect was called Fabian Judson. Fabian? What sort of name was that? No wonder he turned out to be a twisted individual. There was a photograph of him, obviously taken in custody where he was looking directly into the camera with a look of contempt of his face. His skin was far from perfect and he had a scar which dissected his right eyebrow. He was thirty years of age and worked as a delivery driver. Why did so many predators drive for a living? They were almost always cabbies or lorry drivers.

I already despised 'Fabian' and when I read that he had a track record of sexual offending it nearly tipped me over the edge. It always struck me as weird that when offenders were in open prisons and failed to return after a day out, the authorities said that they were not to be approached as they were dangerous. Well, why on earth where they being allowed out for the day if they were dangerous? Surely, they should still have been locked away?

As I contemplated this moral conundrum, I took the opportunity to scroll down the screen to see a list of the crimes he had committed and the victims he had violated. It made for very, very grim reading.

The list was much longer than I had anticipated, and with each attack I read, the angrier I became.

As I scanned the depressing list, I stopped dead in my tracks. Suddenly the whole world, my whole world began to spin. I was dizzy, the room became a blur, and the chatting in the office faded in the distance. The list of attacks Fabian Judson had been charged with and subsequently acquitted of ran to more than two pages, over a period of five years. Below them was a list of other attacks which police believed he was connected to. One in particular stood out from the list.

My friend Rebecca had been a victim seven years before.

Of course, I didn't know anything about it and I'm pretty sure Michael wasn't aware of it either. They'd been an item for the last five years and I jumped to the plausible conclusion that the attack was quite probably the reason that Rebecca often had days when she sunk into depression, if that's what it was.

Wonderful Rebecca. When she was feeling good, she loved making everyone laugh. She was sharp, vivacious and could twist things to make something really boring become hilarious. She was good fun to have around and such a lovely person who wouldn't harm a fly. It has often been said that people who joke all the time were much deeper than they'd have you believe. Was Rebecca's personality a reflection of the trauma? Michael and Rebecca were such amazing friends to me and if I could do anything at all to help, then I would. Absolutely anything.

I was angry, almost shaking with rage at the thought of Rebecca being the victim of such despicable evil. She was kind, considerate, polite and wouldn't hurt anyone. Sometimes, the law was a useless piece of shit. I knew that I had to help the police if I could - especially as they had almost run out of options. I would have to be the law from now on. At that moment I was ready to do what was necessary. Not only for all the victims of Judson's crimes, but for all the future one's too. I was like a see-through Robocop.

I doubted the police had Judson under surveillance and even if they had, there's no way they could do the job as effectively as me. Determined to get the inside information, my mind was made up and this dreadful news had given me a purpose.

As I tried to find my way out of the police station, I took the opportunity to look in on the druggies who were friends of Carl. Their names were Leon and Joe and as I walked down a long corridor, I looked into one of the interview rooms to see what was going on inside. At the fourth door along on the left, I stopped when I saw Leon being questioned by two police officers. I knocked on the door and stood back. When the door was opened, I squeezed inside to witness the session. Leon was refusing to answer most questions: Where were you on the night of December 22nd? Nothing. What was your working relationship with Carl Brooke? Nothing.

After a few minutes getting nowhere, I was beginning to get bored and was just about to contrive another fake knock on the door so that I could leave, when things took an interesting but worrying turn.

'When we recovered Carl Brooke's body from a skip near The Shard, we got access to his mobile. Do you know a female called Lucy Pendleton?' The police officers again waited patiently for a reply.

'You know I do!' laughed Leon. 'You spoke to me while I was there. She's a friend of mine. Are these the best questions you're going to ask me? If you can't do better, then let me go you useless idiots. You don't have anything on me. Or on my boy Joe either...'

I took the opportunity at that point to knock over Leon's plastic cup of water, all over his trousers. The police laughed and Leon protested that it was 'assault'.

'Was Carl involved in drugs?' Again, Leon ignored the question.

'Look, you got the money and drugs he stashed at Lucy's. Of course, he was involved, but we were just friends with him – we had common interests.'

The police officers looked at each other mystified by Leon's claims.

'What money and drugs?'

'The money and drugs you got – that you took. You know man, the gear Carl had hidden at Lucy's. Don't try and fool with me, you told me on the phone when I was at Lucy's...'

'We don't know anything about any money or drugs from Miss Pendleton's...'

A minute later, I could see Leon's brain trying to work out the connotations from his chat in police interview room 207. It was obvious, that if Carl hadn't taken the money and drugs – and he hadn't because he was dead - and if the police didn't know anything about it either, then whoever was on the phone at Lucy's was responsible - and that meant Lucy was implicated too. Implicated up to her pretty eyeballs. The drugs-dealing duo would soon realise that the only way to retrieve the money was to get hold of Lucy before their boss put an electric cattle-prod onto their testicles.

Smiles and laughs were in abundance as I walked London's streets, it was only me who brought the mood down. It wasn't easy mingling with the visible as I was constantly getting bumped into and jostled. People couldn't see me and I was managing to accumulate a selection of bruises around my ankles which meant I had to be on my guard. I must admit I gently pushed people away if they were about to invade my personal space. I just wanted to get home, call Lucy and make her aware of the situation. Suddenly, my day had got very complicated and I was still light years away from fulfilling my objective of making a million. It would be easy to accumulate wealth if I didn't give a fuck, I said to myself as I barged past another group of festive merrymakers.

At midday I looked down Eversholt street. A bus had just stopped a few doors down from where I lived, and a queue of people surged forward hardly allowing any space for people to get off. The big lad who lived upstairs was one of those trying to exit the bus. In his arms he clutched a large package. He always had a package in his hands. What on earth was he doing? The guy was definitely overweight, but I knew it wasn't food he was carrying. For a moment my mind wandered, and I forgot the urgency to get home. I needed to call Lucy and make her aware of Leon and Joe's likely realisation that they would soon put two-and-two together... and make Lucy!

I was tempted to follow my substantial neighbour up to his flat and see exactly what he was up to, but that had to wait until later. As soon as I opened my door, I felt much more relaxed. I could be by myself. I could pick my nose, or trip over my own rug - which I did. Even though no one was ever going to see me, in my own space I could slouch and lose myself without having to take everyone else into consideration. My eyes were tired with constantly having to monitor situations to stop people walking straight into me, sitting on me, or spilling hot drinks over me. I was a walking accident waiting to happen.

As I fell onto my settee, I glanced around the room. For the first time ever, I had failed to be invigorated by the spirit of Christmas. There was no tree or trimmings and even the few Christmas cards I'd been sent were in a messy pile on the mantlepiece. If someone had taken a look at my flat, they'd have said a miserable fuck lived there. At that moment, I actually was a miserable fuck. Supposedly, I was the luckiest man in the world – or something like that. I was certainly supposed to be one of the happiest people alive, with my new super-power. But I was far from that. Everything had got very complicated very quickly. I wished I could have started my week of invisibility all over again.

It was only the third day out of seven and I felt like I'd squandered the opportunity so far. I knew I had to stop feeling selfish. Lots of people were much worse off than me and there I was wallowing in self-pity. I was beginning to hate myself. My sense of humour had gone AWOL. I put the kettle on, attempted to snap out of it and made a couple of phone calls.

CHAPTER TWENTY-NINE:

A call from Switzerland

Michael answered the phone.

'Hi, it's me, calling from Switzerland…'

'Who?' said Michael.

'It's me, for fuck's sake. It's me, Cooper – how many people do you know that are in Switzerland?'

'Ohhh, Coop, it's you! How are you doing?' he replied, 'Are you holding an alpine horn?'

'Well it's never been called that before, but I guess that's why I should be making porn movies and not washing dishes!' I joked. 'Why would I be holding an alpine horn?'

'Why not?' said Michael, seriously.

'How's she doing? How's Lu… er, the girl doing? Has she settled in alright?'

'Yeah, of course she's alright. She's a complete delight! She's upstairs helping Rebecca chose a dress online…'

'Great stuff,' I said, 'well keep your eye on her and don't let her go out on her own for the moment…' The very fact that Lucy was with Rebecca made me feel so much better. I hoped that the two of them would become good friends.

I was trying to keep things vague, as I'd told Michael she was simply a friend of a friend who just needed somewhere to stay, so I didn't want to appear too interested, or know too much about her. As I was thinking about my next question, Michael changed the subject.

'Anyway, stop trying to act all friendly, you've got some explaining to do. What happened with the boxing match? I thought you said you had some inside information? You told me to put all my money on the British guy... and unfortunately, I listened to you...

'Michael, I'm so sorry. I really am' I said, touching the sore part of my face where I took the blow from Dwight Dixon. 'But listen to me, I promise to make it up to you... Everything is going to be fine. Whatever you lost, I'm going to get back, honestly, it's not a problem. Not a problem at all.'

'It's OK, just forget it. Anyway, when are you back from Austria?'

'Switzerland.'

'Whatever, when are you back?'

'In a few days... how's Rebecca?'

'Oh, I guess she's doing OK. She's had a couple of bad days. You know how it is...'

I knew exactly 'how it was'. If there was one thing I was going to fix while I was invisible, it was Fabian Judson. I suspected that Rebecca had seen the news, seen a photograph of her attacker and it had sent her back into a dark place. Poor Rebecca. And poor Michael. It would kill him if he knew what had happened.

Michael continued, 'But Rebecca's been noticeably better today and perked up with Lucy around, they seemed to click straight away. It's good that the girls can chat together. You know, they can talk about girl things and that!'

After speaking to Michael, I had a shower, waited ten minutes and rang Lucy.

As soon as I heard Lucy's voice I was instantly re-energised and affable.

'HG, how's it going?'

'OK. Can I just ask... you haven't mentioned the word "invisible" to Michael or Rebecca, have you?'

'No, I promised I wouldn't. Your secret is safe.'

'Good, well listen, I was at the police station earlier this morning and those two guys who worked with Carl were in there being questioned. They asked about the money that the police had apparently seized from yours - and the police said they didn't know anything about any money. So, it's just a matter of time before they realise we were behind it. And I reckon they'll be coming to look for you. You have to stay inside and keep a low profile. Keep yourself safe at Michael's for the next two or three days. Meanwhile, I'll sort everything out...' As I bigged-up my capabilities, I felt a little more pressure to actually do something right for once.

'I've missed you.' Said Lucy, out of the blue.

I didn't know what to say. But I liked it.

'Oh,' I said, taken aback by the sign of affection, if that's what it was. When I thought about it later, I kicked myself for not saying the same back to her.

'It's weird talking to you on the phone, it's just like you're a normal person. Just like anyone else.'

'I soon *will* be just like anyone else,' I said quietly. It was just a matter of time before I was no longer special. Even though a bit of normality appealed to me, I wasn't bowled over by the thought of it. There was so much to do and so little time.

'How are you settling in? Are the people alright?'

'Yes, it's all good thanks. They're called Michael and Rebecca and everything's really good. I haven't been here long, but it feels like I've known them for ages...'

After speaking to Lucy, I went and laid on my bed. I took some of my clothes off and instantly felt much more liberated. Picking up a photo frame from the side of my bed, there was still a photograph of my ex-girlfriend Sarah on display. I turned the frame face down, as I felt I was being deceitful to Lucy.

My mind jumped to JC Cosmetics. I'd thought it was a dead-end job when I took it – I saw it as something to do until I found something of consequence. I was completely oblivious to what sort of thing went on there. My life then was much simpler: Wash-up, tidy-up, wash-up, dry-up, put away. Simple. All I had to worry about was Ledley's out-of-control romantic desires and what my plans were for the weekend. As I lay there trying to work out what to do next, there was a knock on the door. I could hear crying from the other side. I wasn't expecting anyone.

Obviously, I couldn't answer the door in my invisible state of course, so I just stood there, covering my genitals, wondering what to do. It was definitely a girl and she was crying. I was unable to do anything so just remained motionless.

The crying continued. It sounded like my ex-girlfriend Sarah. But still I didn't do or say anything. I felt guilty doing nothing, but what else could I do?

Our relationship had been quite superficial in many ways. We were just right for each other at the time. It was convenient for both of us, but we also liked each other too. We weren't using each other; we were just like friends with benefits. Neither had any idea of where we would each end up, or what we'd go on to do.

Sarah never dithered when making a decision. She said that ditherers never accomplished anything. And there I was, dithering like the World Dithering Champion.

Contemplating talking to her from my side of the door, an idea flashed into my head was that I could say I was just about to get into the shower. I could have unlocked the door and bolted into the bathroom, quickly turning on the water for that extra bit of authenticity. One thing I knew for certain was that I wasn't going to let her see me. I almost asked her if she'd brought back my Meat Loaf albums, but I thought that might come across as insensitive in the situation.

I found myself getting frustrated with my inactivity. It would have been far easier if she'd just phoned me on my mobile or sent me a Facebook message or something. After what seemed like a few minutes, a folded piece of paper came under my door. I then heard footsteps leading away. Sarah had gone. It was virtually a repeat performance of the last time she left my flat. I didn't see her then, either.

Picking it up, I gently unfolded it before lying on my settee to read the message. This is what it said:

"Sorry to leave you a note like this. I know our relationship wasn't very serious, but I am pregnant and of course the baby is yours. Maybe we can make a fresh start? Please call me when you've had time to think. X"

I folded the paper back into four and then opened it and read it again. It still said the same thing, so I read it again. And then read it again. I could hardly take it in. Me, going to be a father? Was I supposed to celebrate? I didn't feel remotely like toasting a possible Cooper McCrae Junior. My top priority and number one love was Lucy Pendleton! OK, Lucy had never ever seen my face, but I could dream, couldn't I? Was I ready for fatherhood? No. Was I ready to change nappies fifty times per day? Definitely not. My career wasn't exactly putting me in the big league. In fact, it wasn't even putting me in the small league. How could I afford to have a child? What a mess...

Pacing around my lounge, I tripped over my rug again and then slumped back on to the settee, my mind racing with the possible implications Sarah's visit had brought. My life was getting more and more complicated by the hour. Perhaps I'd have been better off just having a normal Christmas holiday like everyone else. I had Carl's druggy mates to stop from finding Lucy, I had a sexual predator to sort out, a million quid to source and suddenly I had a possible new family to cope with. Washing up sounded like heaven when compared to that list. And, of course, I only had about three days to sort everything out.

I looked in the mirror. This power of invisibility was already changing me – and not for the better. I suddenly felt shit about the note from Sarah. Not because of the note itself, but because my attitude was so egocentric. Poor Sarah was carrying a baby and didn't know what to do, yet there I was just thinking I didn't want to change nappies. That attitude really wasn't me.

CHAPTER THIRTY:

Baby blues

Even though I wasn't seriously considering having Sarah back, I flipped open my laptop and googled 'schools in the local area!' Was I going fucking mad? What about Lucy? Lucy, 'the one' Pendleton. She was the one who filled my thoughts, who occupied my mind and gave substance to my romantic hopes. She had even said she missed me just minutes earlier. Did that actually mean anything? There could never be anyone else for me but Lucy. Yes, I was responsible for Sarah's condition, but did I have to get back together with her for the sake of the baby? I was in a difficult position and the timing was terrible. I was making myself tired with the sudden stress of it all. Reading Sarah's note once more, I dragged the duvet over my head.

Half an hour later it was 2pm and I had things to do. I freshened myself up, brushed my teeth and smiled at the toothbrush working itself. I walked briskly from the front door to the pavement, which was exactly ten steps and then looked both ways along my street.

The air was crisp, people were moving slightly faster than normal. My eyes were drawn to next door's cat which was sitting in the window with a party hat on. I stared at it for what seemed like quite a while. Normally, I'd have said it was cruel to put a hat on a cat, but I swear that the cat was enjoying it. He seemed to have a smile on his face. Or was it a grimace? Then I remembered that the next-door neighbours were 'drug-friendly' so considered whether their moggy had been scoffing their secret stash.

Chestnut Avenue. Fabian Judson lived at number 36. He was a delivery driver, so would probably be out on his rounds – although I wasn't sure what he actually delivered or who he worked for. If he worked for one of the big companies like Sainsburys, he could be out until late at night. I decided to go and see where he lived. My thoughts were that he was either a loner, or lived at home with his mother, who doted on him.

As I walked towards Chestnut Avenue, I popped into a convenience store and helped myself to a banana. I hadn't eaten much at all over the last few days, I'd had too many things on my mind to contemplate my dietary needs. I promised myself I'd get a takeaway later on. My own cupboards were pretty bare at home – it was bad planning on my part. It was the haphazard planning of a single twenty-five-year-old dishwasher.

Soon, I was standing outside number 36, under a lamppost. I was hoping the image looked like the original poster for The Exorcist movie. A stranger standing outside a house where sheer evil lurked within. This was such a house. I was on a reconnaissance mission rather than a murder mission. My aim was to learn something about

Fabian Judson. And I was about to find out some surprising information.

There wasn't a vehicle parked on the drive and the lights were on in the lounge, but there didn't seem to be anyone at home. I cupped my face and held it against the lounge window of the Victorian terrace. Fabian was a delivery driver according to the police records, but his house was worth in the region of three quarters of a million pounds. How did that work? He'd obviously been putting in a bit of overtime!

The lounge wallpaper was a retro 1950's style design with lots of flowers and pastel colours. The furniture was all white, shabby-chic and classy. This didn't look like the house where a serial loner or sexual predator lived. Had I got the right address? As I cast my eyes around the lounge, a good-looking woman in her thirties entered the room and was obviously looking for something. I instinctively pulled my face away from the glass in case she saw the vapour from my breath. After half a minute, she walked back out of the room and then returned holding a magazine and a drink. Fabian Judson was certainly not the loner I had imagined, but in a way, it made me hate him even more. Did she know he was guilty of all those evil crimes? Had she provided him with an alibi, or was she completely innocent and being controlled by this monster? I knew I had to get inside and find out.

The front door was locked. I saw the woman peering from the bay window to see who was knocking. She disappeared and a few seconds later I heard a key turning and she stood on the doorstep, looking around. Like a ghost, I was ready to flit past her as soon as there was an opening. She took two steps out of the house and I was

147

inside. The floors were all wooden and painted white. They actually looked great and for a moment I thought I might have my flat done in a similar style. They looked very stylish, but unfortunately, as I walked into the house, I realised they were creaky.

My inspection began upstairs, that way I didn't have to walk around on my tiptoes all the time. The woman eventually closed the door and locked it. By that time, I was making my way well up the carpeted stairs. Halfway up I stopped momentarily to look at a framed photograph. It was one of those outdated images of a young couple shot in soft-focus. The image was obviously of Fabian Judson with an older woman, who I guessed to be his mother. His face sported an impressive array of zits and his eyebrows were totally out of control. My eyes were drawn to them and I put my own face two inches from the glass. He reminded me of a young Fred West – the serial killer who looked like a cross between a special-needs stone-age man and a fucking moron. Yes, just from looking at that photo alone, he deserved a life sentence.

I stepped into the master bedroom and quickly scanned it. Lemon yellow wallpaper with ivory-coloured curtains gave the room an airy brightness. The bed was old fashioned with ornamental carvings on the wooden headboard. The room was immaculately tidy and there were two atmospheric paintings hanging on the walls which depicted Paris in the rain.

A chest of drawers was positioned under the bedroom window and I slowly opened each draw. The first two drawers contained a variety of items such as socks and underwear. The third was folded jumpers, while the fourth was full of jeans, all folded perfectly. My friend Michael with his OCD would have appreciated all the order, I thought.

The bedside cabinet was the only other storage area in the bedroom. I quietly eased open the top drawer to find a selection of sex toys. There were several dildos, a couple of vibrators, some lube, a packet of tissues and some anal beads. Throw in a pizza and that would be a perfect Friday night in, I said to myself. Obviously, I was joking. The pizza wasn't necessary!

In the drawer below, I found a selection of bank cards and official items such as store cards, work passes and old bank cards. A couple of those would come in very handy for an idea which came into my head, so I placed them to one side – as a sort of vengeance souvenir. In my normal day-to-day life, I would never have called myself a person with anger issues, but skulking about in number 36 Chestnut road I felt like a different person.

CHAPTER THIRTY-ONE:

Here she comes...

So, there I was, rummaging around in Fabian Judson's bedroom when I heard footsteps coming up the stairs. Two lots of footsteps and giggling. Was she with Judson? I was invisible, but still had a slight feeling of stress and panic. There was nowhere to hide, so I just stood against the wall like a lampshade at the far side of the bed, whilst trying to breathe as quietly as possible. The woman I'd seen in the lounge was now with a guy – but it definitely wasn't Fabian Judson. Where had he come from? I hadn't heard the door open – he must've been in the kitchen. This was a bald-headed guy who obviously spent lots of time at the gym. His muscles were well-toned and he was about six foot two. He was also a police officer. I had no idea what this woman was up to – apart from the obvious – but by the sexual tension in the room, the police officer was definitely about to take down her particulars!

There was an en-suite bathroom which I'd hardly noticed, and the woman walked inside, saying 'I won't be a sec!' whilst the police officer began to get out of his uniform. He slowly and methodically folded each item of clothing and placed them onto a chair. Once he was totally naked, he laid down the bed waiting for her.

After a minute of me trying to hold to my breath, the woman stepped out of the bathroom. She was about five-foot-seven tall, with dyed blonde hair and a figure like Kate Winslets – which was a very respectable nine out of ten, perhaps even a little higher!

I guessed she was about thirty-to-thirty-five, her lipstick was perfect, and she wore a loose-fitting shirt with a tight skirt.

She stood at the end of the bed whilst the police officer moved towards her and began 'frisking her'. She playfully pushed him back onto the bed and began to take her clothes off. It was a scene of intense eroticism. Even though I was technically the third wheel in the room, it was like my own private dance - although I wasn't paying, and she wasn't dancing. But my fucking heart was – and it was doing the raunchy rhumba!

Once down to her stockings, knickers and bra, she bounded next to her lover and they proceeded to work their way through the Karma Sutra. I almost pulled a muscle just listening as I faced the wall to allow them a modicum of privacy. Edging my way towards the door, I aimed to slowly open it and leave whilst the couple were otherwise distracted.

As I pulled down the door handle millimetre-by-millimetre, I glanced over my shoulder and saw the woman reach for the drawer of sexual enlightenment…

My presence had been much more than intrusive, and I felt uncomfortable being a witness, even though the pair were oblivious to my uninvited company. When I slowly opened the bedroom door, they were too busy to notice. At six-steps down the staircase I heard a buzzing noise. Without going into too much detail, all I will say is that the sound of two AA batteries sounded more beautiful than the greatest symphony ever could.

The scene had been a weird erotic interlude and I felt like I'd done the right thing by leaving as quickly as possible. Their lovemaking repertoire had to remain a private affair, no matter how impressive it was.

I sneaked out of the house and allowed myself to breath easily for the first time in half an hour. Thinking time was needed as there was so much going on and I was finding it hard to prioritise things. At times I wasn't the best organised person, so I just needed to get my head around what I was going to do next. Really, I could have done with an efficient PA.

Around the corner from Chestnut road was a small café which looked like it hadn't been updated since the 1960's. Looking inside, it was completely empty. I thought it might be a good opportunity to have a drink without drawing attention to myself. The old-fashioned bell rang as I entered. The tables were small and made from Formica and there was the most wonderful aroma of coffee. The café was called Sherlocks. I didn't have any money of course, but I had the guile to be creative. When the man walked out of the back, he was surprised to see the café still empty. He took a quick look around and then turned to busy himself stocking up the display counter.

I sat down at a table by the window and gave myself an update on the current situation:

Lucy was safe at Michael and Rebecca's and sworn to secrecy about having an invisible friend. All she knew was that Michael and Rebecca had a friend called Cooper who was on holiday in Switzerland...

Carl's drug-dealing buddies Leon and Joe were free and knew that either Lucy or the fake policeman on the telephone were responsible for the disappearance of around twelve thousand pounds.

Rebecca had been assaulted. I could hardly mention the word 'sexually' even in my mind. The perpetrator was the shittily-named Fabian Judson who had a string of offences. And he was free on a technicality. He had a wife, or girlfriend who had a policeman lover and was living in an expensive house on Chestnut road.

I had no idea if Michael knew of Rebecca's past. It was none of my business, but I loved my friends and couldn't just stand by and let things go on as they were. Surely the police would be monitoring Fabian's movements, but I hadn't seen anyone loitering around in the vicinity - apart from the naked police officer who had just been throwing the lady of the house around like a rag doll.

To stop Judson committing any further offences I was going to have to take matters into my own hands, but I had to be more creative. Forming in my mind was the germ of a devious plan.

The thought of Judson spending life in prison was appealing, but how would Rebecca and the other victims feel about that? If he was dead at least then they wouldn't have to worry about him ever being released. After all, the British justice system was such that he'd probably get twenty years and be out in less than ten.

On top of all this stuff, I had lost all my money, all my friend's money and all the drugs money. My amazing superpower was truly amazing... but it was just in the wrong hands.

CHAPTER THIRTY-TWO:

Can you see me?

'Would you like a coffee?' offered the man behind the counter, completely out of the blue. I looked around to see who he was talking to, but he was talking to me. Could he see me? Was my invisibility wearing off prematurely? Please don't let it wear off just yet I said to myself, beginning to panic a little. I sat in silence as long as I could and then said softly:

'Can you see me?'

'No, but I know you're there… I saw the chair move and you messing around with the condiments.'

'Aren't you shocked?'

'No, I've always known that ghosts exist. Though I must admit that you're the first one I've ever actually spoken to. By the way, I'm Frank.'

'I'm HG.'

'I've always known that this café was haunted…'

'Well, I've lived here over three hundred years and never seen one!' I said, joking on the ghost theme. 'I'm the ghost of HG Wells. I'm the famous author. A coffee would be great thanks – and a sandwich if you don't mind. But, can I just say that in the nether world we don't have money, so could you open a tab for me?'

'No problem HG,' said Frank, who was already pouring me a coffee.

Frank was in his fifties, overweight and wore an impressive amount of Brylcreem on his thinning hair which he had brushed back. He could've got work as an extra in any gangster movie. His rugged features revealed he'd lived life to the full and every experience was etched on to his face. However, it was definitely a friendly face.

'There you are HG,' said Frank matter-of-factly as he placed a cup of coffee on to the table. He wasn't fazed at all by having a real live ghost in his establishment. I was already feeling relaxed. For once I could just be myself.

Frank then brought me over a fabulous bacon sandwich.

'Us ghosts don't normally do food, but it's always been a weakness of mine, Frank,' I said chattily.

'A bacon sandwich is one of life's pleasures – or dead's pleasures in your case!' chirped the proprietor.

As I ate my breakfast, Frank chatted away like it was perfectly normal to sit in a café talking to an apparition. Half-way through, he quickly went behind the counter and took a fresh coffee over to the door, where he gave it an elderly lady who made no effort to come inside.

'Who was that?'

'Oh, that's Elsie. She's got quite a few issues – she's had a shit life, and she loves my coffee. But she never drinks it. She doesn't even like coffee…'

'I don't understand! Why do you give it to her then?'

'Her beautiful daughter Michelle used to call in here for a coffee every day on her way home from work. She was a

156

wonderful girl… bright, funny and friendly… She lived with her mum, Elsie, just around the corner. Then one day, Michelle was killed by a hit and run driver. The aroma of my coffee reminds her of her daughter coming home from work. It's tiny bit of comfort, I suppose.'

Frank's compassion brought a tear to my eye. 'How could I ever sell a coffee to Elsie? And that's the reason I never change my blend of coffee… well, that and it happens to be outstanding!' laughed Frank, but I also detected sadness in his voice.

'Michelle was such a lovely girl, like the daughter I never had. She used to bring me a cake and a card on my birthday… and her mum never got to say goodbye properly. The incident killed her, too.'

The story was devastating. I thought about my mum being taken away by cancer. For a few moments we both sat there in silence.

Frank's coffee was sensational. The bacon sandwich was incredible. Perhaps it was the freedom in which I could eat it which made it so tasty and memorable? I savoured each mouthful and each glorious sip. I made a mental note that when I was back to normal, I would relish every single moment of normalness. And I'd definitely be back for a coffee at Sherlocks café.

'Who do you haunt?' asked Frank seating himself down at the next table.

'Oh, it's a free choice really. I personally love to haunt people who have an element of evil within them. Anyone who has destroyed someone's life is a fair target in my book…' I nodded to myself.

I was enjoying playing the part of a ghost and actually being able to converse with someone. And Frank seemed to be loving our conversation.

Just then a couple almost entered the café, but for whatever reason, they walked on. They were probably looking for a trendy chain café that made triple macchiatos with caramel and cinnamon cream.

'How's business?' I asked.

'It's a bit crap. I know I need to go more upmarket. A coffee or a tea option is not really going to make me my fortune…'

An idea sprung into my head to help Frank.

'Why don't you film me in your café and then post it on social media? That might get you a bit of interest?'

'Are you sure that's OK?'

'Yeah, no problem. But you have to promise me that you won't post it on social media until December 29th. I won't go into detail, but you have to promise me…'

'Yeah, no problem HG. I don't know much about the internet, but my son's coming to visit just before the new year, so I'll get him to do it then.'

'Perfect!'

As Frank went to get his mobile from behind the counter, he asked me what it was like being a ghost.

'For the most part, it's a bit like I'm stuck in a strange world where I wander around aimlessly between thousands of brain-dead zombies…'

'I can't imagine what that must be like…'

'It's a bit like being in Asda on a Saturday morning!'

We both laughed. I then proceeded to let Frank film me moving items around his shop. Knives, forks, spoons, in fact anything I could find which would look good visually.

I moved pictures on the walls, opened and drew the curtains, lifted chairs and poured drinks. We both looked at the footage afterwards and were blown away by how good it looked.

Spending almost an hour at Frank's place, I left feeling the most positive I had for quite a while. A new friend had been made in Frank and I really hoped that business would turn around for him. He was one of life's good guys, no doubt.

'I'll be here if you ever need me for anything!' Frank called out as I left. As I calmly avoided a group of shoppers, I already had an idea of how he could help me…

Walking back down Chestnut road, my timing was perfect as I witnessed Fabian Judson pull up outside his house in a white van. Quelling my urge to introduce an element of violence to Judson's face, I opted to put his vehicle out of action.

Noticing that Judson didn't lock his van, I opened the bonnet. Having checked that he couldn't see from his lounge window, I proceeded to rip out any wires I could see, doing as much damage as possible. I was determined that even if I didn't hurt him physically, he'd be stuck for transport for at least a day or two. He had to be taken off the streets.

By the time I'd finished the engine in his white van was in a terrible state. There were wires sticking out everywhere and for the icing on the cake, I used a screwdriver I found in the glove compartment to slash two of his tyres. A job well done. I took two steps back to admire my handywork and almost got killed by a Tesla electric car. It was so silent it was like a ghost.

Once again, as the draught subsided, I was reminded how finely balanced my existence was. If I'd been hit, no one would have known to call an ambulance. The message was, I had to be more careful - but it wasn't easy to adapt to my invisible lifestyle. After all, I'd had twenty-five years of normal, day-to-day repetition.

Anyway, at least Judson was out of action for a day or two – which meant the women of London were hopefully safe for a while.

A few minutes later, Judson went into the front garden, so I took the opportunity to drift past him. I'd actually forgotten to take some of his I.D, so headed straight to the master bedroom. I hadn't realized it, but Judson had come back into the house and headed straight upstairs. He entered the bedroom as I held a vibrator aloft.

Judson froze on the spot, his mouth open, but with no sign of any speech forthcoming. All he could see was a rampant-rabbit sex toy in mid-air. I decided to say something, as I switched it on:

'Fabian Judson, you're going to be well and truly fucked!' He turned on his heels and dashed out of the room petrified, whilst I followed, waving the vibrator in a threatening manner and making what I thought were scary noises. As I reached the top of the stairs, I saw Judson trip over a few items of laundry which had been placed on one of the steps and he flew through the air not unlike Eddie "The Eagle" Edwards. He crashed onto the wooden floor below. Even though I was no doctor, the angle of one of his arms suggested it was broken. As he moaned, the lady of the house arrived on the scene and immediately scrambled for her mobile to call for an ambulance. Ten minutes later an ambulance arrived and took him away.

Inadvertently, I'd caused Judson to fall down the stairs and, judging his moans and displaced limbs, he wouldn't be driving for a while.

CHAPTER THIRTY-TWO:

Hello Yellow Brick Road

I left the scene quite satisfied that the women of London were a little safer on Christmas Eve. By this time, it was eight pm and the shoppers had all left for home and had been replaced by festive revellers, drinking their way from pub-to-pub. Many were draped in coloured tinsel and I spotted three Santa's, two Elves and a snowman as I made my way home.

Christmas eve and I was pretty much alone. Even though I was beginning to make progress on my mental to-do list, I was still alone. Desperately alone, truth be told. Yes, I spoke to people, but nothing was ever on the level, there was always something I had to withhold or lie about. It was a difficult existence – not quite the dream I'd anticipated. I had been full of bravado and enthusiasm just three or so days before. I was young and innocent back in those days. Christ, it was just three days.

I thought friendship was what I was lacking. My routine had quickly become laborious, despite the unlimited possibilities of the situation I was in. Having someone to share it with was the most important aspect of being invisible, although with my new friend Frank, I knew I had a safe-haven and kind-hearted soul not far away. Not to mention his coffee. With that thought, I headed for the tube station.

On the tube I scanned the posters situated high-up in the carriage. There was a selection of adverts for West End musicals, tourist attractions and the odd-one for financial services. As I moved my eye along the carriage, one event stood out from the rest. Elton John was performing a one-off gig at The Camden Roundhouse. I'd almost forgotten about my wish to meet Elton John as other things had overtaken my thoughts. Elton John. What a singer. What a performer. It had to be fate that he was playing a special show in Camden.

I thought it would be the perfect way to get everything else off my mind and just enjoy myself. Even though this was going to be a free show for me, I fantasised about taking Lucy to shows just like it, as a couple. I excitedly headed straight to the venue.

Camden was buzzing when I arrived. There were street vendors everywhere, the mulled wine was being consumed in vast quantities and there was a smell of smoky roast chestnuts. It was a crisp winter's evening and there was a general feeling of anticipation in the air. I loved Christmas. The evening was actually quite mild for the time of year, but the Roundhouse had fixed a snow machine to their roof, which added a bit of excitement as I entered the building.

Elton John. One of the very few legends left in the music world. There's Neil Diamond, Barry Manilow, Elton John, Billy Joel... Bruce Springsteen, Bob Dylan, Dolly Parton, Cher, obviously Paul McCartney and Ringo...

What an amazing career Elton has had, really amazing. And you can say what you want about Elton, he's been terrific for the floristry industry, if nothing else.

Once inside, it was a bit of a squeeze, with everyone jostling to get to the bar or the merchandise tables. I'd never seen Elton live, but I had a collection his albums which were all really fantastic. Obviously, I didn't have to queue with everyone else, I just walked calmly past the security guards and into the restricted area.

The further I walked, the more distant the chatter of fans became. The corridors were painted a bland grey and the fluorescent lights were those long tubes which flickered when they weren't supposed to.

Eventually I came to a door at the end of a corridor which had a silver star pinned to it. Elton's dressing room. Bloody hell, there I was, just a few feet away from a proper icon. Not one of those shitty reality TV stars - a proper talented, bona-fide legend.

I stood outside Elton's dressing room, a little nervous. After waiting for a few moments, I took a deep breath, knocked lightly on the bright red door and then slowly moved the handle. There was no reply and I slowly entered…

Elton's dressing room was festooned with flowers – pretty much how I'd imagined it. And they weren't chrysanthemums, they were quality, exotic flowers. The displays were stunning, and even though I wasn't particularly a fan of flowers, I couldn't help but admire the amazing displays. They had been designed by a true artist. I looked at the label of one amazing design: "To Elton from David. Your designer was Jim". 'Great job, Jim!' I said aloud as I took a look around.

The room was much bigger than I'd imagined and most of the furniture was hidden by flowers. To my right there was a fabulous ornamental chair and one of those fantastic dressing tables with lights around the mirror. Then I heard the toilet flush and a door to my left opened. There he was: *THE* Elton John. He actually looked better in real life than in many of his photographs.

'Elton, you're amazing!' I said to him without thinking. It was the thrill and excitement of meeting a hero. I just blurted it out.

Without any warning at all Elton fell over in complete shock. I'd not counted on such an extreme reaction and he yelped out dramatically as I brough a chair towards him. Elton pushed himself backwards until he hit the wall and there was nowhere else to go.

'Who's there? Who said that?' cried Elton hiding behind his chair. After Frank's acceptance of me, I had not considered the impact my invisibility could have. I was a freak, a weird anomaly - and it would take some getting used to.

Elton was wearing a shimmery silver jacket with turquoise lapels, purple trousers with silver sequins, and multi-coloured shoes featuring ornamental flowers. His glasses were in the shape of a crown, with diamonds and peacock feathers everywhere.

'I see you've dressed down for the occasion!' I remarked. I couldn't resist the joke.

'Where are you?' said Elton, half-laughing at my last comment. 'What the hell's going on? Am I imagining this?'

Then I simply said, 'Elton, you won't be able to see me no matter how hard you look. I'm invisible. Totally invisible.'

The singer was stuck for words. He just stared in my general direction with his mouth open.

'Fucking hell!' said Elton, eventually. 'You really are invisible!'

'If you're going to behave, I'll let you touch my hand and arm to prove that I'm real.'

Elton moved his hand nearer to me, and I placed my arm underneath his palm. He felt my arm, pulling a face as he did so.

'You are real… my God. This is the most incredible thing I've ever seen, or ever not seen!'

'Yeah, I'm pretty special,' I replied, with my tongue firmly in my cheek.

Elton couldn't stop feeling me and then shaking his head. His reaction was fabulous – I wished I'd been able to film the look on his face. It was absolutely priceless. After a few minutes, he'd acclimatised to me and was much more relaxed.

I continued looking around his dressing room. There were cards from well-wishers, Bottles of water, a portable clothes rail carrying a host of extravagant garments, and an array of hand-sequined underpants. I swished my hand along the rail.

'My husband David sews those on by hand.' Said the popstar, raising one eyebrow.

'I love his attention to detail!' I replied.

'How did you get to be invisible?' Said Elton, shaking his head in disbelief. He reached for his mobile. 'Am I dreaming?'

'It's a bit of a long story, but it won't last forever, it's just a temporary state I'm in…'

'It must be incredible and mind-blowing.'

'Well, that's what I thought too, but to be honest, it's been a bit disappointing. I was really excited by the thought of it, but when you're invisible, you get to see the really negative side of life. Crime especially, and you can't help but get drawn into it, like some moral crusader – but you can't solve everything, so then it starts to stress you out.'

'Yeah, I never thought of it like that.'

'I thought it was going to be all voyeurism and endless fun!'

'My life is!' joked Elton.

'So, to cheer myself up, I thought I'd come and see you do your stuff. I've got a few of your albums.'

'I'm so glad you did! This is just… well, it's completely mad!'

'I'd rather be an international singing sensation than an invisible man any day of the week!' I said, whilst Elton offered me a bottle of water. He watched like a child witnessing a breathtaking fireworks display as the water vanished before his eyes.

'How long is it since you became invisible? What happened?'

I told Elton my story up to date, including my love for Lucy – he was totally engrossed.

'Wow HG… That's a truly incredible story. It could be one of the greatest love stories ever told!'

'I'm not sure about that,' I replied. 'I just want it to end happily.'

'You know,' said Elton, 'I can't help thinking that we're pretty similar, you and I. OK, I might not be invisible, but people never see the real me. They just see the showman and don't *really* know the person behind the distinctive spectacles. But maybe I don't want them to know…'

167

'But you shouldn't live your life for other people – just be yourself and I'm sure you'll be happy!' You've got a lovely family and a life that people dream of…'

Elton nodded slowly. 'Yes, I really have got an amazing life and as I get older, I definitely savour it more. The money is great, of course, but it's the little things in life which make it enjoyable…having a coffee with David, watching the kids laugh… I might be a bit guilty of this myself, but I think a lot of people are so busy chasing fame that they forget to actually enjoy it – and I'm determined to enjoy every second of what I've got now…'

'Good for you!' I said, surprised how the superstar singer-writer had become so comfortable talking to me so quickly.

'Can I get you anything to eat?' Asked Elton.

'No, thank you, I fine.'

'I must say that this is the strangest experience of my life… it's like I'm talking to myself…'

'No, this is definitely real,' I assured him. 'And I'll tell you what – I'm never going to forget meeting *THE* Elton John!'

We chatted for another twenty minutes much to his amusement I tried on a pair of his sequined underpants which he found hysterical. He even filmed me on his mobile – and of course, I told him not to post anything for a few days.

When the knock on the door came to remind Elton that it was fifteen minutes to showtime, we'd discussed our love lives, our families and our hopes for the future. Our heart-to-heart had been a revelation for me – and quite possibly for Elton too. When I left him, it was like we'd known each other for years. He gave me a big hug and asked me to keep in touch.

The show was even better than I had imagined. Truly magical. Elton even dedicated a song to me! He said, "Life is incredible... just when you think you've seen everything, something can happen which is so dazzling and miraculous that it can take your breath away. Today I met someone who is very, very special. And I'd like to dedicate this next song to my new, good friend, HG... and his friend Lucy. It's called, '*Are you ready for love?*'" It was a lovely thing for him to do. I was quite glad he couldn't see me smiling and crying all the way through his rendition as I leaned on his fabulous Steinway piano.

So, there was one definite plus to being invisible and that was I got to mingle with the famous. Elton turned out to be totally fabulous, which was just how I had imagined him to be. I made a mental note to buy every album he had ever made.

As I left Camden Roundhouse, I could see people's breath as they stood around and chatted. My own was obvious to see – but only if you'd been looking for it. I spent a few minutes studying my own breathing patterns and watched the air disperse into the night. It was late. Eleven pm. Just an hour until Christmas Day.

I was just making my way home via the yellow brick road, when I saw the two drug-dealers Leon and Joe. Both touting their wares to the masses. They just had to sully everything didn't they? Those guys were trouble, wherever they happened to be.

Approaching them I casually lifted a wallet from Leon's back pocket. It was the easiest thing I'd ever done. Once away from the public, I went down a side street and searched the contents. Inside was about two hundred pounds cash along with miscellaneous cards – one of which had his address on it. Leon Roderick, Flat 27 Churchill Gardens. My God, Winston Churchill would be turning in his grave if he knew such scum were living on a street named after him. I handed the two hundred pounds to a homeless man I passed as I made my way home and told him to spend it wisely. I'm not sure he fully heard me, but I shouted 'Merry Christmas' as I disappeared around the corner.

Normally, I was an easy-going, even-tempered person, but I was becoming a little concerned about how violence was increasingly the easiest way of sorting out complicated situations. I was not violent in any way at all when I was Cooper McCrae the kitchen technician, but as the invisible man, I had the power to take swift action by side-stepping that awkward negotiating stage.

When I entered the building where I lived, I heard voices coming from the flat where the trendy media couple lived. Tim and Tina lived in the flat immediately below mine and were always very pleasant whenever I happened to meet them in passing. They were both in their late twenties, were always sharply dressed and neither were lacking in the looks department.

As I placed my head silently against their door, the voices were raised and there was an argument in progress. They sounded quite distant, so I gently pushed the handle downwards and the door eased open. The couple were in the bedroom and were talking emotionally about their relationship. Tina was in tears and it transpired that Tim was in the process of splitting up with her. Even though I didn't know them, I was upset at seeing Tina in such a state, as it wasn't what she wanted. And for it to happen on Christmas Eve made things even worse. Why would Tim decide to split up at that time, it seemed cruel and heartless?

It was none of my business, I know, but it was amazing how quickly I became embroiled in the intimate details of other people's lives. Perhaps I was just too sensitive. I couldn't help but feel uncomfortable, yet I also felt compelled to stay. I don't know why - but stay I did.

Tina was sobbing her eyes out as she tried to understand what was happening. How I would have loved to console her in her time of need, but I knew that was impossible. The scene was tortuous, and I couldn't hold back my own tears.

Tina: But why haven't you said anything before if you weren't happy?

I could only just make out what Tina said due to her distress.

Tim: Look, it's just not going to work. You, we want different things...

Tina: Well why have we made all those plans to go travelling in the summer then? You came up with the idea. And now you're just ending it for no real reason. I don't understand. What have I done wrong?

Tim rolled his eyes, which made me want to intervene and shake some sense into him. The girl obviously loved him, yet he was coming across as mean and completely cold-hearted.

Tina: I haven't done anything wrong... have I?

Tim just stared at her. I wanted to put my arms around her and reassure her that everything would be alright, whether it would be or not.

Tim: I'm not going to talk about it anymore. That's it as far as I'm concerned.

He walked into the lounge and switched on the TV. Tina continued crying. She was sitting on the edge of the bed. Her sleeve was wet from wiping away the tears and her make-up was now completely ruined. She looked far from the stunning girl I saw leaving for work most mornings. She was devastated by Tim's revelation and his unsympathetic manner. Eight years invested in their relationship for nothing.

As Tim watched TV, his attention turned to his mobile where he began to send a text message. It was obvious as I looked over his shoulder that he was contacting another girl. I felt so sorry for Tina. There was nothing I could do. I was emotional and helpless, standing there like an idiot. I shouldn't have been there at all. I was just like a burglar. I'd violated their personal space, their home - and seen Tina at her most vulnerable.

All over the word, in every country, town, and street, people were living out their lives in the privacy of their own homes. People were being loved, crushed, mis-treated, spoiled, seduced, comforted and a million other things. They were entitled to do that without me watching. At that very moment, I hated myself and just wanted to get back to my normal, insignificant everyday existence. My days seemed to be nothing but highs and lows, with nothing much in-between. Plus, I was starting to annoy myself with all my whingeing.

I returned to my own flat, tripped over my rug and went straight to bed. Christmas Eve had provided me with more things to think about. Staring upwards, I laid on my bed and examined the patterns made into the plaster on the ceiling. The swirls reminded me of the way the artist Van Gogh painted his skies. My mind drifted from one thing to another, I was tired and could feel myself nodding off. I had a very weird dream that night which involved me working at Nasa where I was responsible for pushing the launch button. Just before take-off was due, the mission was aborted due to technical difficulties. I remember being very frustrated and saying, 'C'mon, it's not rocket science!' The weird thing was, I could remember laughing in my sleep.

CHAPTER THIRTY-THREE:

CHRISTMAS DAY

My flat looked anything but Christmassy. In fact, it was actually looking quite neglected. I normally went out and bought a few discounted decorations in the last few days before Christmas, but with the excitement of my forthcoming invisibility, it had all been overlooked. I rummaged around in my desk drawer and found a single red bauble sitting at the back. I removed a photograph of a Banksy mural from my wall and hung the bauble from the small nail left behind. With my new display, I instantly felt more Christmassy.

On the draining board beside my sink in the kitchen, was a plastic Tuppaware container. It looked empty, but it wasn't. Inside were two things which I had taken from Fabian Judson's house. A credit card and a store card for Marks & Spencer. The cards were now invisible and they would be a crucial part of a plan which had formed in my mind. I took both cards and placed them in my left inside jacket pocket until I needed them.

Normally on December 25th I would go and see my dad and we'd argue our way through one of his lacklustre Christmas dinners. This year was different. My dad thought I was in Venice or somewhere – all part of the ruse so that I could spend my week of invisibility in isolation. It was 8.30am and I decided to phone him straight away, as I knew he'd have been up since 6.30. After thirty years It was a habit he wasn't going to break.

Me: 'Hi Dad, it's Coop'.

Dad: 'Hi there, Cooper. Merry Christmas!'

Me: 'Merry Christmas to you too. Have you got anything planned today?'

As soon as I'd asked the question, I wish I hadn't. I knew he wouldn't have anything planned. Since my mum died of cancer, he didn't do anything on Christmas Day – apart from have me round for Christmas dinner so he could criticise everything about my life. It had almost become a traditional part of Christmas in the McRae household.

Dad: 'No, I've decided to just have a quiet one this year, you know…'

Me: 'Yeah, it's nice to have a quiet one…'

The reality was that my dad had become more and more withdrawn. His best friend Mark had moved to Scotland with work, his job as a school caretaker was a challenge and his life had become boring. It was no wonder that he clung on to the potential excitement of ghost hunting on TV. I may be being too dramatic here, but I often thought he was winding down to death. Whereas once he took absolute pride in his appearance, now he did the bare minimum. Basically, he lived for my mum. I missed my mum every single day – in fact before I had even woken-up properly I was reminded of her, because she always told me off for brushing my teeth in a particular way. I'd bought a Mickey Mouse toothbrush holder which was basically Mickey holding a toothbrush. I'd cut a photo of my mum and stuck it over Mickey's face. Ever since doing that, I'd brushed my teeth how my mum wanted me to.

At times I felt like my dad's carer.

Dad: 'How's Venice?'

Me: 'Pretty good… it's not great for driving though.'

Dad: 'Is there a lot of pigeon shit?'

Me: 'Yeah, loads'

Dad: 'I thought there would be… they're vermin, pigeons.'

Me: 'What are you doing for Christmas dinner?'

Dad: 'I've bought a turkey crown from M&S as a bit of a treat and I'm doing some roast parsnips, Brussel sprouts and Yorkshire puddings.'

Me: 'Sounds great. I thought you didn't like Brussel sprouts?'

Dad: 'I don't, but your mum does…'

I don't think he even realised he said it. It was probably a habit ingrained in him over twenty-seven Christmases with his late wife.

After informing Dad I had a present for him, I promised to pop over and visit him as soon as I got back from Venice. He told me he was looking forward to the Christmas Special of Britain's most haunted. I knew that he would record it and watch it several times. It was good that he had an interest in something – even if it was something which didn't exist.

We ended our call and I decided to plan my own Christmas day. It was going to be the weirdest one ever. I was anxious to know how Lucy was getting on at Michael and Rebecca's – were they all keeping up their ends of the bargain, without each other knowing?

My mind was made up, I decided to head over to theirs at around one p.m. and see exactly what was going on. I was desperate to see Lucy's beautiful face again. As her features became etched in my mind, I was actually starting to forget what my own looked like, so I took the opportunity to look at some photos of myself on my mobile.

My day would be a chilled out one, relaxing with a beer and I'd try and come up with a method to make that million pounds I'd promised myself.

I switched-on the TV to see what the schedulers had planned for me on that Christmas morning. It was the same old stuff. Celebrities handing out presents in a children's hospital, Some clips of old movies, a church service and Miracle on 34th Street, the movie – Richard Attenborough version. Everything was just as expected.

My solitary bauble stood out a mile on my lounge wall and even though Christmas was not the same event as usual for me, I still felt the excitement. Gone were the days of me having a pile of presents to open. The only gift I had this year was a "Secret Santa" gift from work. Ledley and I were the only two people in the kitchen department who opted to do it, so in actual fact, it wasn't very secret at all. This year, Ledley had got me a self-help book to buff up my confidence and I'd bought him one of those special combs to buff up his afro.

As I left my flat a few hours later, I stopped briefly outside Tim and Tina's door. There wasn't a sound to be heard. I recalled the night before and the uncomfortable experience I had listening in on their private conversation. I hoped Tina was alright.

Christmas Day in London. Frost was still on the ground and the roads were quite busy. Most of the shops were closed, but London was still laden with tourists searching out the classic landmarks such as Buckingham Palace, Nelson's Column, Leicester Square, The Houses of Parliament, Big Ben and the rest. I must have unofficially photo-bombed a thousand images as I made my way through the tourists, but no-one would ever know. The only shop open was one of those tourist meccas which sold miniature red telephone boxes and t-shirts with slogans like: I [heart] London and Mind the Gap.

If I'd been a professional pickpocket, I would've made a fortune in just a few minutes. There were endless mobile phones hanging out of back-pockets, wallets and purses in open jacket pockets and bags left unattended whilst owners posed for selfies and festive group shots.

Walking through the crowds, I suddenly saw Wyngard the boffin and he was alone. The man who'd created the invisibility oil didn't seem to be heading anywhere in particular. If only he knew the impact his invention had already had on people's lives. I walked alongside him for a minute, thinking about how I could make him aware, without giving the game away. I toyed with his scarf for a few moments and made it wrap itself around his face, so each time, he had to remove his hands from his pockets to adjust it. I made it rise and dance like a snake charmer on the top of his game. I had no idea what Wyngard's plan for his invisibility oil was, but I guessed it would be something much more serious than making a scarf act like a snake.

Wyngard stopped to buy himself an ice cream and then sat on a bench to attend to his '99'. What was he doing out on his own on Christmas day? Didn't he have anything else better to do? Maybe his huge brain couldn't cope with things such as relationships, it was probably always preoccupied with the bigger picture and sciency-stuff. I watched him, in awe of his capabilities. People wandered past him, oblivious to the fact that there sat one of the greatest minds in the world, one of the greatest minds the world had 'ever' known, making a right old mess with his ice cream. He smiled to himself as he wiped drips of ice cream from his coat. Was it just a coincidence that I'd spotted Professor Wyngard in the crowds? It seemed improbable, yet I never gave it any more thought.

Outside Michael and Rebecca's on Penbridge Crescent, there was total calm. There were no cars in sight, no people and the only movement came from a little robin who was perched on the low-level wall of number forty-nine. He sported a magnificent red breast and was enjoying a moment of peace on Christmas Day. I'd never been so close to a robin before and I hardly dared move in case I frightened him off. It would have made the perfect Christmas card image, so serene and beautifully calm. I didn't have a morsel of biscuit or any treat to give him, but he continued to look around, completely harmless and gentle.

Until, that is, another bird landed on the same wall of number forty-nine and then all hell broke loose. The innocent little robin I'd been admiring suddenly turned in to a vicious little creature determined to cling on to his territory. That wall, that tiny garden which was home to a single bush was his domain. I had to move out of the way as the two birds fought in mid-air. I might have missed out on the opportunity to be wildlife photographer of the year, but it was still an exhilarating experience being privy to nature at work. My robin won the fight and with a shake of his head, normal, peaceful service was soon resumed outside number forty-nine. I just hoped that nothing so dramatic was going on *inside* number forty-nine.

CHAPTER THIRTY-FOUR:

Christmas dinner

At the first opportunity, I entered the home of Michael and Rebecca - unannounced, of course. They had done a great job decorating the whole place with festive tinsel and ornaments. The tree stood majestically in the corner of the lounge, where the angel's halo brushed the ceiling. Their home was the opposite of my festive-free flat. Christmas cards hung on the walls and piles of gifts – which had already been opened – were stacked neatly beneath the tree. My friend Michael was on the cusp of having OCD. In fact, to be honest, he was well over the cusp! The place was spotlessly clean with everything neatly in its place. All traces of wrapping paper had been removed and the carpet in the lounge showed the recent track marks of the post-unwrapping vacuum cleaner. But, that didn't stop Michael going back over it, again and again. Every shelf and surface was pristine, every nook and cranny had been explored and every cushion had been immaculately buffed. I was actually in two minds about entering my friend's house without permission. Technically I was an intruder and I had a very uncomfortable feeling about inviting myself into their home. Once the week was over, I would definitely be confessing all my actions – good or bad.

Michael and Lucy were both sitting in the lounge and each had their hands clasped around a posh, frothy coffee. The TV was on, which enabled me to move around without having to be deadly silent.

'Thank you so much for my necklace, it's so cool,' said Lucy, cupping it in both hands and holding it near her face.

It brought a tear to my eye that Michael and Rebecca had been so thoughtful towards Lucy. They were just so, well, they were the best friends an invisible man could ever have.

After a few minutes of general chat, I came up in conversation.

'I wonder how my friend Cooper is getting on in Switzerland?' asked Michael

'He's probably skiing down a mountain at break-neck speed as we speak, clutching a half-eaten Toblerone in his big, puffy gloves,' replied Rebecca.

Lucy laughed and almost spilled her coffee. Michael was up like a shot to help avoid any spillage on his well-looked-after Berber carpet.

'Yeah, well wherever he is, I hope he's enjoying himself.' Replied Lucy.

'I think we're expecting him back in a couple of days...'

'I can't wait to meet him...'

Yes, I was 'due back' from Switzerland in just a couple of days or so. My week was moving frighteningly fast and it would be over in double-quick time. It was highly likely I would never have the opportunity again. If I blew it, then I'd never forgive myself, so I had to make it count.

Lucy was in good hands, and I could rest assured that she was not only cared for, she was also in the cleanest and tidiest environment anyone could wish for. Howard Hughes would have felt quite at home, I thought.

'I'd better get cracking with the vegetables. The turkey's been in for three hours already…' announced Michael.

'I love a Christmas dinner with all the trimmings,' replied Lucy. 'I can't wait!'

'I'm going to eat so much that I explode!'

'Me too. This is my best Christmas ever.' Said Lucy.

Even Michael, was visibly moved by this and attempted to give her a hug, but he pulled out at the last minute to avoid a clash of coffee cups.

It was heart-warming to see Lucy so relaxed and happy. Each time I'd seen her previously there had always been a threat of danger hanging over her and even though it was good that I had one or two moments of closeness because of it, I never got to see the real Lucy. I'd really only got to see Lucy with her make-up all smudged with crying.

I stayed for Christmas dinner and watched the Queen's speech. Her Royal Highness made no mention whatsoever of her Scrabble success, which was a little disappointing, but nothing gave me so much joy as seeing my friends and Lucy laughing, chattering away and pulling Christmas crackers. They even gave a toast to me. I ate my own Christmas dinner secretly in the kitchen and even though no one was aware of my presence, I still felt like I was a part of it, quietly groaning at the terrible jokes inside the Christmas crackers, to laughing at Rebecca's stories about her student days. At one point it was almost impossible to suppress my laughter and I couldn't wait to see my friends again in the flesh.

After their Christmas meal, Michael and Rebecca handled the washing up duties, whilst Lucy read a book in the lounge. I took the opportunity to take a Santa figure off the Christmas tree and float it in the air to catch her attention. When she caught sight of it, she gasped and covered her mouth to hide her excitement.

'Is it you?' she whispered, holding one hand over her mouth.

'Yes, it's me. Keep quiet, I'm just checking up on you all to see if you're OK.'

'Yes, we're all great, thanks. Michael and Rebecca are so cool. And very tidy!'

'Yeah, Michael is extremely tidy.'

'Extremely.' She repeated.

I hadn't mentioned to Lucy that her own place would be extremely tidy too, as I'd asked my new friend Frank, the café owner to help remove all Lucy's stuff from her flat. I'd told him that the place was haunted by ghosts who just didn't appreciate the clutter - and Lucy needed to move to a ghost-free location and have a fresh start. I wasn't sure what the plan was beyond that, but at least it was a step in the right direction. That was just one of a couple of favours Frank was delighted to help out with. But who wouldn't want to help out their friendly neighbourhood ghost?

Lucy's parents lived in Spain and so she wasn't expecting to see them over the Christmas period. She phoned them and they were ecstatic to hear that Carl was no longer a part of her life. They said she could now get on with her future and find herself a nice young man who had a steady job and fewer tattoos.

'Right Lucy, I'm going now as I have a few things I need to sort out,' I announced after a quick catch-up.

Lucy held out her arms for a Christmas embrace - and held me for several seconds. And that still wasn't long enough for me.

'Be careful.' She said, looking more or less into my eyes.

CHAPTER THIRTY-FIVE:

A strange choice

Making my way towards 27 Churchill Gardens, where the drug dealer Leon Roderick lived was more difficult than I'd imagined due to a blister on my left toe. I wasn't particularly keen on making this trip on Christmas Day, but I doubted that drug dealing stopped on a national holiday. Even though Lucy was safe, I still needed to know what Leon and Joe were up to. Were they intent on finding Lucy to get the drugs money back? I could tell them exactly where it was - it was sitting comfortably in the bank account of a bookmaker, that's where – all thanks to my misguided foray into the world of professional boxing. And my face was still almost as sore as my pride.

Leon's flat was located five miles east of the city in the crime hotspot of Newham. Even I didn't feel completely safe and I was invisible! Knife crime and moped related thefts were very popular with the criminal fraternity in the area and so I kept my eyes peeled as I walked carefully through the borough.

Leon's flat was actually in one of the more upmarket areas of Newham, which showed that in most cases, contrary to popular PR catchphrases, crime actually does pay. And it doesn't pay minimum wage, either. I would have loved to have had a one-week blitz on crime in Newham, but sadly my diary was pretty full. Perhaps once Wyngard's wonder oil was ready to be launched, it could be used by the police and security forces to crack down on crime? The statistics would instantly plummet, as long as there were enough places for the villains to be incarcerated.

I knocked on Leon's door and almost half a minute later, the drug dealer himself answered, blatantly holding a small bag of cocaine. That's how blasé the dealers were about the police and the chances of them ever being held to account. He stood there with a stupid look on his face, a spliff in his mouth and wore a T-shirt which boasted 'I'm acting under the influence!'

I had to squeeze past him to gain entry as he seemed glued hypnotically to the spot on his doorstep. Once inside I went straight into his lounge where drugs were currently being packaged ready for sale. Leon's partner in crime Joe was sitting at a table with his own little production line going on. On the walls were framed photographs of Michael Bublé, which made me stop in my tracks. If anything, I'd expected some posters of 'gangsta rappers', not the housewives favourite crooner. The world is full of surprises.

It was really the first time I'd had the opportunity to see their faces properly. Leon was Jamaican, with intricate patterns cut into his hair. He had a jewel stud in his nose and was wearing a black leather jacket and skinny blue jeans. On his feet he wore a pair of designer trainers which had electric-blue markings down the side.

Joe was a white lad who tried to speak like a black youth. It was his attempt to sound cool, but it didn't actually make him sound that cool, it made him sound like he had special needs. He also had a face that you'd never tire of hitting. His eyebrows had been coloured purple, he had a three-inch scar across his forehead and he constantly sported a mean-spirited look on his face. His eyes were narrow, he possessed high cheek bones and a huge Adam's apple. They were the sort of people you wouldn't want your mother to meet. Still, even the most vicious and depraved people had another side to themselves. I noticed that Joe was half-way through writing a birthday card to his grandma.

The card was positioned so that I could see his message: Grandma Smith, miss you lots and can't wait to see you, Love Joe. X

I read it once more and looked at him again. He obviously wasn't all bad, was he? It was a lovely message and it struck me that even evil people couldn't possibly be evil 24/7. When they weren't committing evil deeds, they still had to go shopping, probably held the door open for old ladies and probably still said their please's and thank you's. Yes, even evil people were capable of just being nice.

Then Joe casually tucked a bag of high-grade cocaine in with his grandma's birthday card, licked the strip and sealed it.

Placed beside the drugs on the table was a huge pile of money which had attracted my attention. There must have been at least thirty or forty thousand pounds. They had a very lucrative business, though I suspected they paid very little tax.

I was busy thinking about how I could take all the money stacked neatly on the table, when Leon's mobile rang. It was obviously someone important, as he signalled to Joe and then put the call on speaker mode.

'Hey Leon, how's it going?'

'Good, man. Everything's as it should…'

'What's happening with my money, bro?' The voice sounded like a public schoolboy trying to be 'down with the kids.'

Leon looked towards Joe and pulled a face. It transpired the voice on the other end of the phone was the boss man who Leon and Joe worked for.

'Yeah, look, everything's cool man, We got the money just give us a day and we'll get what's due to you…'

I couldn't quite hear the rest as the signal became weak and Leon unexpectedly turned away with his mobile in his hand. I struggled to get near enough to him as he went and stood behind Joe. Whatever was said, was enough to make both guys scared of the consequences if they didn't produce the goods - and quickly.

After the call, Leon was silent. He was thinking.

Joe: 'So, what is da plan?'

Leon: 'The plan is this. We've got the money here for that last batch, but we're still 12K short and we've got to get it A.S.A.P. We've got to get to Lucy and find out where she's hidden it…'

Joe: 'Or where her friend's hidden it. He's the one who's behind all this…'

The mystery 'friend' being referred to was me.

Leon: 'We've been summoned to the 'W' tomorrow at 3pm…'

Joe: 'But, I was gunna watch the Michael Bublé Christmas Special tomorrow! That is got to be a Christmas priority, my man.'

Leon: 'That man can certainly sing, we knows that. His voice is part Sinatra, part Matt Munro innit…'

I stood there trying not to laugh as the dealers discussed the merits of Michael Bublé's voice. I certainly hadn't expected the Canadian crooner to be such a feature of their afternoon. And I was quite impressed with their knowledge of classic vocalists from the 50's and 60's. Matt Munro had the most amazing voice and had been a favourite of my mum's – and of course, my dad had every album on vinyl.

Joe: 'Dat boss man can be a bit harsh sometimes, but one good ting he 'as done is introduce us to Mr Bublé. We gotta be ever grateful for dat. He seen 'im over thirty times live and he says he's the consummate pro. An' I can believe dat.'

Leon: 'Amen …But if we don't get to the 'W' by 3pm tomorrow, it'll be the last thing you ever watch.'

Joe: 'Couldn't we do 4.30?'

Leon: 'You's being a bit unrealistic man. Even though The Bublé is certainly worth stayin' in for, no doubt, no doubt, but on this occasion, I think we're gunna have to put our lives first. You hear what I'm saying? C'mon, we got things to do, we'll carry on with this later…'

The Michael Bublé fan club stashed the cash and drugs away under the sink and hastily left Leon's flat. Thousands of pounds had fallen right into my lap. And then it suddenly hit me. If these two small-time criminals were capable of collecting such large amounts of cash, then what amount was their boss going to have in his possession? Probably a hundred-thousand or even more. I was starting to get excited at the prospect of making some headway with my financial aspirations. At last, things seemed to be looking up.

'It's Christmas!' I sang aloud as I dumped the cash on to the table and began to count it. There was a lot of money. Much more than I'd guessed. When I got to the last few twenty-pound notes I had counted over fifty thousand pounds. Jesus. Fifty thousand pounds, just like that.

Within an hour, my ghost-friendly friend Frank had collected my haul and it was safely deposited in a secret location at the back of his café.

I'd suddenly got a spring in my step again. The rigors of my special circumstances had worn me out in the seventy-two hours or whatever it was since I became invisible. Now it was all to play for again.

CHAPTER THIRTY-SIX:

Am I delusional?

My thoughts turned to Leon and Joe's boss. If I could find out where his headquarters was all my problems could be solved, at least financially. The Bublé twins were due to meet him the following day at 3pm. The location was the "W" whatever that was. These were the options I had:

I could hang around with Leon and Joe and then tag along to the meeting place. But, there was always the chance that they might not be going to the meeting directly from Leon's flat so I could turn up, say at 2pm and there could be no one home to tag along with...

Or, if they were driving, there was always the possibility that there might not be room for me, so I could be left behind at the last moment. And being stuck in a car with two criminals was asking for more than trouble.

Time was starting to run out for me because the following day, Boxing Day, would be my fifth day - so the pressure was beginning to mount. I needed to get things sorted, even if it meant I had to be more ruthless. Normally my day consisted of planning whether to put the cups into the dishwasher first, or the saucers. Now I was saddled with admin!

There were several things I had to do in the next two-to-three days: Make decisions regarding Fabian Judson the sexual deviant, meet with - and benefit from - the unknown drugs lord whilst also ensuring that Lucy was safe from Leon and Joe, as they were likely to do anything to save their own skins, if it came to that. There were also a few other items on my wish list.

I headed home to chill out on Christmas evening. But then I wondered whether a night in front of the TV would be a waste of time, as opportunities could be out there? I picked up a free copy of the Evening Standard newspaper and browsed the pages.

The first page that stuck in my mind was an advert for prams. I had completely forgotten that I was going to become a father. The last few days had given me so much to think about that I'd had trouble processing all the events. Normally I had little to think about, other than Ledley's love life.

How could I have forgotten about such huge news? The note from Sarah had asked me to get back in touch once I'd had time to think about things. I was definitely against getting back together with her just for the sake of the baby – it was a relationship destined to fail. However, I knew it would be a tough decision – when it came to it.

Nothing had changed in my head about Lucy Pendleton, she was still the object of my desire and the object of my love – even though it was slightly unorthodox. She'd never seen me, or in actual fact, knew much about me. I thought that my lowly position at JC Cosmetic Developments would be a negative for someone like her. What was I even thinking about? Was I delusional? Could someone fall in love with someone that they had never even clapped eyes on? I berated myself for even thinking about it. I knew deep inside that it was highly improbable that I could ever have a real relationship with Lucy. A friendship would have to suffice, but could I live with that?

I was definitely confused about what I should do. The small, mature part of me knew that I had to take responsibility for my actions – getting Sarah pregnant – and everything else should take second place. I decided to email Sarah and arrange a get together on December 29th. Then, I'd be back to my normal self and would be able to see things more clearly. I'd inform her that I was away at the moment and we needed to chat on my return. I already felt pleased with myself for thinking the situation through properly like a mature adult.

As a twenty-five-year-old single man, with high testosterone levels, I had been somewhat disappointed with a certain aspect of my invisibility so far. At the start of my adventure, my mind was full-to-overflowing with thoughts of sexual escapades and unlimited erotic encounters which would have been impossible to fulfil as a normal person. Yes, it's shallow, but most single men would have gone down the same shallow and murky path. My own plan was to see Perfect-Ten Pendleton is all her naked glory, but that never worked out. As it turned out, I was actually feeling joyous that I hadn't been given the opportunity.

I had planned all sorts, from skulking around the dressing rooms in the West End theatres where dancing girls might be in abundance, to finding out the location of adult movie studios to watch the action unfold, live! Unfortunately, the nearest I'd come to a sexual experience was seeing Elton John's selection of home-made glittery underpants. It wasn't the fantasy I'd had in mind. Just because I'd hoped to see more flesh than in the Walking Dead Christmas Special, didn't make me a bad person, did it? I know I should have been aiming for world peace or at least something more ambitious than peeping-tommery!

It was Christmas Day. Yes, Christmas Day – and I was determined to give myself a treat. I decided to end the evening by visiting The Green Lounge, the hippest adult entertainment club in Soho.

Of course, I wouldn't have to pay a penny to get in, I just hoped that my impressive erection would fit through the door.

Located on Brewer street, The Green Lounge was probably the best strip club and lap dancing establishment in London – at least according to their own advert in the Evening Standard. I looked online and it had great reviews, so I was anticipating a thrilling evening.

Back in the old days. Soho had a reputation as the sleazy part of town. It was then full of sex shops selling everything from complete rubber outfits and gimp masks, to hardcore porn mags and chastity penis locks. I remember my friend's dad had a decent collection of adult movies from the 1970s and the fashions were quite extreme. Turquoise eyeshadow, frizzy perms and huge earrings were all the rage – and that was just the men.

Much of Soho had changed since those days and Brewer Street -which was once down-market, was now trendy and vibrant. As I approached the bustling street, the pubs were so full that people spilled out on to the street. Many were sporting Christmas party hats, and other revellers were draped in coloured tinsel. Music blared out and even the doormen seemed to be in good spirits. I was looking forward to my 'night off' and couldn't wait to see the treasures within the confines of The Green Lounge.

I stepped sideways at their front door to gain access between an up-market bouncer and a young lady who was on her mobile.

The interior of The Green Lounge could be described as boutique hotel-esque. The wallpaper was dark green with swirling floral and botanical images, the light fittings were extravagant, and the leather settees were shades of aqua. Miniature palm trees divided the seating areas and added a touch of exotica to the surroundings. The floor was wooden and mostly covered by lush rugs that you could lose a fluffy kitten inside.

The clientele was quite classy, and the ladies were some of the finest specimens of the human race. Well-toned and tanned, they looked stunning. I noticed on the tables there were menus, offering different specialities. This was not your common-or-garden menu where burgers and chips were seductively described to tempt you. This was a different sort of menu altogether. The starters and main courses looked so good, that I doubted I would have room for a pudding!

As I scanned the tasty starters on the menu, an attractive young woman barged into me. She'd obviously had a drink and was with a friend. Instinctively, I said, 'Pardon me!' She looked around in a surprised manner. It was someone I knew - Julie, who I'd been to sixth form college with. I remembered she'd been to university and it transpired she was now a qualified teacher. I'd had a bit of a crush on her at college, but was so shy that I never actually said anything even though we socialised together and I had several opportunities to confess my feelings.

Julie always wore unusual boots and tended to wear black clothes – hence she was often mistaken for a goth. She had jet-black hair and a fabulous smile, which in my opinion was her best feature – although she also had a brilliant figure.

'Who's that?' laughed Julie, who was slightly giddy due to alcohol consumption.

'It's me, your guardian angel!' I replied 'I'm here to protect you…'

'Well we might need you tonight then…' Both Julie and her cool, tipsy friend Kath were totally non-plussed by the sudden attention given to them by a heavenly presence. Julie reached out and luckily grabbed my arm before I had chance to pull away. They escorted me into a VIP private party event, whilst in the background, Elvis Presley sang 'Young and Beautiful'.

Julie seemed to brush off my invisibility so easily that I was quite shocked. Reactions by other people had been much more dramatic. Whilst Julie hardly battered an eyelid, Kath was way too far gone to care. To be quite honest, both of them were lost in the twilight zone – a place located somewhere near 'Planet Gin'.

As we danced our way to the VIP area, I glanced at the female dancers – and recognised one of them as Fabian Judson's wife or girlfriend. The very one who I'd witnessed being well and truly frisked by a police officer in her bedroom the day before. She was a beautiful woman and was on form as she gyrated impressively for a group of businessmen who casually tossed ten-pound notes in her direction. After her stint around a well-polished pole, she began talking to a middle-aged guy dressed in a parka coat. He seemed a little out of place and he also seemed familiar, but I couldn't quite place him.

Then it suddenly came to me, I was sure he was the police officer I saw when looking for information at the station. The two were standing away from all the other dancers and customers, in a quieter part of the club. I snatched myself away from Julie's vice-like grip and quickly joined them to see what they were discussing.

I caught the woman mid-sentence: '...so we're fortunate that he's currently out of action.'

'What exactly happened? It seems so bizarre!' asked the undercover police officer.

'I honestly have no idea. It's fucking weird. I went out to the shops – so I could make a call to the station, and when I came back, he was on the floor in agony. He said he didn't know what had happened – but no one had forced their way in or anything. Anyway, it's been a stroke of luck for us. I do have some info about why he's been making life difficult for us though – a contact of his called Gary runs a van hire business and every day, he's been using a different vehicle and swopping them back last thing at night…'

'OK, I'll look into that, but at the moment, we've got him exactly where we want him. Look, just be careful, this guy is still dangerous – even in his current state.'

'I know, anyway, got to go, time for my next dance!'

So, it seemed Fabian Judson's girlfriend was either working for the police or tipping them off. It was encouraging to see that there were still people intent on bringing Judson to justice, one way or another.

I made my way to the VIP area and located Julie and Kath who were attempting to take a selfie. They took and re-took their selfie several times before deciding on one which was suitably good enough to be published online. They actually had the camera facing the wrong way, so the results weren't fantastic, but they were definitely enjoying themselves.

A 'VIP' show suggests that you are entitled to something that you wouldn't get if you weren't a VIP and I surveyed the room enthusiastically. About twenty seats were allocated for the show, with a miniature stage barely six feet in front of the nearest seats. I was determined to get a good, close-up view of the forthcoming spectacle.

The level of excitement in the VIP area was raised when I heard the door close at the back of the room and the lights were dimmed slightly. I noticed that there were more women to my left and a group of men with fashionable moustaches to my right.

The women in the room probably felt more at ease than I did when the dancers came out – as they were all men. As a man at ease with my own sexuality and that of others, I could certainly appreciate the sight of a well-toned male body, but it wasn't the sort of sight I hankered after during a night out. The small, but perfectly-formed troupe began by mimicking The Village People and performed a slightly lacklustre version of YMCA, but the more clothing they discarded, the more enthusiastic both they and their audience became. And for what it's worth, I noted that the gentleman playing the construction worker had a very impressive tool belt.

Despite my open-mindedness when it came to sex, I wasn't overly keen on having young men's genitalia swung in my face. I soon realised that this was an uncensored gay revue and I couldn't escape it as Julie had a vice-like grip on my arm. The doors were also patrolled at the back, which meant that I was basically a sex-hostage.

The small VIP crowd loved every minute of it. The gay boys cheered every position, whilst Julie and Kath just cheered everything because they were drunk. I must confess that it was that particular evening and the over-sized body parts I saw, which put me off ever going to a German Christmas food market again. I think you know what I'm saying.

Suffice to say, it wasn't the sort of evening I'd anticipated, but I couldn't help but laugh as Julie and Kath both continued to talk to me as if it was totally normal to have a guardian angel beside them as we watched the boys getting up to - and down to no good. I saw things that night which were technically unbelievable - and quite possibly illegal. But, I'm pleased to report that all the performers received – and produced a standing ovation.

Julie and Kath shared a flat about twenty minutes away and invited me back for drinks. After a kebab in the taxi on the way back to theirs, I actually felt quite normal - and now look back on the experience as a 'bloody good night out!' It provided a little bit of much needed normality in my abnormal world.

The two girls quizzed me as to what I thought of the show. 'Well, it wasn't as good as Joseph and his Amazing Technicolour Dreamcoat!' I said, although to be fair, some of the group scenes were brilliantly choreographed…'

The girls continued to be in laugh-at-anything-cos-we're-drunk-mode. We drank for another hour and all fell asleep in the lounge. I vowed to keep in touch with them, although I suspected they wouldn't be able to remember anything from the night before. I left before either of them stirred the next morning. I placed a note on the kitchen table which read:

"Dear Julie and Kath,

Thanks for a great night out at the live male sex show. You two are awesome!

Best wishes, The Invisible Man."

I was sure that the excessive amount of alcohol the pair had consumed the previous night would cloud their minds to what really happened. There's no way that Julie or Kath would ever believe that someone could be invisible – although, the videos filmed on Julie's phone of me writing the letter might persuade them otherwise.

CHAPTER THIRTY-SEVEN:

Ledley & Laughs

As soon as I got home, I grabbed my mobile. No messages. I thought about the night before and recalled the fantastic kebab I had with Julie and Kath. I started laughing because it reminded me of the day Ledley came in to work and said, "Coop' you'll never believe this. It's bad news, I found my first ever grey pubic hair last night!" That's not so bad, I said. "No, it is – it was in a kebab."

I fell back on to my bed and laughed at Ledley's kebab story from months before. Tears ran down my cheeks and towards my ears, as I laid flat. The ceiling blurred with my tears. I was already missing my normal, boring existence. Julie and Kath had reminded me of what life was like without a super-power: Ledley falling head-over-heels after one date, me trying to give him advice and getting annoyed with him. My friend driving me up the wall with his OCD, going around to my dad's house and getting frustrated with him, burning the roof of my mouth when I had a pizza – even though it was a basic schoolboy-error, having a laugh with my friend Muzzy who ran a vintage clothes stall in The

Stables market… There was so much to enjoy about mundane daily life – and it was so much easier to appreciate when I didn't have it.

I focused on the intricate swirl pattern on the ceiling once more and began to wonder how it was put on there. My eyes followed the pattern, my mind drifted and I gradually felt everything go blurry and I was off to sleep. I had a strange dream which involved 'Perfect Ten' Pendleton, a spatula and a jar of Nutella chocolate spread. It was one of the most enjoyable dreams I'd had for ages - and quite frankly, I didn't care how many calories were in Nutella – in my dream I licked it off like my life depended on it.

Boxing day was going to be a big day. I phoned Frank and asked him to take a few thousand pounds from the secret drugs money stash and go to the shops for me. He was provided with a shopping list for a few specific items which were an important element in my plan. It wasn't going to be easy for him to find the items, but I told him to spend whatever he had to. Frank was enthusiastic and completely reliable and I knew he wouldn't let me down. He was rapidly becoming indispensable. Good old Frank.

Boxing Day was my fifth day of invisibility and it all started so positively. Refreshed after a good night's sleep, I'd washed and dried all my clothes. They smelled like a glorious summer meadow. I'll let *you* decide what a summer meadow smells like. The process of cleaning my clothes was an achievement itself and I smiled as I put them on. My mum always used to warm my clothes through before giving them to me on a school morning in winter. My clothes had become an extension of my body, an extension of my skin - they were my own personal space suit which I had to wear.

All the items I wore were amongst my favourite clothes, yet I pined for the chance to wear something different, or nothing at all. Still, just a few days to go.

At that moment I missed my mum more than anything in the whole world. She had died when I was a child, so it seemed strange that suddenly I had an overwhelming desire to be with her again. She always held my hand a little too tightly for my liking, but I would have given anything to feel that uncomfortable experience once more. Despite not having other siblings, and an uncommunicative father, I had managed to survive on my own into my mid-twenties without any major catastrophes. I pined the closeness that only a mother could provide. Removing my invisible wallet from my invisible jacket, I opened it and knew what was in store. I awkwardly removed the only photograph I had of me and my mum. It was invisible. It would be back and visible in a few days, but in my moment of need, it had vanished.

Whilst I had lost my mum at a young age, Ledley had suffered the heartbreak and trauma of his parents splitting up when he was ten years old and almost fifteen years later still hadn't come to terms with the event. His mum had a long-term drug addiction and he hadn't heard from her for years. We always said we were bonded by tragedy, which may seem a little melodramatic, but we really were like a surrogate family to each other.

I peered into my fridge and saw several rashers of bacon wrapped in cling film. Despite being severely tempted by a bacon sandwich I opted for boiled eggs and soldiers – an old favourite from my school days. I enjoyed slicing the tops off my two boiled eggs, the yolks were perfect and the simple pleasure I got from dipping my soldiers cannot be understated. With a nice cup of tea beside me, I lifted myself out of the maudlin mood and felt altogether more relaxed. I filmed myself eating breakfast and turned on the radio.

I knew that in a secret stash at the back of Frank's café was around fifty thousand pounds in cash. That amount of money would more than compensate myself, Michael and Rebecca for the loss of our savings from my boxing disaster and I was now well in profit.

As I tried to get my mind on to my activities for the day ahead, I was listening to the radio when the new single by Michael Bublé was introduced. Immediately I thought of Leon and Joe - the Michael Bublé Fan Club as I'd nicknamed them. The pair had lost well over fifty thousand pounds – and that was on top of the original twelve thousand. They must have been so pissed off - and their boss even more so. Well it served them right – it was all illegally earned, so it's not like they could report it missing or stolen. I wish I'd been a fly on the wall when they returned to discover their money had gone.

The plus side was that I was back in the red, but of course, on the minus side, the drug dealers would be going all out to find the culprit.

Before I set foot outside, I called Lucy. She was still my number one priority on my to-do list. As much as I put my mind to it, I realized that to woo someone while you're invisible is much harder than you'd imagine. It's so much more complicated than buying a girl flowers and chocolates. As quite a shy individual and lacking in general confidence, the task was made even harder. OK, girls had commented in the past that I was cute, but I wasn't sure if that was actually a compliment or not? Cute seemed a little bit like a cop-out. Like saying a baby was pretty instead of beautiful.

Lucy was the sort of girl who looked great in every photograph, whether posed for or not. There was one thing in particular about Lucy which I really liked – and that was she was always just herself. She never pouted, she often wore little or no make-up and if she had a chocolate biscuit, she always folded the wrapper neatly. If it was a KitKat, the piece of foil would be almost surgically removed and then lovingly re-folded. Michael would definitely appreciate that.

It was the little, normal things which endeared me to Lucy. As things had been so hectic in the four days so far, I'd almost lost sight of my goals. Lucy was still the one for me and with every additional day I knew her, I was more in love with her. But, was it really love? Can you fall in love with someone in what was actually just a few hours? As the Supremes once sang, 'You can't hurry love!' But, with only three days and counting in which to win the girl's affections, I just hoped that the Supremes were talking crap!

I called her.

'Lucy, it's HG! How are you doing?'

'Great thanks. How are you?' she said. I thought I could trace excitement in her voice. Maybe it was just wishful thinking.

'All good with me thank you. Have Michael and Rebecca driven you mad yet?'

'No, not yet, but if I have to kill Michael at some point, the courts will treat me leniently won't they?'

I laughed and agreed.

'I'm really in need of some fresh air and exercise, but I've been very good and done exactly as I was told. I haven't taken a single step outside of the house…'

'Excellent!' I replied. 'It really isn't safe – not yet anyway. But the good news is that if you can hang in there, I'll be over to see you later – and maybe I can get you out of the house for a bit?'

'That would be great. Rebecca and Michael are going out this afternoon to take advantage of the Christmas sales, so you won't have to skulk about.'

'Good. I'm getting fed up of sneaking about, yet people can't even see me. You'd think that I wouldn't have to sneak anywhere…'

'I've missed you!'

Did Lucy Pendleton, actually just say she'd missed me? She had said those very words once before, which in my mind meant she really liked me. Or did it mean she was a bit fed up of being stuck in exile?

Was that the major breakthrough I'd been waiting for? Or was she just being polite? God, I wished I was more educated when it came to signs and signals from girls. Was I supposed to say: 'Well I miss you too, Lucy, I find it hard to sleep because you're on my mind all the time…' Lucy wasn't on my mind *ALL* the time, but that was because of my extreme circumstances. However, she was there every time I had time to think. I was drawn to her and had to stop myself from contacting her all the time. That was the hardest thing of all, but I didn't want to come across as some sort of needy freak. The more time I spent being invisible, the lonelier I was becoming.

My mind shifted on to what was probably just an unrealistic dream – that once I'd got a million pounds, I could buy a place for myself and possibly Lucy. Or maybe it would be for me and my ex and child.

I was running out of time fast. How could I procure the funds I needed for the lavish lifestyle I'd imagined? I liked the word 'lavish' – it was a word the newspapers always used when talking about celebrity's lifestyles. All I really wanted was just to have a life with love and no immediate pressure to pay the bills.

Would it really be so terrible to steal a few diamonds from a jewellers which would be heavily insured anyway? Or what about doing a number on a bank? If I stole from the Bank of England it would be no big deal – the royal mint would just print more notes to cover it wouldn't they? They might not even notice that a few bundles of fifties had gone. I mean, how often do they do a stock take? Or, what about stealing from people's personal security boxes held in their vaults? I'd recently watched a great movie starring Jason Statham and Keeley Hawes called The Bank Job. Statham's character does a bank job, but the underlying reason is to steal one particular security box. In the movies, at least, the mega-rich people who used those facilities were often shielding possessions or money from the authorities. The money might not even be reported stolen.

There were various possibilities, but I didn't have much time to mull them over. In one way, a million pounds wasn't that unattainable – Elton John probably earned that in one night, but that was because he was as talented as fuck. Unfortunately, I *wasn't* as talented as fuck, although to be fair, not many people could fit as many plates, dishes, cups and utensils into a dishwasher as I could.

My position was quite difficult as on the one hand I had the invisibility factor to amaze people and do incredible things, but on the other, I had to keep my profile low or I'd be arrested and probably receive a lengthy prison sentence for industrial sabotage or something like that. I'm sure the authorities would have a field-day with me and would enjoy setting me up to receive a much larger sentence than I really deserved. Oh, what to do?

However, at that time I did have fifty thousand pounds. Was there something happening where I could have more of an influence than I'd had in the boxing ring? Could I get some inside information from somewhere? A tip off?

I felt like I was on a quiz show – should I stick and keep the money? After all, fifty thousand pounds was not a small sum – or should I gamble it all on a much bigger prize? At that moment I had no idea what that bigger prize was.

The time was just after 9am. I had already been up for two hours and I decided to pay another call on the Bublé brothers. I needed to find out what they were up to, were they actively seeking Lucy, and did they have a plan to recoup the lost cash?

'Boxing day' was traditionally the day of sales in the shops, and even though online sales had made large dents in their businesses, the crowds still delighted in saving money where they could. I cut through Covent Garden and stopped when I saw Nigel the busker who was already performing his routine as The Invisible Man. In his hat were a few coins, probably amounting to six or seven pounds.

A couple of unimpressed teenagers stood in front of him, smirking. One of them leaned forward and pretended to put coins into the hat, but actually I saw him take coins out. This was quite a common little trick with unruly would-be fraudsters. What on earth was wrong with people? Without the teenager realising, I lifted the culprit's wallet from his back pocket, searched it and removed all the notes. There was a total of sixty pounds. I then deposited the wallet into the nearest rubbish bin. The two young men walked away in a superior fashion, laughing to themselves at their little con. Meanwhile, I floated the notes through the air and deposited them safely into Nigel's breast pocket. As his head was tucked-down into his jacket, he couldn't quite see what had happened.

'Excellent! Here's sixty quid. And that's a great outfit,' I said, attempting to disguise my voice.

As I walked away, I heard a voice say: 'Hey, thanks a lot HG – you're the man!'

I laughed as I made my way up Neale street.

CHAPTER THIRTY-EIGHT:

Lucy says something bad

There was no-one in when I visited the flat where Leon and Joe lived. I presumed they were either out dealing or were crumpled up in the boot of a burnt-out car somewhere for failing to find the money they'd lost. I really hoped they were OK, as I'd actually got a little bit of justice planned for them myself. The big question for me was, who is Mr Big? He was the key to all this. To be honest I wasn't too bothered about the Bublé brothers themselves, because I had bigger fish to fry.

It would have been easy to break into Leon and Joe's flat, but I decided not to bother. After all, I didn't think there would be anything else to find and I was eager to see Lucy as soon as possible and spend some quality time with her. Michael and Rebecca were going to the sales – Rebecca was after a coat she'd had her eye on for ages in H&M, whilst Michael was desperate to get his hands on more cleaning products.

When I realised it was too early to see Lucy, I took a detour through central London, taking a look at the sights.

I also wandered along Oxford Street and looked through the window of Costa. I really needed a coffee, but it was too difficult to get one without the whole world watching me. A coffee would be the first thing that me and Lucy would do, I told myself. A simple coffee.

Each time I thought about Lucy, I instantly recalled her saying that she'd missed me. I was like a teenager at school after catching a girl looking at me. It probably meant nothing, but I was hanging on to the hope it did.

When I got to Michael's, Lucy was peering out of the window, looking for me. I got her attention by shaking the bushes in the front garden, I didn't think she's notice but by now she knew what to look for.

Lucy made us a both a cappuccino and opened a packet of pink wafer biscuits. In one swift movement she passed me a treat and dropped a bombshell. It was a devastating phrase which was much more painful than a weighty kick in the balls.

'I've joined a dating site!'

The bottom dropped out of my world right there and then. I couldn't even speak. Nothing. I was quiet for so long that Lucy thought I'd left.

'HG? Are you still there?' she asked, looking around the kitchen.

'Yep, still here.'

'It's been a disaster so far though. Not a single guy has swiped me…'

'What dating site are you on?' I enquired, completely disinterested, but trying to act mildly enthusiastic for Lucy's sake.

'It's called Grindr…'

'Grindr? I think that's for gay men isn't it?'

'Oh, that'll be why then.'

Despite my secret discomfort, I couldn't stop laughing. But, Lucy then told me she was winding me up – of course she knew that Grindr was for gay men.

'Have you really joined a dating site? I asked, desperately hoping it was all a big joke and that the answer would be no.

'What do you think? Yeah, I've joined Tinder!'

Apparently, it was Michael's idea. Fucking brilliant! Even my best mate was conspiring against me. Michael's idea for Lucy to join Tinder made me realise one thing though; he probably didn't know that the love of his life, Rebecca had been sexually assaulted in her past. In the police records, it noted that she'd met her attacker on a dating site. If he'd known that, I figured, there's no way on earth that he'd be recommending one to Lucy. Could things get any worse? Apparently, yes, they could.

'I've already been on and got quite a bit of interest…'

Quite a bit of interest? God, what torture that was for me. I had to go through the whole process pretending to be enthusiastic about possible suitors, whilst hoping they would all die! OK, I am exaggerating about them all dying. However, there's nothing worse than unrequited love.

Lucy seemed pleased that she was already proving very popular on Tinder, which was another arrow straight through my invisible heart.

'Be careful on those dating apps though, there are some very dodgy people about.' I said seriously. 'I haven't been on myself, but my friend Ledley has…'

As soon as I said Ledley's name I knew I shouldn't have. I didn't want her to be able to place me. But, she never gave me any indication of knowing anyone called Ledley.

Actually, I was quite surprised she hadn't been engaged to him, as he had something of a reputation around London!

'He says that people tell out-and-out lies on there. How they describe themselves on their profile is not what they're like in real life. There's like a secret code you need to know about.'

'What do you mean a secret code?' asked Lucy sampling a wafer.

'Well, for example: if someone says they are "jolly" – That doesn't mean they're jolly!'

'What does it mean then?

'It means: "type 2 diabetes". Lucy laughed.

'And if someone says they're a "professional" – It doesn't mean they're professional...'

'What does that mean?'

'It means that they work in a call centre on a zero hours contract!'

This time we both laughed uncontrollably. It was like when you're with your best friend and you're both in a bit of a stupid mood. It was the happiest I'd been since I'd left my spectacularly normal lifestyle, the previous week. Unfortunately, even though I wanted to, I couldn't go and give her a hug or anything as that might have come across as a bit weird. I was beginning to crave the human touch. And I couldn't think of anyone I'd rather touch than Lucy Pendleton.

'What about this guy?' she asked, showing me a photo of a guy aged in his late twenties with an immaculately groomed beard.

'Beards are bad!' I stated. 'It's a hygiene issue I'm afraid. Imagine all that bacteria hidden in there on bits of crisps and pastry. And I don't like his eyes...'

'Oh, I do, especially the blue one!' replied Lucy. Her sense of humour was winning me over even more, if that was possible.

She showed me another guy. His eyes were vacant - he looked like he'd been doing lots of drugs. His profile said he was an actor.

'I wonder what he's in at the moment...' said Lucy.

'Hopefully, rehab!' I replied.

'Look, here's one who's a company director!'

'Are you attracted to money, power and success?' I asked, knowing that I possessed none from the list which I'd just reeled off. I understood that women might want some sort of security and stability in a relationship, but in the modern world, surely it was just as possible for the woman to be the successful or powerful one?

'Who isn't attracted to money, power and success?'

'I can see how that would be appealing,' I said, pacing up and down the kitchen, 'but, most people don't actually have money, power and success. And anyway, I personally think that all that stuff is all overrated.

'Personally, I just want to find somebody to love - and who will love me. I want someone who will tell me when they're troubled or will wake me up in the night if they feel anxious and we'll talk about it. Just someone who'll want to hold my hand, laugh at stupid things and get just as much pleasure sitting watching Come Dine With Me together as they would climbing Kilimanjaro!

'It might sound corny, but I think that if you find true love, you *are* rich.'

Lucy didn't respond.

'Oh, er, sorry for ranting Lucy!'

Eventually she just said: 'That was a beautiful rant.'

After a few moments of complete silence, I swear that Lucy wiped her eyes, but she turned away, so I may have been mistaken.

Lucy then continued to scrawl through lots more images of guys, many who had forgotten to put any clothes on. As Lucy raised her eyebrows at some of the images, I had to restrain myself... as jealousy was in town.

'God, this guy is just a complete wanker.... And look at this poseur... who in their right mind would have a tattoo of...' she stared closer. 'Of Bradley Walsh on his arse...?'

I'd moved away from Lucy to compose myself, but this comment certainly got my interest. She angled her mobile towards me to give me a look. Making the screen bigger, I said: 'That's not Bradley Walsh the TV presenter... that's Michael Bublé!'

'How do you know it's him?'

'Because he says in his profile: "I have a tattoo of Michael Bublé on my arse, although, I've been told it looks a bit like Bradley Walsh. That sounds pretty definite to me!'

'Yeah, that is pretty conclusive,' admitted Lucy.' Just look at him, posing with his flash car!'

We both laughed at the sheer madness of it, but my mind was already putting the clues together. This character in the photo wasn't Leon or Joe – but could it possibly be the drugs kingpin himself? His profile boasted that he had his own distribution business and had a network of freelance people who delivered "stuff" for him all over London. That all seemed to tie in with him being a drugs-lord of sorts.

Whoever this guy was, he didn't actually look like a kingpin in the narcotics industry, he looked more like an accountant in local government. His profile revealed he was over 6ft, with short hair and little round John Lennon glasses. As he was pretty much naked, I couldn't get an idea of his dress-sense, but his profile was enough for me to make a bold statement:

'That's Mr. Big!' I announced.

'Well, God knows what size *YOU* are if you think that thing's big!' said Lucy, pulling a face.

Our chat had not only been productive in the search for my future benefactor, but it also drew Lucy and I closer together as friends. She was witty, sharp, intelligent and didn't take herself too seriously. When she casually said she had no intention of actually going on a date with any of the Tinder parade, I felt instantly energised.

CHAPTER THIRTY-NINE:

The facts about Mr. Big

So, these were the facts; Mr. Big lived in London, had a tattoo of Michael Bublé on his arse and virtually admitted he was running some sort of street-level operation. These snippets might not have been definitive proof, but they were a very big coincidence.

'How long do you think I should stay at the safe house for?' enquired Lucy.

'That's a good question. Probably just a few more days and everything should hopefully be back to normal.'

With the best part of three days left before I reappeared to the world, I hadn't given too much thought about what was going to happen with Lucy. She couldn't go back to her old flat, she would always be at risk due to Carl's drug connections. If I could just make that elusive million pounds, I could rent her a place or something.

Admiringly, I looked-on as Lucy made us a second cup of tea. She was casually dressed in a Green Day T-shirt which covered her knickers and She looked incredibly sexy.

From going into the cutlery drawer for a teaspoon, to reaching into the top cupboard for the tea bags, I watched her every movement. She placed two cups onto the unit top and looked at the kettle as it neared boiling point. In preparation, she removed the milk from the fridge. All the while she had her back to me. She obviously felt totally comfortable having an invisible man in the same room. Never had the mechanics of watching a cup of tea being made looked more alluring. Yes, that was the word. Alluring. And I was one hundred per-cent allured!!

'When will Michael and Rebecca be back?'

'Er, they'll probably be another hour or so. All those cleaning products will take some packing!'

'How are you finding everything. Are you comfortable?'

'Yeah, all's good thanks. They really are lovely. Anyway, tell me something about yourself... we've had quite a few chats, but I don't know much about you, apart from your obvious talent...'

'Haha,', I said, 'Apart from my obvious talent, I'm pretty boring, so there's nothing really amazing to find out, to be honest.'

'Aww, you're just being modest.'

'Ok, you're right, I'm amazingly interesting and just down-right awesome in every department!'

'See, I knew it.'

We were both completely on the same wavelength when it came to humour. I knew that the more I liked her, loved her and wanted her, it would make it more difficult for me when it turned out she didn't fancy me. Deep inside, I knew that there was a possibility I'd effectively be dumped, without Lucy really knowing who I was.

219

We both took sips of our tea, so there was a momentary silence. Then Lucy said, 'Rebecca has a lot of medication in the bathroom cupboard, do you think she's OK? I don't like to ask, as I don't know her well enough, but sometimes she just wants to be on her own. Michael said she's not been herself for the past few weeks and he's been worried about her. And I know it's none of my business…'

I slowly sipped my tea whilst considering my reply.

'I'm not sure. I know less than you to be honest.' That was my reply to Lucy. Of course, I knew much more, but I had to keep everything close to my chest. It was really none of my business, but what *was* my business was the fact that I had managed to put Fabian 'shit-name' Judson out of business for a few days.

'You know that in three days I am going to disappear. Or should that be: I'm going to appear. I'll be normal again and I'll just be like everyone else – for good. That will be it. The novelty will have completely gone. You wouldn't look twice at me if you passed me in the street. I'll just be another person on the tube, or at work, or wherever…'

'I'm so excited!' replied Lucy, like a schoolgirl looking forward to a birthday party. 'It'll be amazing to see you. It's alright for you – you've been able to see me, but it's been all one way…'

Even though a part of me was now looking forwards to the end of one-week adventure, it would be difficult facing Lucy in normal circumstances. Since nearing the end of primary school I had generally lacked confidence. I was taunted for my clothes and dishevelled appearance, which didn't help. That was because my dad refused or was unable to take on the role of my mum after she died, and the phrase I always remember him saying was, "You're a man now, you've got to do all these things by yourself!" Countless times I recall trying to hide stains on my unwashed clothes from pupils and teachers at school as my dad neglected this role. I wasn't a man at all. I was just a little boy. Mrs. Thompson my teacher took pity on me at one point and began secretly washing my clothes for me. She saw how embarrassed I was and she used to discreetly leave them for me in my desk. It was our own little secret.

The clock was ticking and I needed to do something with my day. Lucy had enjoyed watching me drink my tea and eating several pink wafer biscuits, but now it was time to make things happen.

Our hands brushed each other's, and we almost held hands, but not quite.

'Oh, by the way, did you get rid of your old mobile?' I asked as I opened the door to leave. It was imperative that Lucy was untraceable and that the Kensington drugs cartel had no method to contact her.

'Yes, don't worry, I've got rid of it...'

The architecture in Kensington looked so amazing that I stopped in my tracks to admire it. My gaze was frozen as I stood right outside the Royal College of music. A stunning red-bricked structure with countless arched windows with an impressive dual entrance. 'They don't build them like that anymore,' I muttered to myself. As I was standing there enjoying the spectacle, I was suddenly knocked flying. I was left sprawled out on the pavement.

'Watch where you're going', I called out whilst face-down on the pavement, with tiny pieces of gravel stuck to my chin.

Slowly rising to my feet, I looked around, to find a vicar standing there. And to make me feel even more guilty, he was disabled. I tried to improvise, but I'm not sure if I made things worse or not.

'Is there someone there?' asked the vicar.

'Yes, it's God here,' I said off the top of my head, not realising the impact it would have to a man of the cloth.

'God??'

'Yes, you know, that old fella who lives above the clouds! Don't be alarmed, I've just come down to earth to see how everybody's doing. How are you doing personally, vicar?'

The old gentleman was stunned. He fell to his knees with his hands clasped together.

'My lord,' he said, 'My sweet lord!'

'I'm not George Harrison!' I replied, pretty pleased with my answer.

'Is there anything I can do to assist you here on earth? I'm the Reverend Potter... but you probably know that already...'

'Yeah, er, you don't happen to know if any drugs dealers live around here do you?'

'There are many people in this area who need help and direction with their lives... but I don't know any drugs dealers personally...'

'OK,' I said, 'keep your eyes peeled.'

'Yes mighty one, I am here to serve...'

But, just when I was beginning to enjoy the chit-chat with the Reverend Potter, the conversation suddenly turned from my flippant manner into something altogether more serious.

'My lord, I'm not sure if it's appropriate to ask you this, but do you perform miracles?'

'Oh, well, I certainly have a reputation for doing them… it's been widely reported…' I replied. 'Why? Have you got something specific in mind?'

'Yes. They're a lovely family who attend the church regularly and they have had a tough time over the last twelve months. I wondered if you could help them?'

'Do they need money?'

'Oh no,' said the vicar looking skywards, 'money is not the issue. Their little daughter Keisha has cancer, I'm afraid. She's a beautiful and positive soul who loves to sing… she's only eight years old, but her time is running out – and it's the most painful situation one could ever imagine. The doctors say they've done everything they can to help her now - and I've been praying for her every day… If miracles can indeed be done, I'd appreciate it if you could enable me to switch places with her.'

I was stunned into silence. It made me feel instantly ashamed of myself for making fun of the vicar. How do you answer a question like that? I was stuck for words. The vicar meanwhile rummaged into his wallet and removed a picture of the family in desperate circumstances. Keisha, the little girl was pictured in hospital. She was clutching a soft toy of Pumbaa from The Lion King and had a huge grin on her face, despite being connected to pieces of medical equipment. So how did I answer the vicar's question?

After my silence, I said, 'Vicar, you're a very special man. Please continue to help and support these people. I'm not God at all, but if I had any power at all, I would use it to help them…' That was all I could think of to say.

My day had been mixed, with definite highs and lows. Lucy had revealed she wasn't going to go on a date with anyone from Tinder, we'd had a great laugh together and then I'd impersonated God for a minute or two with mixed results. I saw some kids playing football in the park and took the opportunity to take the ball and dribble around about seven players before scoring a terrific goal. The opposition hardly moved. They stood there dumfounded, watching the ball weave its way around them. I even did the TV commentary as I dribbled. I was like a kid again.

For half an hour, I wandered around Kensington without really achieving anything. Not sure what I'd hoped to find, but at least I got some fresh air and I scored what had to be a contender for goal of the season.

After a while wandering aimlessly around the posh part of London, I decided to visit Frank at his Café. It would be good to have a catch up. Plus, I wanted one of his amazing coffees and I knew there would be a fantastic full-English breakfast on offer.

As expected, when I looked through the window, there was Frank, scanning the Daily Mirror newspaper with a coffee in front of him. There was not a soul in the café, but Frank never seemed too concerned about the situation. Apparently, he always had a very busy spell between 7 and 8.30am as people made their way to work nearby.

'HG!' he called out as I opened the door and he saw that there was no-one there. 'How's it going? Let me get you a coffee…' He stopped mid-sip and headed for the coffee machine.

It was great to be looked after.

'What can I get you to eat? Bacon sandwich? Toastie? Full English?'

'I opted for one of his special coffees and the full-monty, full-English with toast. It had been ages since I'd had a full English and my mouth was already watering in anticipation.

'How's the haunting been going HG?'

'Not so bad, thanks Frank. I've been looking to put the frighteners on a drug dealer over in Kensington, but I haven't had much luck tracking him down. Anyway, how have you been getting on with those chores?'

Frank was busy preparing my lunch and kept turning his head to talk to me as I flipped through his newspaper.

'I think I've done pretty good, HG. I've managed to get everything you were after apart from one item.'

'That's great Frank. Well done. I honestly didn't think you'd be able to find any of the things on my list. That's brilliant, thank you so much!

'What have you done with the stuff?'

'Exactly what you said, HG. And financially it cost me – or should I say you - just under seven hundred quid. I've put your change back with the rest.' Frank nodded towards a door which led to the back of the café.

I was elated. Frank had been a godsend - and I knew, because I was God! Well, at least I had been, a little earlier.

'You're doing a brilliant job Frank, I really appreciate it.'

'No problem HG, I'm glad to help, you know that.'

'You've helped me so much so far, is there anything I can do to help *YOU*? Just name it and I'll do my best…'

Frank said, 'Nope, HG, can't think of anything. Why would I want more than this?' It's just nice to have someone in my café.'

Reminding Frank that I couldn't pay, I suggested he take a wad of cash from the kitty hidden in the back, but he wouldn't hear a word of it.

As I drank my coffee, I told Frank about a friend of mine who I thought he'd get on with – my dad! With their passion for ghost hunting, I guessed they'd hit it off straight away.

225

'Have you bumped into any other ghosts recently?' Asked Frank, sitting himself down opposite me. 'Do you ever meet any other celebrity ghosts?'

I'd previously told Frank that I was the ghost of HG Wells, the author of The Invisible Man.

'Yeah, I bumped into Elvis yesterday.'

'Fantastic – how's the fella doing?'

'He says he's got a lotta living to do. Whole lotta living to, ana-who-lotta-livin'-ana-who-lotta-livin'-ado' I replied in my best Elvis impersonation.

'Yeah, that definitely sounds like Elvis!' acknowledged Frank without laughing.

I loved how he took it all as being perfectly normal.

'Frank, while I remember, can you make a note of this telephone number? 07849 216559. That's the mobile of my friend Lucy…'

'Is she dead as well?'

'No, she's one of my 'living' friends. You might need this so just hang on to it.'

Two hours later I was in Leicester square watching the tourists take selfies in front of famous landmarks. It was busy and I got bumped and jostled quite a few times – I felt like a jumper in a tumble drier. As I headed towards Covent Garden, I hoped that one day Lucy and I could walk together as a normal couple enjoying everything that normal couples did. That hope seemed a world away at that very moment as someone else accidentally grazed my ankle.

Before long, I had drifted into the kitchens at Joe Allen's restaurant on Burleigh street. This was my favourite restaurant in all of London. It had originally been opened for all the actors and workers in the West End to have good food after the theatres closed each evening following a performance. This was the one place I was determined to take Lucy, once everything had settled down and I was back in the land of the living.

Even though it wasn't the busiest time of day in the restaurant, the kitchens were a hive of activity as preparations were underway for that evening's diners. As a big fan of Masterchef on TV I loved watching the chefs in action. The skills on show were mesmerizing. I had previously worked in several kitchens and some of the chefs I'd worked for had almighty egos. In Allen's the atmosphere was positive and encouraging, it was a real team effort. This was exactly how I imagined the atmosphere in Michel Roux Junior's kitchen. The aromas were out of this world. I was in heaven and took the opportunity to sample a few of the dishes being prepared. I felt like a fox must feel rummaging through the dustbins of a suburban semi. For a moment I thought I was going to be rumbled, but my timing was getting better, so I managed to avoid detection. If I'd had any money to give them, I would've left a massive tip.

In the restaurant area itself, there were plenty of empty seats, so I took a table to give myself some thinking time. I wondered what Leon and Joe were up to. Were they still looking for Lucy? And what had happened to the missing fifty thousand? Going to visit the police would be a waste of time as I really had no idea where to look and no clues to try and piece together. Everything was much too quiet for my liking.

With nothing else planned for the rest of Boxing day, I made it my mission to try and make some money. Some honest money. Or at least some 'reasonably' honest money. I figured that there had to be an element of cheating or dishonesty if I was to get some money quickly. For example,

227

if I went into a casino and got someone to play blackjack, and I secretly told them when to stick or twist. Then it wasn't stealing money directly off someone, but there was definitely an element of deception in play. You could call it cheating. And of course, you'd be right.

I toyed with the idea of asking Frank if he'd be up for a spot of gambling, but tried to think of something less complicated than casino-fraud. The more I thought about how I could make money from my skills, the harder it became. It would be easy to make a few hundred pounds here and there – such as when I stepped in to help Nigel 'The Invisible Man' busker – but it would never make me rich in three days.

It was obvious I needed inspiration. And then help arrived – as if God was providing me with a plan. To be honest, I was just glad he wasn't pissed off with me for impersonating him earlier on.

A gentleman on the next table was reading a copy of The Times newspaper and it contained a story about how the flamboyant President of Guinea, Papa Marape, was attending a dinner in London that very night. He was acclaimed as the most corrupt leader in the world and there was a big uproar about him even getting permission to enter the UK. He was President, but he acted like a King. In an online survey, he'd been voted 'Most corrupt leader in the world'. That was enough for me. It would be a pleasure getting the better of him. And from the photograph in the newspaper, his ego could be his big downfall. There he was, surrounded by beautiful young ladies, at a private party at his palace.

Communications were extremely difficult, and I regretted not putting more thought into the area pre-

invisibility. I needed Frank's help that evening, although only as a driver – I wasn't going to rope him into anything dodgy. We arranged to meet outside the Grosvenor House Hotel at 9pm, by which time I should have done what I had to do.

The President of Guinea and his wife Uta, would be dining with the UK minister for Overseas Aid and the Minister for Business. There would be other guests there too, all no doubt eager to be handed some lucrative contracts and the like, which would probably include a variety of inducements – which was the way to do business with the president. But, that isn't what drew me to the high-flying fraudster.

The fabulously corrupt couple had a well-known reputation for flaunting their wealth. They loved to be photographed wearing their jewel-encrusted gowns, crowns and necklaces. They really loved their 'bling'. My aim was to take a few of their jewels and share them equally between the charities: Thewaterproject.org to provide fresh water in African communities and the unregistered charity of CooperMcRae.com (me).

My dad told me that ever since he was a kid in the late sixties, the TV series Blue Peter had been raising funds to dig wells and provide clean water in Africa. Alongside the outstanding efforts of Blue Peter viewers, many countries had donated billions of pounds - and yes - you've guessed it, they still needed fucking wells and clean water! It made me so angry that this was still going on. How much does it cost to build a well? Africa should have had a well every hundred yards from all the money they've been given. And guess what? Yes, countries like ours will still be sending money to get those wells dug, fifty years from now.

Where exactly has all that money gone? Well, it's a fair bet that a lot of it has been used to buy luxury houses in Chelsea and places like that. And grand palaces owned by people such as the President of Guinea.

So, any way that I could get one over on the corrupt was a worthwhile cause. This was the best opportunity I'd had to make some big money and the good news was that I didn't have to wear any boxing gloves to do it.

CHAPTER FORTY:

The Jewel Heist

That evening, there was high security at The Grosvenor House Hotel. An hour before the guests were due to arrive, a group of around one hundred protestors – many originally from Guinea – took position as near as they could to the hotel entrance. They held placards and banners aloft which included phrases: "The President is Corrupt", "Stop Stealing from the People" and "Guinea Pigs!". I spotted one which really appealed to me. It was held aloft by a man originally from the West African country, who had fully embraced the English language and sense of humour. It said simply: "Wankers!" I thought it was a perfect example of an immigrant making the effort to be really British.

The dinner was in a private room, which with my skills I had no trouble accessing. As the time for the President's arrival drew closer, all the guests were seated at their respective tables. The room held ten tables, which in turn seated ten guests. The waiting staff were immaculately turned out and stood in pairs, with their hands held behind their backs.

A Master of Ceremony announced the entrance of the VIPs.

"Ladies and gentlemen, please be upstanding for The President of Guinea, Papa Marape and the First Lady, Uta…"

The president was a small, dumpy fellow with a huge grin and a single gold tooth at the front. He sported an impressive double-chin and wore a suit which looked fifty years out of date. His lady wife Uta was tall, slim and quite attractive. She wore large gold earrings and a nose stud. Her lipstick was the reddest of reds and she had a beauty spot painted onto her cheek. Her cleavage was impressive and was almost popping out of her red silk dress as she walked.

They – that's the President and his wife – not her breasts - received a warm round of applause and there was a buzz of expectation around the room. No doubt the privileged guests expected lucrative contracts to be forthcoming, so were all extra-welcoming. The whole event seemed in bad taste. Why be so respectful to two of the biggest crooks in Guinea? Two of the biggest crooks in all of Africa. They were happy to laud-it-all-up and live the flamboyant lifestyle whilst their people struggled for food and water. I felt ashamed that Britain had welcomed them at all.

My eyes were instantly drawn to the exquisite, yet totally over-top jewellery worn by the pair. They'd certainly been busy robbing their own citizens by the look of it.

As drinks were being served and the noise of chattering became louder, I moved as close as I could to the President and his wife. The President was wearing some sort of head-dress which had several diamonds on display, he also sported a chain, similar to those worn by Lord Mayors. The piece also boasted a selection of diamonds surrounded by an impressive assortment of pearls. A wristlet finished off his outfit which again was studded in precious stones. I didn't know what type of diamonds they were, but even I could tell that they were expensive.

The President's wife Uta sported even more jewellery than her husband. There was so much sparkling going on that I almost went and bought myself some shades to protect me from retinitis. Uta also donned a sort-of tribal hat which looked like a triangular Fez. It was encrusted with at least half a dozen diamonds and finished off with gold sequins. Even Elton John would have said it was a bit over-the-top! Uta's hat was perched quite high, as she obviously had a lot of hair. She also had a selection of jewelled bracelets and wore three rings on each hand – all featuring impressive jewels. They were a right couple of show-offs.

Whilst the guests were fawning over Guinea's premier crooks, I took a closer look at their 'bling', making a mental note of which diamonds I would try and take. It wouldn't be easy, but it was a much more agreeable task than getting my ass whupped by Dwight Dixon, the reigning World Middleweight Champion.

As I contemplated on how to remove precious stones from their housings, I remembered that I had a penknife with me – the one which I'd found in my jacket pocket a few hours after becoming invisible. It was fate. My golden future was getting closer and closer - and my lucky penknife was going to help me accomplish one of the targets I'd set myself a week earlier.

As far as valuations go, I had no idea what the diamonds were worth, but with no experience whatsoever, I had to presume that the stones were the real thing. I guessed that the President and his wife wouldn't be seen dead wearing imitation stones or cheap crap.

As the starter was being served, I removed my penknife and felt for the little groove on one of the blades so that I could pull it open. My thumb nail fitted perfectly, and the small blade was extended.

The first course of the evening was soup. A creamy chicken soup which almost had me drooling. Getting the jewels out wasn't going to be easy – I had to try and engineer the moves whilst my hands, *and* the penknife were invisible.

I didn't want to hang around all evening, so I got stuck in to removing the first diamond from Uta's hat, but because she had so much hair piled beneath it, she obviously couldn't feel me manipulating it as I stood behind her, like a demented hairdresser at work. The main difficulty I had was that Uta had the habit of lowering her face to be almost level to her soup bowl to eat and then raising her head again. It was the sudden movement which made me slip forward as I was just about to remove the first stone. It popped out and dropped straight into Uta's soup. She never even saw it.

Deciding not to try and retrieve it, I endeavoured to pluck a few more jewels out as quickly as possible and then get out of there. Frank was waiting across the road in his car, which was an ideal set-up. I didn't really need a getaway car, but it was much more convenient than traipsing around London on my own with diamonds.

As I continued my operation, I realised that each stone was clasped into a small metal holder, which in turn was sewn into the hat. Despite the potential value of all this jewellery, they seemed relatively easy to dislodge.

After a few minutes, a security guard arrived to talk to the President. I couldn't hear what they talked about, but the President and his wife both got up and left the room, surrounded by security personnel. My hand plunged into what remained of Uta's soup and rescued the diamond from within. I'd also managed to get one more diamond. As a non-diamond expert , I had opted for the ones which were the prettiest colours. I got one blue diamond and one red one. They actually looked really cool.

As I held the two diamonds in my grasp there was a commotion in the room as several protesters gate-crashed the party. That marked the end of my stint as a diamond thief. I needed to leave as quickly as possible, as I didn't want anyone to see the diamonds floating through the air, or anything suspicious. When I got to the main doors to leave, the crowd had grown and there were now around two hundred protesters in full voice. The police were holding them back and preventing anyone else from entering the hotel.

Across the road I saw Frank sitting in his car, exactly where he said he would be. As I passed the protesters and began to cross the road, I thought I saw someone I recognised and so stopped in my tracks just for a brief moment. Out of the blue I was clipped by a moped, spun around and left spread-eagled on the freezing tarmac. It all seemed to happen in slow-motion, I saw a swirl of lights and a light breeze crossed my face as I swivelled. The diamonds were jolted from my grasp as I hit the ground and somersaulted under Frank's car. The chanting from the crowd covered my cries as I felt my chin scrape painfully along the tarmac. I scampered up as quickly as I possibly could, as I could hear cars approaching fast. It was then I realised I had what is known as a 'dead-leg' which severely hampered my movement.

Frank was reading a newspaper totally oblivious to the incident which had just taken place. I knocked on the window which he quickly wound down.

'Frank, it's me.' I said with pain in my voice.

'Alright HG?'

'Frank, I've dropped something under your car, could you just move it about ten feet so I can have a look?'

'No problem fella.'

Frank moved his silver Citroen Berlingo car forward and then stuck his head out of his window to see what I was searching for. Almost straight away I found one of the diamonds, but there was no sign of the other. Unfortunately, Frank had been parked over a sewerage grate. I placed my face so that it was touching the grid. My cheek was still sensitive after my failed boxing match and now I had a chin which provided me with an added dimension of pain. All I could see was the movement of water flowing past beneath the metal drainage cover. The other diamond was lost.

'What are you looking for?' called out Frank

'It's OK Frank, I've found it…'

'What is it?' he said, as I opened the passenger door and slowly dragged myself in.

'It's a diamond,' I replied. 'I've no idea what it's worth.'

'Well I've got a mate in Hatton Garden who could put a price on that little beauty. It looks like a pretty thing.'

And it was worth a pretty thing too. The next time I saw Frank he told me it was worth over twenty thousand pounds.

So, my night which had been so full of potential had resulted in a lost precious stone and one worth 20K.

Later that night I decided to treat myself to a stay in a top hotel. The Savoy was delightful, even through the pain I was experiencing, but once again I was scavenging for food. By the time I crashed into my free five-star bed I found myself wishing I had just gone home where I could relax fully and stick a pizza in the oven or something. I was really pissed-off with myself for not being able to do anything right, or for just not having much luck.

Years ago, as a child, on countless occasions I recalled my mum saying that she was very lucky and I remember thinking that it was a strange thing to say because I'd never, ever seen her win anything. It was only after she died and at her funeral, I mentioned it to my aunty that I understood. My aunty Jen smiled and told me that my mum meant she was lucky to have had a little boy like me. I realised that 'luck' actually wasn't about winning anything. It was about being part of a family, being healthy and in a position to enjoy life. Unfortunately, little Keisha - the girl with cancer, and her family were not in that privileged position.

CHAPTER FORTY-ONE:

Long live The Sex Pistols

I woke early, had a five-star shower and a five-star breakfast, albeit secretly, then I left my five-star hotel without paying my five-star bill. That bit felt pretty good. I had almost forgotten what had happened the night before with the President of Guinea.

Walking through the streets of London at 7am was quite invigorating, and my dead-leg seemed to have rested nicely. I loved watching businesses come to life, deliveries being made and people enjoying a coffee on their way to work. A group of pigeons gathered behind a young lady eating a croissant and drinking a coffee as she walked along. It was as though she was the Pied Piper of London. When she glanced behind her and noticed the line of pigeons, she laughed to herself. I also smiled to myself.

A young man watched too, from a nearby bench. He smiled and a few moments later they were chatting and laughing. Maybe they'd get together and make a go of it? They were obviously attracted to each other and it gave me hope that one little interaction could lead to something more substantial. Or alternatively, knowing what I'd seen since I became invisible, he'd probably beat her up and treat her like shit. At that moment I gave the benefit of the doubt to humankind. For a moment it gave me a faint hope that me and Lucy could also have a chance of romance.

It was great to see the building where I lived. No five-star hotel could replace my home comforts. I retrieved my key from on top of the door frame and made my way straight to the kitchen after tripping on my Rylan Clark-Neal rug. I decided to make a posh coffee from my machine and checked my mobile for messages. There were none. I really *WAS* invisible!

Another day had passed without me getting any further – although that was entirely my own fault. I flipped through my vinyl records and put on the 'Never Mind the Bollocks, here's the Sex Pistols' album. I sat in my favourite chair and sipped my coffee whilst listening to Johnny Rotten and the boys.

The Sex Pistols were probably the coolest band ever. My dad introduced me to them officially after my mum died. He said she never liked them… She was a Clash fan.

My dad's record collection contained a load of stuff that I'd borrowed, but had no intention of returning because it was so brilliant. I had 'borrowed' albums by The Jam, The Skids, The Stranglers, Stiff Little Fingers, Elvis Costello and lots more. I think they were all from the late 1970s and early 80s. Apart from talking about 'ghost' shows on TV, talking about music was the thing which sparked my dad into life. He loved the fact that I liked the same music as him and he kept all the tickets to gigs he'd been to in a frame prominently displayed in his lounge. I felt completely relaxed in my chair with The Sex Pistols doing their thing. I closed my eyes, and all was good.

Afterwards, I phoned Lucy and arranged to meet her a few hours later. Hearing her voice was wonderful, and I enjoyed the fact that she always seemed pleased to hear from me.

Michael and Rebecca were out visiting Michael's parents in Surbiton when I arrived, so we had the house to ourselves. Lucy was dressed in tight pale blue jeans and wore a pink sweat-top with the phrase 'Ain't No Stoppin Us Now!' across her chest. She looked as amazing as usual.

'So, you keep talking of not being invisible for much longer – how do you know? I don't understand?'

'I'm going to be completely back to normal in two-days-time at 9.15am. I don't know why, because I'm not a scientist, but all I know is that from then on, I'll be completely normal. Of course, there is a chance that this calculation is about as accurate as a weather forecast – and I could be invisible forever. I don't think it's ever been properly tested to be honest!'

'My God. What are you going to do if you stay invisible?' said Lucy, obviously concerned for my future welfare.

'Fuck knows.'

'That would be awful, wouldn't it? I couldn't begin to imagine that…'

'Yeah. Being invisible sounds pretty cool, when you're visible… and it does have its advantages, don't get me wrong, but there are also some big downsides.'

Lucy had the TV on in the background. It was one of those daytime discussion shows and one of the guests being interviewed was nursing a baby. It caught my eye and it suddenly reminded me of my soon-to-be fatherhood experience. I really didn't want to mention anything to Lucy, for obvious reasons, but I thought it was best to be honest and just tell her.

'Lucy, I have something to tell you. It's been on my mind for a few days, and I've been so caught up with other things that I haven't really had time to think too much about it...'

Perfect Ten Pendleton, sat up on the settee and looked at me. I thought she was going to say something, so I paused. But she never spoke.

'The thing is... er... well, before I was invisible I erm, was seeing this girl – Sarah Jemson. It wasn't serious or anything, and she decided that it wasn't going to work, so she left...'

'Oh, she left you?'

'Yes, and not that I'm bothered, but you'll never believe this, she took my Meat Loaf albums with her...'

'You *ARE* bothered, aren't you?' commented Lucy

'Yes, I am bothered as it happens. I cannot tell you how good those albums are! Especially 'Bat Out Of Hell!'

'Haha... anyway, so Sarah left you...'

'Yes, that was a couple of weeks ago and then the other day she left me a note – she slipped it under my door. I'd become invisible by then, so I couldn't answer the door – anyway.... That's it.'

'What do mean that's it? She left you...OK, I thought it was going to be something more important than that. Not that Sarah leaving you isn't important enough...'

'Oh yeah, there is one other thing...' I continued slowly. Lucy waited.

'Hmmm, I'm going to be a dad.'

Lucy sat there and didn't say anything, at least not for a few seconds. I kept my eyes on her trying to pick up on how she was taking my news. Was she showing signs of being upset? It would've been great if she'd cried, "Oh no, that's the worst news I could ever hear, because I'm madly in love with you and I was just about to take you upstairs and shag your brains out!" Unfortunately, she didn't say that, or anything remotely like that at all.

She said something that took me completely by surprise. It was a question that I, and probably anyone else could have predicted:

'Will it be an invisible baby?'

I started to laugh and then she did. And we didn't stop for quite a while. Well, it was probably just a few seconds.

'NO, it will NOT be an invisible baby.' I eventually replied, 'And I won't be getting back together with Sarah either. The relationship was over.'

'What does Sarah say?'

'She wants to get back together with me. I've no idea why...'

'Me neither!'

'That's charming,' I replied. 'My friends will tell you that I'm quite a catch!'

I was giving Lucy the opportunity to give me some sort of compliment, but I didn't get one. It made me think that if Lucy wasn't going to be interested, then maybe I really should consider having Sarah back? At least the baby would have a proper dad.

'Do you love this girl?' asked Lucy, getting up from the settee and pacing around and tapping her finger against her chin. For a moment she lost track of where I was - and when I replied, she was actually looking in the wrong place.

'No, I can only love one person at a time.'

'What does that mean? You don't love her then?'

'No, definitely not. She's quite nice really, but she's not right for me.'

'It would mean you get your albums back…'

'You're right. I'll deffo get back together then! We can get married, and then I can whisk her away for a honeymoon in Devon – that's her favourite place.'

'Oh, I've never been to Devon,' said Lucy

'Great pubs and beautiful scenery,' I said enthusiastically. 'The last time I was there I sampled the local honey. She was a lovely girl!'

I couldn't resist the joke. Lucy came over to me and accurately thumped my arm. 'You're mad!' she said, with a big smile on her face.

'What do you think you'll do?' She said playfully pushing me. Was I detecting a hint of jealousy? Oh, I desperately hoped so.

'What do you want out of life?' I asked, deflecting the questions away from myself. 'What do you *really* want, Lucy?'

'Well for starters, I know what I don't want - and that's someone like Carl. I just want someone who will love me. I hope I'm not asking too much…'

'I don't think you are.'

'I'm not materialistic at all. As long we love each other and care for each other. Money is not important. I think it's all about whether you feel comfortable with someone and you can just be yourself.'

Lucy was saying everything I wanted her to say – apart from saying she wanted to do it all with me. At that moment I could have grabbed her and asked her to marry me. The very fact that I hadn't used my powers to watch her getting undressed said it all to me. I was really in love.

CHAPTER FORTY-TWO:

My big mistake

Lucy hadn't been out for a few days and so when I suggested a walk to get some fresh air, she rushed excitedly to get her coat. She wore a bright red knee-length number and a pair of black leather boots. We stepped out of the house and she searched for, and then grabbed my arm, like a couple would. Or maybe how just good friends would.

'This is great,' remarked Lucy, looking up at the sky. 'It's like I'm free at last. I feel like I've been a prisoner.'

'...But in a very clean and tidy prison!' I pointed out.

'Exactly. And with really good food...'

We ambled down Gregson street and then Parker avenue. What I hadn't realised was that we were being followed. I was so taken with having an attractive woman on my arm that everything else blurred into insignificance.

'You know, I think some girl's going to be lucky having you in their life. And I have the feeling you'll be a great dad.'

I really didn't want Lucy visualising me with anyone else or as a father. It seemed to mean that she would be willing to accept that we would never get together. It looked like she had kicked a possible happy ending into touch.

'I don't even want to think about that.' I replied seriously, desperately trying to think of something so I could change the subject.

As we passed the small red post-box on the corner of Watts road, the sound of a car-engine revved and a black BMW car drove past us, much more slowly than one would have expected. A hundred yards further along, it parked between a white Fiat500 and yellow Volvo. I didn't think anything of it as I was pre-occupied by Lucy. If I'd been more alert to the situation, I would have changed sides with her, as she was nearest the roadside. As we got nearer to where the BMW was parked, a guy opened the driver's side door, got out and lit up a cigarette, all with his back towards us.

As we walked within twenty feet, I noted his demeanour and a thought ran quickly through my mind.

'You did get rid of your old mobile phone, didn't you?' I asked quickly. Carl was the sort of person who was so controlling, he would have definitely put a tracker on Lucy's mobile. And it was possible that the Bublé brothers, twins or whatever they were, had Carl's mobile in their possession.

'Where did you get rid of it?' I continued.

'I put it in Michael's dustbin.' announced Lucy innocently.

'Oh fuck…'

As we got alongside the BMW, the passenger door opened and a second guy got out. Both were dressed as if to hide their identities, but I knew who they were. It was Leon and Joe. They dashed towards Lucy. I tried to move her to safety behind me as Leon made a grab for her. I managed to grab his arm and hit him in the face. His other arm wrapped around me, so I was effectively useless in stopping Joe grabbing Lucy as she attempted to get away.

I thrashed my arms about like a demented aircraft controller. Leon had no idea what was really going on, as he had his arms wrapped around something that he couldn't actually see - me. After a brief struggle, I managed to break free and kicked him in the balls. He certainly never saw *that* coming.

He fell to the ground and tried desperately to crawl towards their car. Joe meanwhile was holding a cloth against Lucy's face as he dragged her to the vehicle. He was using some form of drug from a turquoise bottle to render her helpless and I heard him say, "C'mon, let's get her to the 'W'" as he bundled Lucy unceremoniously into the back seat. As soon as she was in, he slammed the door shut and instantly spun around – in the process unknowingly headbutting me in the face. I heard a dull thud. Everything went blurry and I passed out on the pavement. I just had time to register the faint whiff of freshly-laid tarmac before I lost consciousness.

After a few minutes I slowly opened my eyes and noticed steam rising from my face. I then felt heat on my cheeks and my face seemed to burn. A dog was having a piss on me. A little old lady, said, 'That's it Georgie, who's a good boy?'

What happened? I was with Lucy and... Lucy was gone. Taken.

I registered it in my mind, Lucy was gone. I was going to look for them, find them, and then I'm not sure what, but I was definitely going to do something to them!'

The car used in the abduction was a black BMW, I knew the two culprits and where they lived – but they weren't going to take Lucy there. That's right, Leon said something about the 'W'. What the fuck was the 'W'? As if it wasn't bad enough, all I had was a stupid clue that even Sherlock Holmes would struggle with. What was the 'W'?

What could I do? I had the equivalent of a superpower but couldn't do anything 'super' with it. In the circumstances it seemed like a gimmick rather than a superpower. I possessed a superpower where I could get into the cinema for free. Whoopee! It was only a fiver for non-superheroes.

While I dithered on the pavement of Watts road, Lucy could've been in a ships container somewhere being sex-trafficked to exotic places such as Amsterdam, Oman, or Huddersfield. Just a few minutes earlier we had been bonding and actually getting to know each other. Now that was shattered.

Angry with myself for letting two dim druggies take Lucy away from me, I once again chastised myself. I was useless and I'm sure that when she found herself sitting next to a horny Sheik on his huge luxury yacht off the coast of Wolverhampton or wherever, she'd be pretty pissed off with me. Unintentionally, I'd let down the girl I loved. Life didn't get much shitter than that.

I was getting carried away. Lucy wasn't kidnapped in order to be sex-trafficked, she was taken because they thought she had their drugs money. That's the only reason they would want to talk to her. They may have suspected the original 12K could be due to Lucy, but the other 50K which went missing from Leon's flat was obviously nothing to do with her. But then again, they might have concluded that Lucy had an accomplice to do the dirty work for her. Either way, she was in big trouble. And I was responsible.

What on earth could I do to find her? I didn't even have a mobile to call anyone. Frank was really the only person I could think of to call, but what could he do to help?

The big question was, what did the 'W' stand for? Was it someone's name, or was it the town where she was being taken to? God, I hoped not, I couldn't imagine anyone ever wanting to go to Walsall. Not even semi-conscious.

Was it a venue? A restaurant? An area of London? I was already driving myself insane trying to think. Why the hell hadn't I put a tracker app on her mobile – especially as I knew that people might be looking for her. It was an innocent oversight.

The best thing to do was visit the Bublé Brothers' flat to see if I could find a clue to where they were heading. The twenty-five-minute journey seemed to take hours as my mind was working overtime trying to figure out what 'W' stood for. I hoped they weren't taking her to a Westlife reunion concert, as I wouldn't wish that on anyone.

Back at Leon's there was no one around, so I managed to kick the door in quite easily. Their drugs den was in a reasonable state. It looked like they'd made an effort to tidy up, yet there was still a selection of drugs paraphernalia lying around, waiting to be discovered by the authorities. There was even a dusting of powder on the table and some on the carpet too. 'They obviously don't have a 'Dyson' I thought.

Rummaging through the drawers of the one piece of furniture which carried any sort of paperwork. I'd hoped to find a mobile number, a name – beginning with the letter 'W', or an address. Just a tiny little clue would be better than what I already had. If those goons laid a finger on Lucy, then I would do indescribable things to them – but I'd probably have to look away while I did them, as I was a bit squeamish. I once fainted when a friend of mine put too much ketchup on his chips. Not the best trait for a potential torturer, I know.

Nothing in the top drawer other than a few unpaid bills, and the usual crap: biros, rubber bands, paperclips, old bank cards, knuckledusters…

The second drawer down was completely empty apart from an empty crisp packet. Ready salted.

The bottom drawer was more interesting. Beneath a piece of material was a notebook. It was a cheap, tatty book which had obviously been in someone's back pocket at some point because it had an exaggerated curve to it. I opened the book and flipped through it, quickly scanning the pages, but not really taking notice of the fine details. Then I stopped on a page which had a title above a list of dates. The title said: 'Shipment in'. I took this to mean a consignment of drugs. It also gave a list of what were obviously ports, and then a series of code numbers. 'These could be containers' I thought to myself. Whatever they were, they weren't the sort of thing that a non-drug dealer would have in their notebook. Perhaps Leon and Joe were a little bit higher up the food chain than I thought?

If these were drugs shipments, they'd obviously been very busy boys, as the list ran to hundreds of lines. Despite their skills as dealers, they were pretty crap at keeping their activities a secret. Perhaps the police were in their back pockets? They definitely had the knack of leaving drugs and even money out in the open.

I made my way home as quickly as I could, taking the notebook with me. It wasn't a particularly easy task taking any object, but I slipped the notebook down my sock. Yes, if people had been especially alert, they might have seen a little book hovering near the pavement, but nobody seemed to see anything. And if they did, no one tried to do anything about it.

My mind was processing everything as quickly as it could. What should I do next? As I reached for my mobile to call Frank, I remembered that Lucy had her own mobile with her, so I decided to call her. I was just about to press the last digit when it struck me that I needed an angle. It wouldn't be Lucy who answered the phone – or if it was, there would be someone listening and prompting her. Sitting on the edge of my bed, I quickly formed a plan before making the call. Should I pretend to be a police officer? Would that have them quivering in their boots? I just needed to come up with something that would stop them touching, hurting or even, God forbid, killing Lucy. I scratched my chin nervously. After all, I didn't have a good track record of saving someone's life.

I needed to call as soon as possible, before anything bad happened to Lucy.

Over the next hour I tried calling her mobile several times, and each time it rang out and went on to the answer machine. I didn't leave a message.

I thought I'd try one final time before giving up. The phone rang. It rang four times and then it was picked up. Silence.

'Hello, this is Lucy…' I could hear that it wasn't the relaxed, happy Lucy who I was with an hour earlier.

'Hi, this is detective HG from Scotland Yard…'

I don't know where 'Scotland Yard' came from, but it sounded more important than anything else I could think of. The druggies would be listening anyway, so I wanted it to sound as formal as possible.

'We need to see you as soon as possible. Can you get into the station in the next half hour?'

'…I don't think so,' she said, whilst obviously being distracted by someone in the background. Then the phone went dead. I wasn't sure what their game was, but it was certainly frustrating me. There was not the tiniest glimmer of a clue to go on.

For the next hour, I tried to get my head around what had happened. There was nothing I could do to locate Leon and Joe. I knew their boss man lived in the Kensington area, but knew nothing more than that. I paced up and down my lounge, kicking out every now and again into thin air. In my hour of need I was getting no help. 'God, please help me!!!' I called out.

A few moments later I heard a series of noises outside my door. It sounded like someone had fallen over and dropped some packages. It was definitely the sound of boxes hitting the floor. I presumed it was the big guy upstairs with his mysterious obsession. For some reason, it overtook my thoughts and I decided to see just what he was doing up there. My mind was all over the place and it was giving me a headache.

CHAPTER FORTY-THREE:

Breakthrough

As I eased open my door, there was my upstairs neighbour, trying to carry more boxes than anyone should. I followed him up the stairs, leaving plenty of room between us, just in case he dropped everything again. He duly did so, right outside his own door. I'd never been any further up than my own floor and I noticed the residents above had made an effort to make the landing look friendly and colourful. Two large exotic plants in dark-blue pots were strategically positioned in each corner and the walls had been painted in a very light shade of orange, giving the landing a hint of the Mediterranean.

The big guy eventually opened his door, gathered together his boxes and stacked them just inside. That gave me ample opportunity to walk straight in like I owned the place. There were boxes and boxes, and more boxes everywhere.

There was a long hallway before it opened out into a large and impressive open-plan living space. The sight which greeted me was not what I was expecting. I was awestruck by what was in front of me. No wonder he'd needed box after box of stuff. The view was fucking unbelievable. I stood their trying to take it all in… He'd been busy alright.

The big guy was not a serial killer at all. It turned out big guy was a serial Lego builder. He'd cleared out his complete lounge - and it was a big lounge – and had built himself a complete replica of London. I'd read an article online about adults who were obsessed with Lego, and my neighbour was definitely one of them. They were known as AFOLs - Adult Fans of Lego.

Everything was there before me. The London Eye, The Shard, Nelson's Column, The Houses of parliament, Big Ben, Buckingham Palace and more. And it was all there in perfect scale. No architect could have done it better, it was almost a tourist attraction it its own right. But, despite all the undoubted skill and quite possibly years of toil it had taken to construct, this was a work destined never to be seen by the public.

The city landscape was too vast to see from ground level, I needed to see it from a higher vantage point. The big guy had a step ladder positioned so that he could plan and monitor his vision from on high.

I took no notice of him moving around in the kitchen making a cup of tea and climbed his decorator's ladder without taking my eyes off the city landscape in front of me. Why would anyone go to the extreme of replicating the whole of London in Lego in his lounge? It was a beautiful thing. And judging by the many boxes mounting up in his hallway, he had expansion plans.

It was whilst I was precariously balanced two steps from the top of this shaky aluminium ladder that a most wonderful thing happened. The answer to my prayer was there, right in front of me. I stared and yes, it was still there right in front of me. Sometimes, miracles do happen.

My eyes were drawn to the Kensington area of the city. I was looking for…well, I don't know what I was looking for, but my eyes found it. The road system in Kensington from above was quite an unusual design. Most roads ran parallel with each other, but one smaller section stood out as I looked down. It looked like the letter 'W'. That *had* to be it. It had to be what the Bublé brothers were referring to.

'Take her to the W' that's what Leon said as Lucy was pushed semi-conscious into the car. And now, right in front of me was a 'W' as plain-as-day.

That's where they'd taken Lucy and I had to get there without delay.

My own personal 'Clarence the Angel' had appeared and shown me the way. My own Clarence wasn't an angel dressed in white, he was fat, bald guy with a Lego fetish, dressed in a David Bowie t-shirt.

Without him ever knowing I'd been there, I left the big guy's flat. I knew I'd be back to introduce myself when all this was over, but at that moment, I had a damsel in distress to save. Yes, I was a bit pretentious, but fuck it, I still had two days of my superpowers left, so I was going to make it all count. It was HERO time!

As I hurried back to my flat on the floor below, a young woman almost knocked me over as she made her way up the stairs. She seemed upset, but I didn't have time to find out what the reason was. The house I lived in appeared to be some sort of emotional hub.

CHAPTER FORTY-FOUR:

On the road with Frank

'Frank? Yeah, it's me HG, your friendly neighbourhood ghost.'

'HG, lovely to hear from you, how's it going?'

'Not great Frank. I need a big favour - and normally I wouldn't ask, because I know you've got a business to run...'

'Look HG, just tell me what you need, a mate of mine, Roger, is helping me out today, so I can make myself free right now. I'm at your disposal.'

'Brilliant!' I said, like a weight had been lifted off my shoulders.

'I need you to pick me up and take me to Kensington...'

'Oh, haunting the well-to-do now are we?' he joked.

'Yeah, something like that Frank...'

Twenty-five minutes later, Frank drew up and I got straight in without any pleasantries. I had been pacing up and down the pavement waiting, like a caged, ravenous tiger ready to attack a baby pig. OK, that's probably a bit of an exaggeration, but I was definitely impatient.

I patted my pockets – was I prepared for any eventuality? I thought I had everything I needed. The most important piece of equipment in my armoury being the power of surprise.

We travelled through the streets of London in silence. I could feel Frank casting glances towards me every now and again, but he didn't say anything. And neither did I. All I could do was shuffle uncomfortably in my seat as I thought about the situation and what might lie ahead. Frank seemed to sense that something was wrong, but he didn't pry for details.

In my mind I was trying to work out some sort of plan, but then I wondered whether it would all be a waste of time, as yes, we were going to Kensington, to the 'W' on the Lego map, but once there, I had no idea where or which house they were holding Lucy. And, of course, there was a chance that I'd got things completely wrong and we were on some sort of wild-goose chase. The thing was, I had no other lead to follow, so had to put my faith in the only option there was.

Soon we were in Kensington at the junction between Richmond road and Adamson terrace. We were at the 'W'. Frank parked the car and I asked him to wait until I'd had a chance to do a quick survey of the scene.

The houses were all immaculately kept three-story buildings and the gardens were as neat and tidy as you could wish for in winter. I looked all around me, walked a few hundred yards and turned 360 degrees. Everything was a perfect picture of the privileged London lifestyle. Every house I could see in any direction was probably worth millions. It told me that there was big money in the drugs trade, I just needed to find the kingpin and free Lucy.

When I returned to Frank's car, he was busy reading a copy of The Times newspaper. He was engrossed in a story concerning insider trading. I knocked on the driver's side window which startled him for a second. He wound it down and asked if I'd found what I was looking for?

'Unfortunately, I haven't.'

Explaining my mission to locate the possible top man of a drugs organisation, we both set our minds to work.

'Does he have a car?' asked Frank, unwrapping a toffee.

What a brilliant question and it was something I had completely overlooked. Did he have a car? The streets were designed in such a way that few houses had drives or garages – which meant that most of the resident's cars were parked on the streets.

I thought back to Lucy showing me the profile on Tinder. Yes, we were gambling that the guy we saw with the Michael Bublé tattoo was the man we were after, but not only did he fit the criteria, I also remembered the comment I made to Lucy as I looked at his profile: "Look at him, posing with his flash car." He was draped over a white Mercedes car. If it really was his car, then this was a vital clue. All I had to do was find his car and the chances were, I would find him too – and Lucy.

'Frank, we're looking for a white Mercedes!' I announced enthusiastically.

We both went separate ways in search of the vehicle which might lead us to Lucy. I scoured my designated area but found nothing, but as I turned to walk back to Frank's car, he walked briskly around the corner, with his thumb in the air pointing behind him.

'I'm here. Have you found something?'

Frank had to wait a moment to regain his breath.

'Yeah, I've found a white Mercedes…'

I followed Frank until we reached the vehicle. The doors were locked and I as I peered through the windows, I could see that it was a real mess inside.

'I might have to smash the window,' I said, half looking around for a brick.

'There's no need for that,' replied Frank. 'There's a parking permit in the window. It's registered to number 68 Adamson terrace. The house was opposite, the one with a deep red door and frosted windows on the ground floor.

I told Frank to stay with his vehicle, and if he hadn't heard from me in thirty minutes, he had to call the Police. Hopefully half an hour would be more than enough time to handle this situation. I also suggested that if he was needed – and hopefully he wouldn't be needed– that there was a chance it could be dangerous. He seemed OK with that possibility, but putting Frank in danger was definitely a last resort.

Frank returned to his car, and I stood outside number 68 wondering how to proceed. For a moment, I considered ringing the doorbell as a ruse for entering the building, but I decided to try the doorknob first. I'd seen so many movies where they broke into a house only to find that the door wasn't actually locked. I turned the doorknob and slowly pushed open the door. I was in. Ta-dah!

The entrance lobby which was not how I'd imagined it. A huge crystal chandelier dominated the space and there was a long, swirling staircase immediately ahead of me. The whole place was tastefully decorated, and the walls were covered with paintings in a classic style. This didn't seem like the sort of sordid drugs den I'd imagined it to be. Perhaps this *was* the wrong house after all?

I decided to have a look in the downstairs rooms first. Each room I entered was the same as the entrance hall. It was more like the residence of a little old lady rather than someone who possessed a tattoo of Michael Bublé and malicious intent.

The lounge was home to a grand piano, exotic pottery, plants, and furniture which looked like it should have been in a museum. The kitchen was unremarkable and empty, another sitting room was draped in what looked like decorator's sheets and a further room housed a thousand books and an old oak desk. So far, so bad.

I was just beginning to think I was on the wrong track entirely when I opened a door off the kitchen. It was a utility room. On the floor were a selection of wellingtons, riding boots and outdoor items, but hanging up was the one thing which didn't quite fit with all those things. Hanging there was a hoodie.

Taking it from its hook, I opened it out fully to reveal that it had wording on the front. It said: "Lil Baby" and there was a picture of a skull smoking some weed.

Lil' Baby was a rapper from Atlanta, Georgia and was said to be one of the best rappers of all-time. Either the 'little old lady' of the house had a very unusual taste in music or there was more to this Kensington residence than first met the eye. For the first time, I was pretty certain I was in the place where Lucy was being held.

It was time to venture up the staircase. Even though I was invisible, I still tried to tread carefully to minimise noise as I moved.

I quickly scanned the first floor, but there was nothing to give me any hint of illegal behaviour. As I stood still to listen, I heard the smallest creak of a floorboard above me. Someone was home.

As I reached the top floor, a light, open corridor led to a room at the very end where I could see someone deep in concentration. I gently walked along, trying not to make a sound. There was a framed black and white photograph on the wall of notorious drugs dealer Frank "Superfly" Lucas a former heroin and organized crime boss, whose life was dramatized in the movie American Gangster starring Denzel Washington. Not the best role model.

At the end of the corridor was large open plan area. This looked like it was the very hub of their illicit operation. Sitting around a large round table were Leon and Joe, both measuring out cocaine like contestants on The Great British Bake Off, measuring out ingredients for a cake. Their concentration was admirable – I bet they never showed the same commitment when they were at school.

Another face at the table was the guy from the profile Lucy showed me on Tinder. He had a stupid moustache which looked like it belonged to Salvador Dali and he wore a pink shirt and purple bow-tie. His inaccurate tattoo of Canadian crooner Michael Bublé was hidden from view, but it was definitely the guy from Tinder. Whoever he was, he was not the sort of drugs lord I had imagined. When he spoke, he had the accent of a public schoolboy. I'd expected a guy brought up on the dirty streets of Tower Hamlets, not the well-coiffured streets of Kensington.

So, there they were, the three people I hated the most in the world – apart from sexual predator and general scumbag Fabian Judson.

In the far corner of the room was Lucy.

My Lucy. Love-of-my-life Lucy. She was tied to a chair and had a bruised cheek. She'd obviously been hit. Other than that, she looked OK. I'd managed to get her out of one terrible life-threatening situation and plonked her right down in the middle of another. Witnessing her in her pain and discomfort, I was extremely angry and becoming more and more agitated by the second. But, I knew I had to try and remain calm. I just couldn't fuck this up.

The room was quiet. There was no music, so it was imperative that I moved around as silently as possible. Any noise would draw attention to myself. Worryingly, there was a firearm on the table too, which I presumed was loaded.

At least Lucy was OK, so I just had to make the right call. Even though I had the big advantage, I still I had to consider my options wisely *and* select the right one. Outnumbered three-to-one, it was a situation which could easily get out of hand.

Fixed to the spot and breathing inaudibly, I surveyed the room. On a shelf near the door was the distinctive turquoise bottle of something – probably Rohypnol or Chloroform – and a cloth. Probably the same one that had been used on Lucy.

It seemed like using the Rohypnol or whatever it was, would probably be my best option. The open plan area was like two sitting rooms knocked in to one. Nearest to me was an open door which I could see led to a small kitchen area.

'Look you guys, watch me do this. You've got to be terribly accurate when you're weighing out the goods – I'm trying to put together a quality international operation here…' said Mr. Big. Leon and Joe both moved from their chairs and began to watch intently at the delicate weighing process. I took the opportunity to remove the bottle of drugs and cloth and re-housed it into the kitchen. On the kitchen table was an unopened letter. It was addressed to Jeremy Tockwith-Smith. Not the first name I would have guessed for an International drugs dealer.

After Leon and Joe had finished their impromptu tuition, Jeremy said, 'Let's put some music on, shall we?' Instantly, I felt more relaxed. No longer would I have to be completely silent as the music would help cover my movements.

For the music selection, I fully expected it to be Michael Bublé, but the popular choice was British rapper Stormzy. As soon as the beat began, I knew I could breathe easily as it gave me the freedom to move around the room. My plan was to render each gang member unconscious when the opportunity arose. The music would help drown out any noise, well, that was my quickly thought-out plan.

After about ten minutes, I was beginning to get impatient. The trio had hardly said a word and Lucy had been completely silent. Then Joe got up.

'Let's get some brews on, shall we?'

'Good idea that man!' said Leon holding a bag of cocaine in each hand.

As soon as Joe went into the kitchen, I carefully doused the cloth in the liquid drug. Then, in one swift movement, grabbed him from behind, clasping the cloth over his mouth and nose. After a brief struggle, the drug worked, his body went limp and I slowly lowered him to the floor before dragging him to the far end of the kitchen.

All I had to do then was wait for someone else to investigate and I'd give them the same treatment. Maybe I should have just run in to the room and battered the others with something, but there was always the risk of someone picking up the gun and firing indiscriminately. The last thing I wanted was for Lucy to be harmed, so I decided to stay put in the kitchen and let the trouble come to me.

Whilst I waited, I knew that the clock was ticking – I'd given Frank the instruction to call the police if I hadn't come out in thirty minutes. Of course, I didn't want the police involved unless absolutely necessary, as I was hoping to get myself a huge cash bonus to go towards my pension fund. But it wasn't just about getting my hands on any cash I could find, I didn't want Jeremy and his cohorts to be arrested just yet. I had plans for them.

Then Leon called out, 'Where are those drinks Joe? Joe?'

The plan was working like a dream, and when Leon made his way to the kitchen, he immediately saw Joe slumped on the floor and went over to see his friend.

Without looking, I reached for the bottle and covered the cloth in liquid. From behind, I leaned over and clasped it around Leon's nose and mouth, hoping for the same result. I clung on waiting for the drug to take effect as Leon struggled, but nothing happened. With a burst of energy, Leon threw me backwards. He was shocked and freaked-out. He said shakily, 'I know there's someone there... what's your problem, man?'

'You're my problem!' I replied, still clutching the cloth.

'Well if you're trying to knock me unconscious, then I think you'll find that Fairy Liquid isn't as effective as Chloroform, brother!' said Leon, wiping his mouth and nose. His eyes darted around the kitchen

Looking around, I realised I'd picked up the wrong fucking bottle. I was so stupid sometimes. I replied with the only line I could think of at that moment.

'Well, your face has never looked cleaner. And now you smell like a delightful Alpine meadow!'

After a brief, surreal stand-off, Leon suddenly lunged towards me, but I instinctively grabbed a sturdy wok which was on the work surface next to me and smashed it against his face. The impact propelled him backwards and he dropped to the floor semi-conscious. As soon as he hit the ground, I rushed to give him the proper 'medicine' while he was still dazed. Leon and Joe were both out for a while, which just left their boss.

The rapping track ended, just as Leon fell unconscious. There was total silence for few seconds before the next track began. Two down, one to go.

Just as I made my way out of the kitchen, Jeremy, the last man standing, made his way in and we bumped right into each other. He felt that someone was there, he instinctively reached out and grabbed something - me - and we began an intense struggle. I could tell that the guy was terrified, after all, he was grappling something that wasn't there. We fell backwards into the open lounge area.

Lucy twigged that it was me and called out my name.

'HG, is it you?'

The struggle continued, and we both rolled across the floor.

'HG? HG?'

As Jeremy broke free and tried to get to his feet, his arm swiped the table, sending a cloud of cocaine dust into the air. It was the only thing I was afraid of. Within a few seconds, the dust was coating me, making my shape more and more visible. I was rapidly becoming a target which was easy to see.

'Jesus Christ… what the fuck are you?' said the Jeremy Tockwith-Smith, drugs baron.

'I'll tell you what I am,' I replied, as dramatically as I could, 'I'm the one who's going to put a stop to everything you do. So there!' I wish I could have come up with a snappier answer or catchphrase, such as Hasta LaVista, Baby! or something more Clint Eastwood-esque, but it was the best I could do at that moment.

All I was to him was an outline, a transparent shape formed by a smattering of cocaine dust. No wonder he looked like he was in a state of shock. Whilst Jeremy stood there looking at me like a kitten watching a fly, I reached inside my jacket and got hold of my lucky pebble. In one quick movement I threw my stone which hit him square between the eyes. I expected him to fall dramatically to the ground like in the movies, but he didn't.

'Ahhh!' he cried. 'That really hurt!'

I was stunned by the stupid response. Jeremy looked across to the large, ornamental mirror and rubbed his forehead. I could see that he had noticed something in the mirror and for a split second it was like the whole scene was frozen in time. What had he seen?

The gun.

There was an almighty scramble for the small firearm. I could see him lunge towards it, but I'd got the same idea and dived forwards across the table. If I didn't get to it first, then it was the end for me.

Whilst Jeremy and I flew through the air heading for the gun, the rapper belted out the lyrics which were quite apt for the situation:

*"It's a time to lie and it's a time to die, don't ever start to trust…
cos you never know who's gunna take you down and your life will end
in dust…"*

It was like a parody of a Quentin Tarantino movie, shot
in slow motion to the coolest music.

I got the gun, but the other guy got me in his clutches.
We rolled around trying the get the advantage. Lucy was
screaming by this time and her cries spurred me on.

Even if I'd had the opportunity, I couldn't have killed
him, as I just wasn't capable of doing something so… final.
As we struggled, I began to lose the initiative and frantically
grabbed anything that was within reach. All I could find was
an electric cable and I instinctively pulled it. The result was
that a huge ghetto blaster came hurtling down from a shelf
and struck Mr. Big on the head. As he lost consciousness,
the CD became damaged in the fall and played itself out at
an increasingly slower speed until it eventually came to a
stop. The dust settled and all was silent.

Slowly, I raised myself up and dusted my myself down,
gradually returning to my state of invisibility.

'Don't do that just yet,' called out Lucy. 'I want to see
you… you've no idea how weird it is talking to something
or someone that you can't see. At least you've got an outline
now. It's like you really exist.'

'I think you'll find that I really do exist.'

'Well, you know what I mean. Can you untie me?'

'Erm, well… I'll think about it…' I joked

'Pleeeaassseee!'

'Ok, go on then, just this once.'

Lucy's hands had been tied with zip-ties. I found some
scissors, but the blades were too dull to cut through the
thick plastic. Luckily, I had my penknife with me for just

such an eventuality. Just like my lucky pebble, at last they had both proved their worth.

Once I had cut Lucy free, she threw her arms around me which created a ripple of cocaine dust. At last I was being squeezed by someone I actually wanted to be squeezed by. And I enjoyed every second.

'You're incredible.' She whispered.

Actually, I was incredibly lucky I hadn't got my head blown off. I knew I had to act fast. Firstly, I gave Leon and Joe an extra dose of Chloroform to ensure they didn't come round for a while and I also gave Jeremy a good dose too, so he was going to be out for an hour or two.

'Lucy, have you got your mobile?'

'Yes, do you need to make a call?'

I sent Frank a message telling him to hang-fire. And then I began to put my plan into operation.

'Lucy, we need to get these guys sitting around the table, generally weighing drugs and involved in illegal activities.'

'I don't get what you mean… they're unconscious?'

'Yes, I know… but we're going to manipulate them, so it looks like they're not!'

We managed to drag all three from their locations and get them propped-up in their chairs at the table. Fortunately, the seats had quite high backs, so it actually looked like they were conscious and active. I grabbed some sunglasses from a nearby shelf and placed them on Jeremy, whilst Lucy got her camera ready.

We took a variety of photographs of them working, weighing drugs and close-ups of their hands holding drugs. The set up looked perfect as two of them had identifiable tattoos on their wrists and hands. Lucy found another pair of sunglasses, which we placed on Leon. It was incredible how realistic the photographs were. No one could possibly tell that the people in them were unconscious. But however, I had an even better idea. A video.

CHAPTER FORTY-FIVE:

Puppets on my string

Lucy filmed as I animated the guys in action. I moved their arms and had them doing the thumbs up. You name it, we filmed it. We laughed so much that at times we had to stop to control ourselves. In all the shots, we made sure there were plenty of drugs on display and we even thought to get in every identifiable object we could, including the letter with Jeremy's name and address casually placed to one side.

We quickly watched back some of the shots, and they looked brilliant – it was exactly what I wanted. OK, it wasn't Steven Spielberg quality, but the clips were for the police, not the Oscar nomination panel.

Before we left, we collected several bags of cocaine which I'd planned to leave hidden in Jeremy's Mercedes. My plan was complete, apart from the money. There were drugs all over the place, but no sign of any cash.

Keeping one eye on the gang we searched everywhere we could think of. But we failed to hit the jackpot. At one point we thought we'd found the treasure – Lucy found a rucksack which contained a few thousand pounds, but it was nowhere near what I'd anticipated. I was sure Jeremy was sitting on a ton of cash, but where could it be?

We had to leave without the million pounds in cash I'd dreamed of, but at least everything else had gone pretty much to plan. Lucy was free, we had a few thousand in cash, but more importantly, we had footage of the gang, which would help the rest of my plan come together. Before we left, I also remembered to leave a 'special' invisible calling card which was vitally important if everything was to work. I also left a nice, dramatically worded note for them which read:

"Dear drugs gang,

If you make any effort whatsoever to find Lucy or myself, then my gang of invisible beings will put you through an industrial mincing machine and you will be fed to the pigs. That's after you've been mercilessly tortured, of course. And just to make sure you don't do anything stupid - we have lots of video footage of you weighing drugs, doing deals and more. We have a mountain of evidence which is ready to be handed to the police.

You will not hear from me again, unless it's to kill you all.

Yours sincerely,

The Invisible Man.

P.S. Michael Bublé is shit!"

I didn't really think that Michael Bublé was shit, I thought he was pretty good, but I just wrote it to annoy them.

Later, I sent a couple of videos of them measuring drugs. If they tried anything, the police would receive the footage, and they would be fucked, basically.

Before Lucy and I left, I drugged the gang a little more so that we could remove our fingerprints, we took the keys to the Mercedes and left.

Once out of the house, I quickly ran to see Frank, gave him the bag containing the money and told him to head back to the café and I'd meet him there later.

Lucy drove the Mercedes with me as her passenger.

'Thank God you're alright!' I said, breathing out in an exaggerated manner. 'I was starting to think we'd never find you.' Only when we were outside and in the fresh air did it seem like we could de-stress properly.

'Yeah, me too…'

'Do you remember being taken from the street when we went for a walk?'

'Yeah and then the next thing I knew, I was tied to a chair in that house.'

'What did they say to you?'

'They said they had some work to do - and if I hadn't told them where the missing money was by the time they'd finished, then they'd tie weights to me and drop me in the Thames.'

'Jesus.'

'That Jeremy, is a vicious, violent, nasty piece of work. 'He told me they'd done that before – several times. He might look pretty harmless with his crap 'tash and bow-tie, but I reckon he's a psychopath.'

'Well my plan should sort those guys out once and for all.'

Lucy dropped me a ten-minute walk from where Fabian Judson lived. She didn't ask why I wanted to be dropped off there and I didn't tell her. I was curious to see if Judson was still incapacitated.

As I didn't want the vehicle to be associated with anyone else apart from Jeremy Tockwith-Smith, I asked Lucy not to park too near Michael's house when she returned. Before she left, I stashed some bags of drugs into the boot – these were bags I'd made sure had plenty of the gang's fingerprints on before we left.

'My life has been mad ever since you happened to be walking past my door five days ago,' said Lucy shaking her head. 'I'm not sure that anyone will ever believe my story. It's the sort of thing someone on drugs would come out with…'

'I know, maybe we'll wake up and it's all been a weird dream, what do you reckon Lucy?'

'I hope not.'

The plan was for Lucy to stay inside and she handed me her mobile. I told her to keep hold of the Mercedes keys for the time being and I'd be in touch later - but if there was anything suspicious, to phone the police straight away. Next on my list was Fabian Judson and his delectable piece of fluff. After that I needed to visit Frank and tell him some very important news. For once I felt relaxed, in control and relieved.

CHAPTER FORTY-SIX:

A heart-warming sight

My day had been successful so far. Lucy had been located and freed, I'd got some recordings of the gang in action, and made a few quid along the way. I was starting to think that making a million was going to prove too elusive, but in some ways, I didn't mind going back to my normal existence without the riches I'd hankered after. At least I was alive, healthy and had become friends with Lucy – if nothing else. Yeah, things weren't so bad, all things considered.

It was late afternoon on December 27th and I had until 9.15am on the 29th before I reappeared.

It was beginning to get dark as I stood outside Judson's house. When I looked through the lounge window, I saw a heart-warming sight. There was Fabian, sitting on the settee with both arms in slings. Merry Christmas Fabian! And, if my plan worked, he had a lot worse coming to him than a bit of trouble with his arms. Along with Lucy's mobile tucked into my sock, I'd stored a couple of bags of cocaine from the Kensington drugs factory and I waited until the time was right to discretely place these around Judson's house.

As much as I'd enjoyed my previous visit with the sexually frustrated lady of the same abode, I couldn't hang around as I needed to talk to Frank – it could possibly be the last time I ever spoke to him, at least in my ghostly form.

When I arrived at Sherlocks café it was already dark and the coloured lights from inside gave it a warm, welcoming glow. As I entered, Frank was deep in conversation with someone. The very fact that there was a customer in the place took me by surprise. What was more surprising was that it was my dad.

Frank stood up as soon as he realised there was no-one there.

'That you HG?'

As my dad was there, I was in two minds whether to put on an accent. For all he knew, I was on holiday in Switzerland and wouldn't be back for a few days, so I guessed there was absolutely nothing to worry about. And even if he thought our voices sounded similar, there's no way he'd think his son was a ghost.

'Yes, it's me, HG. How did you know?'

Frank laughed and introduced his new friend.

'HG, this is my new ghost-hunting buddy, Geoff!'

'Hello Geoff, please to meet you.'

Geoff – my dad - was speechless. He just stood there incredulous. The look on his face was priceless. If there was one single memory that I was going to remember from this whole invisibility thing, it was my dad's face at that very moment.

'So, I'm guessing you haven't met a real ghost before then da... er, Geoff? Well here I am, your friendly neighbourhood ghost.'

'Unbelievable! Just UNBELIEVABLE!'

Frank was enjoying watching my dad's reaction as much as I was.

'You know, Geoff, life... or should I say death is not easy for us ghosts and we need all the help we can get. I must say that Frank has been brilliant – as dependable and as helpful as a best friend could ever be. So, thanks for all your help Frank. You is da man!' I added, remembering what Nigel the busker had called out the last time I saw him.

Frank was almost moved to tears. I could tell he was trying his best not to become too emotional.

'I've always believed in ghosts all stuff like that,' said my dad, 'but I'm being honest when I say that you're the first ghost I've ever seen – or experienced - in my life. So, you really do exist... it's just, well, I don't know what to say, I really don't. You don't happen to have bumped into the ghost of Buzz Aldrin do you?'

'No, because he's still alive.'

'Oh, that'll be why then!' My dad was determined to get to the bottom of the moon landings and whether they actually happened or not. I decided not to fool around and tell him anything.

'So, how did you two meet? I asked.

Geoff replied. 'It was my son Cooper who said he'd heard of a fella who ran a café and he was into ghost hunting and it might be good idea to start a club or social evening... Cooper's a good lad, doing really well for himself these days... he's such a hard worker.'

Did my dad really think that? Well, at least it was great to see him so chirpy and out socialising. I hadn't seen Dad so animated and enthusiastic about anything for ages. And now he was experiencing a real ghost, there was no stopping him.

'How was this afternoon's haunting? Was it the success you thought it would be?' enquired Frank, pouring coffees all round.

'Not really. I had to go and haunt some drugs dealers — and one of my "living" friends was in a spot of trouble, so it was necessary to go and have a word or two with them. I think they've got the message.'

'Frank, I need to tell you something - and it's very important.'

'Oh, what is it HG?' said Frank holding his coffee mug several inches from his mouth, dramatically.

'In just over a day I have to move on. I've been summoned by a higher power and I've been given, well, I've been given a new case to move on to. Once I've done my next "project", hopefully I'll get my final promotion and move on up to heaven.'

'Wow, I didn't realise there was a system like that in place?'

'Yeah, and it takes ages to get to heaven. They've had me haunting people for years. Honestly, sometimes it does my head in trying to help people… but it looks like my time has come at last. I'm pretty sure that this is my final stop, so the reason I called to see you is to say goodbye.'

There was silence in the café. And then I was asked a question which I'd never anticipated. A question which brought tears to my eyes. Normally I wasn't an emotional person in the sense that I cried easily. I don't think I'd cried

276

since I lost my coat when I was ten, but as I stood there, I couldn't help but wipe the tears off my cheeks.

Geoff – my dad – said: 'Would it be possible for you to help me out if you possibly can?'

'Yes, I'll do my very best,' I replied, having no idea what was coming next. 'How can I help you?'

'Thank you. When you get to heaven, will you check to see if my wife is alright?'

I couldn't answer. Emotionally I couldn't handle the question. My mum. His wife. We'd both missed her massively, but neither of us had spoken much about her, both afraid to cause the other distress. How I missed her. And as I watched the tears well-up in my dad's eyes, I knew how affected he'd been by her death. The pain right then was indescribable for me - and I suspected it was the same for him too.

In the background, Frank was also wiping a tear. All three of us connected with one simple question.

When I finally found the courage to say something, I simply whispered, 'I'm already sure she's doing fine.'

Never in a million years did I envisage that my new-found invisibility would bring me and my dad closer together. Yes, I know that he didn't realise I was the 'heavenly ghost', but it gave me an insight to who my dad actually was and what he'd been through.

Bidding farewell to my new-found friend Frank I told him that I would send a couple of my other friends to meet him one day soon to sort out the finances and enjoy one of his amazing coffees. And I told Geoff to be strong, live life to the full and take care of things.

It was quite a strange departure really. I'd definitely be seeing both my dad and Frank in a couple of days once I was my old self again, but at that moment, it felt like the end of something, like a real goodbye. It definitely felt like the end of one Chapter and the beginning of a brand new one. Yeah, it sounded – and it was – a cliché, but there was no better way of describing it.

As I left Frank's café I was feeling a little deflated and I have no idea why, as I was heartened to know that my dad had finally got out of the house and was making an effort to socialise. There was hope for him yet. He'd be even more pleased when he knew the company I worked for had finally given in to modern-thinking and were planning to change my job title to "Happiness Technician". That definitely sounded like a step up.

My mind wandered on to the fact that I had one full day left of my powers. How was I going to fill it? I'd crammed so much in to my five or so days it was hard to believe it was all coming to an end. From seeing the Queen – and I'm not talking about Elton John – but I saw him as well (and he was ace) – to fighting drug dealers… I'd done so much yet still had a bit of time left.

Should I go and see Elton again? No, I knew what I was going to do. I'd call Michael and tell him it was now OK for Lucy to get out and about. She was safe and could go out alone. I would arrange to meet Lucy and we could have nice day out together. That sounded like the perfect way to spend my last day of invisibility.

'Michael, is that you?'

I could hardly hear his voice.

'Michael, turn that vac off – your house is clean enough. I said it's clean enough!'

'Alright, keep your hair on,'

Silence at last.

'It's Cooper, how's it going?'

'Yeah, all good with me thanks. Rebecca's busy making a cake and Lucy's asleep. I've no idea why she's so tired, she's not done much. She was asleep on the settee when we got back from our shopping expedition…'

'Well, there's good news my old mate, Lucy's safe now. Everything's been taken care of. She can go out without having anything to fear.'

'Great news, Coop. She'll be ecstatic! You know what, you and Lucy would be great together. Something to think about, eh? Do you want me to put a good word in for you?'

Michael was loving the idea of being a matchmaker. And I liked the idea, too.

'Anyway, how's Switzerland going?' he asked.

'To be honest, I'm getting a bit bored of it all now. There's only so many Toblerones you can eat…'

'Oh well, you'll soon be back. Do you need picking up from the airport?'

'No thanks, I've got that all sorted.'

What I hadn't got sorted were the arrangements with Lucy. She couldn't realistically stay with Michael and Rebecca much longer as they'd already done more than I could have asked for. Lucy's flat was now empty and she couldn't go back there again, that was for certain. Was it realistic to offer her a room at mine? She had no idea who I was, although I would have to tell her at some point. As far as I was concerned, if she moved in with me, that would be awesome!

As my mind worked overtime trying to figure out what to do with Lucy, I suddenly felt very tired. It had been a very long and exhausting day. Plus, I think I inhaled quite a bit of cocaine during the fight with Jeremy Tockwith-Smith and it had taken its toll on me.

I carefully removed all my clothes and laid them out in a certain order so that I could find them easily in the morning. God, it would be so good to wear whatever I wanted, whenever I wanted. Just one more day to go and it was a day I was really looking forward to. Some quality time with Lucy was the perfect antidote to all the intensity of the last few days.

After placing my eye-mask over my face, I laid myself out on the bed like an Egyptian mummy. I thought about the pattern on the ceiling and as before, it seemed to have some sort of hypnotic power over me - and in what seemed like a minute, I had drifted off to Narnia.

The sun was shining on me when I eventually woke up on the morning of December 28th at just after 9.15am.

'This time tomorrow, it'll all be over.' I said aloud to myself and I smiled. Most people would love twenty-fours of invisibility, but I'd had enough. The novelty of looking in the mirror and breathing on it to frost it up had more-or-less worn off. The toothpaste and toothbrush still looked like an incredible movie special effect when I went through my ablutions, yet it was just a novelty aside, not an earth-shattering moment. Each time I walked past a mirror or looked at a window for my reflection it just emphasized that I was nothing. Just an entity which could move around anonymously yet which couldn't change things of importance. Perhaps I should have gone down the super-spy route after all. It may have been beneficial to the UK government to know exactly what the Russians and Chinese were really up to. However, that all seemed too much like

James Bond. Kitchen porters aren't really cut out for espionage and the likes.

My creativity had let me down due to a lack of serious planning, but then again, how could I have known that this special substance would actually work?

With a whole day ahead of me, hopefully most of it with Lucy... I was looking forward to it more than anything I could imagine. I decided to start the day off with a bath rather than my favourite shower and as I laid in the water, covered in soap suds, I planned what else I needed to do before my invisibility wore off.

If the plan I'd put into action worked out, the problem with the drugs gang would be solved and Fabian Judson would be well and truly sorted out. On the monetary side, Frank had about 60K stashed away somewhere, awaiting my instructions.

As I got out of the bath, the soap suds clung to my body and the remaining bubbles began to pop themselves. My legs and torso had a rainbow-like sheen to it, the light captured the reflections of the soap film and I stood there like some sort of Marvel superhero.

My plan for the day was to see Lucy and then in the evening, break into JC Cosmetics and return the oil phials. Following that, I'd head back home to bed ready for the effects of invisibility to wear off at 9:15 am the following morning.

Unfortunately, as I shaved I cut myself several times. It wasn't easy shaving when you couldn't see anything. A few small specs of blood appeared in the air. Little globules of red, suspended in nothingness. I stared at them, then smeared one of them to see what the effect would be. It was quite a magical moment, even though it was normally a mundane and annoying occurrence. I tore a piece of toilet paper and ripped it into a series of tiny pieces, placing a piece over each cut until a spot of blood seeped through, holding the tissue in place. In the mirror, there were just four small pieces of tissue with a red dot in the centre of each.

Once I'd stopped bleeding, I removed the tissue, splashed on my favourite aftershave and stepped outside into the corridor where I could hear noises from above. I suspected that was the big guy expanding his private metropolis. What an amazing sight that was. But it filled his whole flat, and there was barely any room to sleep. I vowed to ask him the question: Why? Especially as Legoland was not too far away on the outskirts of Windsor. And *they* had a café and toilets!

CHAPTER FORTY-SEVEN:

Perfect Pendleton

Christmas week in normal circumstances was my favourite time of the year, but this time I was on the periphery of the festivities. I had seen it almost from above, like an angel looking down on the masses, seeing things I didn't want to and mixing with people I normally wouldn't be seen dead with. It had been a thoroughly troubling experience in many ways, yet the number one goal – along with goal number two, had yet to come to fruition. As an expectant father, at least one of them never would, but still, I was determined to enjoy my last day and 'go out in style' as they say.

Boasting my new, positive demeanour and with a light at the end of the invisibility tunnel, I fairly skipped through the streets like a dandy of London. I was going to see Lucy. And that was more than enough to put a spring in my tired step.

Our rendezvous was arranged for 11am and I waited outside for her as I didn't want to do the usual 'knock and sneak in' tactic. It felt a little disrespectful to do that at my friend's house on my last day for some reason, so I opted to wait. I waved at her as she stood in the lounge window, but of course, she was never going to see me. When I realised, I felt a little embarrassed by my action and lowered my hand, as if the whole world could see my faux pas.

Lucy was dressed in black jeans and donned a thick winter coat with a fake fur collar and wore a white bobble hat. She looked stunning, like a model for a winter catalogue. My plan was for us to make our way to the Thames and then head towards Southwark as I needed to re-visit The Shard, where I had something to collect.

We stopped along the way for a coffee and the guy serving in Costa thought it was slightly odd that Lucy ordered two coffees and two cinnamon swirls. We sat in a quiet part of the café, away from the toilets, where I could enjoy my coffee and bun without having to be too secretive.

'Guess what?' asked Lucy excitedly.

'Er, you've been asked to star in a Hollywood movie about me?'

'Haha, no, Michael made me breakfast in bed this morning! I had bacon, eggs, sausage, beans, mushrooms and a hash brown! Wasn't that lovely of him?'

'Yeah, I suppose so. He's never offered to do that for me when I've stayed there!' I replied, sounding miffed.

'They've been so lovely, I need to get them both a present while we're out today if that's OK?'

We discussed what would be a good present for Michael and laughed as we came up with an array of cleaning products from Dettol to bleach, from dusters to floor polish. Thinking of gifts reminded me that I also needed to purchase the biggest Toblerone I could find, some Lederhosen and a cuckoo clock – as I was expected back from my fabulous Switzerland skiing trip in a couple of days. However, I couldn't buy the gifts whilst I was with Lucy or she'd know that I was their friend Cooper.

'So, are we still going to keep in touch when you suddenly reappear?' asked Lucy, completely out of the blue.

'Well, yes, I hope so…' I replied, trying not to be so enthusiastic, as I was hoping Lucy might be a little more forthcoming with her feelings.

'It's just that with you going to be a dad, you might be too busy. Children take up a massive part of your life. My friend's got a little toddler and I hardly ever see her these days… anyway, what are you going to do when you're back to normal, are you going to get a job? I don't even know what you do?'

These were questions I hadn't anticipated – but I should have! I couldn't tell her I worked in the same place as her and was in charge of the fucking dishwasher. It wasn't something I was prepared to brag about.

'Well, I suppose I'll have to get some sort of a job, but I don't really have any skills, not that I can think of, anyway.'

'Aw, you must be good at something? You should've gone to a publishers and shown them you're invisible - they might have wanted to do a book about it, you…'

'That's a great idea,' I said genuinely impressed with her idea. Why hadn't I thought of that? I'd been wracking my brains for ages to try and come up with a money-making idea which didn't involve doing a bank job. And that would've been good – apart from the fact that Samantha Penhaligan and Christopher Wyngard the boffin would've known straight away what I'd been up to. But, it really was a great idea.

'You should see if the place I work has any vacancies!'

I nearly dropped my cinnamon swirl.

'What do they do?' I asked, as innocently as I could.

'It's a cosmetics company – they develop all sorts of oils and creams for people who've suffered burns and stuff like that. But I'm just in admin, so it's pretty boring... I'm just on a computer all day.'

I was dying to ask if there was a canteen and how many people worked in it, to see if she mentioned anything about Ledley or me, but I decided not to, for fear of her giving a negative review of the section.

A few days later I'd be back at work, doing what I did best. It would be great to see Ledley and take him for a pint. But what did the future hold for me? The sixty grand Frank was saving for me wasn't going to propel me into any sort of grand lifestyle. It would be nice to have some money in the bank, but it fell far short of what I'd imagined I could get my hands on originally.

'What about you and your future?' I said, turning the conversation to Lucy.

'Well this might seem strange, but while I was with Carl, I didn't see any future for me at all. As stupid as this sounds, I thought he'd end up killing me.'

'Fuck' was all I could think to say.

'I was just a meaningless object to him - and all his mate's girlfriends were treated the same. There was not an ounce of respect or anything. Once you're invested in that sort of relationship, they control and manipulate you until you feel worthless. I know people say, "just walk out" but it's so much more difficult than that. It happened to me and I don't believe I'm stupid or unintelligent... anyhow, it sounds corny, but you've opened up the world for me and I'm getting pleasure from the small things which I was restricted from doing before. Just having a coffee with you here in Costa has been so amazing… and I can't even see you. Think how great it would be if I could look at you, actually look at your face…'

'Yeah, but who'd want to look at *my* face?' I laughed.

Lucy reached out and I eagerly moved my face forward so she could find it.

'I'm very intrigued…' she commented as she stuck her face a fraction from mine. I swear I could have kissed her right there and then, by moving just an inch. She wasn't teasing me, but looked at me in a quizzical way. It was sheer innocent curiosity. With her lips almost brushing mine, I just couldn't resist. I felt myself slowly moving forward and made a fumbling play for her heart. I kissed her so lightly that perhaps some people wouldn't even describe it as a kiss at all.

There was complete silence from both of us. Had I ruined everything? Had Lucy even noticed my lips brush hers? It was the most delicate kiss imaginable, maybe even too delicate for her to even notice. Neither of us said anything.

After our coffee we strolled along the South Bank arm-in-arm and headed for The Shard, where six days earlier Lucy's boyfriend had ended up in a skip. It was still the Christmas holidays and lots of tourists took advantage of the mild weather to pose for selfies every two seconds. Lucy was even stopped and asked to take photographs several times – usually for groups of Japanese teenagers eager to capture London's most iconic sights on their iPhones.

'Shall we do lunch somewhere nice?' I asked.

'That would be lovely, but to be honest, I haven't got much money with me and I've left my cards at home…' she replied.

'Well that's not a problem. Not a problem at all!' I announced, seeing The Invisible Man busker in the distance: 'Watch this…'

I said hello to Nigel the busker, who was delighted to see me, or at least hear me. Once more, I asked him if I could take over for a few minutes as I needed some money to take a pretty lady for lunch. He was more than happy for me to take centre stage.

'Come here Lucy, let's make some money!'

I proceeded to float her in the air, like the world's best magician. 'Even Dynamo can't do this!' I said, as large numbers of people immediately came to see the incredible sight before them.

After the incredible levitation Lucy then stood still while I removed her bobble hat… and put it on my own head… and then her coat, which I just managed to squeeze on. And then I put her gloves on too. And then I borrowed her sunglasses. With each item, I was taking shape as the Invisible Man – and the crowds loved it. There were shouts, cheers, people filming, it was quite chaotic. The atmosphere was fantastic - and the great thing was that people were volunteering to put money – and lots of it - into the hat positioned on the floor in front of Lucy. In just fifteen minutes we had accumulated over two-hundred pounds. A businessman handed Lucy a fifty pounds note – along with his business card and signalled for her to call him. Business opportunities were presenting themselves right before my eyes, it was just a shame it was my last day in my current state.

For my - and *our* - finale as impromptu buskers, I removed the clothes and accessories and gave them back to Lucy, who was having simply the best time. A huge grin never left her face for a single second. She turned her head to me and said: 'You're amazing!' I was ecstatically happy. If I could have frozen the moment for ever, I would have done so. I actually cried with joy but wiped the tears away before anyone could see them form properly.

'Ladies and gentlemen,' I called out, like a circus showman, 'in a few moments, I have to go, but first, we'd like to leave you with this...' I was making it up as I went along, with no real idea of what I was going to do. My eyes were quickly scouring the crowd to see if anything sprung to mind. Glancing down to my side I noticed that Nigel had brought his lunch with him, so I quickly asked if I could help myself. 'Go for it!' was Nigel's reply – he was loving every minute of it too.

Lucy held her hands out and I floated Nigel's well-prepared lunchbox on to her waiting palms. Removing the items one by one I proceeded to eat and drink them. First, a packet of crisps. The crowd could not believe what they were seeing. Crisps floating in the air and then being eaten. My invisible coating meant that nothing I ate could be seen. Professor Wyngard had done a superb job developing the key to invisibility and I was taking full advantage of it.

Then I needed a drink. I reached for a bottle of Diet Coke and unscrewed the cap to cheers from the onlookers. When I poured the Coke down my throat – thus making it completely disappear into nothingness – people jumped up and down, screamed and cheered. I was in my element and if people hadn't already been standing, I would have got a standing ovation without any problem. I said: 'Give the sensational Lucy a round of applause...' and as they clapped and cheered, I picked her up and floated her sideways before returning her to her original upright position. Finally,

I borrowed Nigel's bowler hat, put it on my head and then said, 'This is Lucy... and I've been the Invisible Man – goodnight!' And I doffed my hat to our adoring fans.

I had always wanted to use that final phrase, as if I was just coming off stage at Wembley Arena or something, so it seemed an apt end to our performance.

The money poured in and we felt like successful international cabaret artistes as we took a final bow. Nigel was blown away and insisted that we took all the money, as we deserved it. Lucy picked up two hundred pounds and left another two hundred or so for Nigel for letting us borrow his pitch. 'Get your mum something nice!' I said as we hugged him and left. We were buzzing with the thrill of what we'd just done. Lucy hugged me, I hugged Lucy and we strolled along hand-in-hand, laughing together at the surreal experience we'd just created. I had never taken drugs, so couldn't really base my experience on that, but what we'd just done was perhaps the equivalent. We both felt an incredible adrenalin rush and it was something that would always connect us.

CHAPTER FORTY-EIGHT:

What's the time?

As we approached The Shard, all the memories of that horrific evening returned to me. It was only a few days earlier, but I'd already forgotten many of the details. I smiled to myself as I fondly recalled Ledley getting accidentally tazered. I couldn't wait for him to tell me all about it when we got back to work on January 2nd. I knew his telling of the story would be absolutely hilarious.

My trip to revisit The Shard was for one particular reason – and that was to retrieve a gold Rolex watch - the watch I had removed from Carl's body as he lay dead in the yellow skip after his fall from the top of The Shard.

My aim was to give the watch to Ledley as a gift. I knew that a genuine Rolex watch was worth quite a few thousand pounds and as Ledley had been showing off his fake version with such innocent enthusiasm, I wanted him to have the genuine thing. Ledley was pretty ace – and he'd become a good friend in my time at JC Cosmetics. Plus, anyone who took pride in showing people his fake Rolex when the word 'Rolex' was misspelt as 'Rowlex', deserved better. Even if he just decided to sell it, I didn't care as I knew he'd appreciate the gesture.

A few hundred yards from the glass building there was building work in progress. In a wall cavity, behind a piece of tatty polythene was the watch I'd carefully hidden.

Once there, it struck me that I hadn't actually considered how Lucy would feel as I retrieved Carl's watch. For a moment I had an awful feeling that it would bring back terrible memories of her relationship – if you could call it a relationship – with Carl. I needn't have worried. When she saw the watch, she just casually said: 'Carl was so superficial, he was all image and no substance.' That was music to my ears.

The pair of us then had a fantastic lunch at a cosy restaurant named Ballentyne's. We selected it specifically as it had booths which were almost private where I could eat peacefully without looking around before taking every mouthful. We thoroughly enjoyed our time and chatted about everything from conspiracy theories to Masterchef to the latest documentary on Netflix. A couple of times, a waiter came over and asked if everything was OK. He probably thought he was going mad, over-hearing voices yet never seeing anyone, but Lucy.

We parted at 6pm.

'This is it!' I proclaimed. 'This is the last time I will be invisible.'

'How was it?' responded Lucy dramatically.

'It's been emotional,' I said, mimicking an old TV advert starring ex-football star Vinny Jones. 'Well, actually, it's been much more than that. It hasn't been anything like I imagined it would be and I'm not sure that if I was ever given the opportunity to be invisible again that I would take it.'

'What time will you be visible again?'

'9.15 if all goes to plan, but who knows? I'm guessing there must be a chance that it might not work. I'm just hoping that everything will happen how it's supposed to. There's always the possibility of a glitch!'

'So, the question is: what are *WE* going to do?'

'What do you mean?' I asked.

'Well, we are going to see each other again, aren't we?'

'Yes, you try stopping me! It'll be really weird though. Jesus, I hope I can adapt to normal, everyday life again,' I laughed. 'If I fail to materialise as I'm supposed to, then I reckon we'd make a great double-act and we'd have to turn pro. I mean, just think about the reactions we got earlier on. It was amazing.'

'I know, that was just… well, I can't describe how great that was.'

'OK Lucy, you've been incredible… but I really have to go as I have a couple of things to do…' This was the last time I'd see Lucy in my invisible state and I had no idea how to handle my goodbye.

'Do you think it would be possible… well, do you think it would be possible to kiss you?'

After a stunned pause, I replied.

'Yes, I think it would be *VERY* possible.'

'Thank you for everything you've done for me. No one has ever been so kind…'

And with that, Lucy's lips puckered ready for the moment. Her hands found my shoulders and we moved towards each other for our goodbye. Our lips slowly met. It was a tender, exploratory type of kiss. Whilst our lips tenderly touched, I looked at Lucy. Her eyes were closed, but she was crying. I felt one of her tears touch my nose.

CHAPTER FORTY-NINE:

Baby blues

Lucy headed inside Michael's house. She stopped at the door and looked back towards where she had left me. I had one hand raised in the air to wave her goodbye. The moment was poignant, like a pivotal moment in an old black and white movie. I headed home.

Occasionally stopping to look in a shop window, my journey took much longer than I intended. I decided to vary my route and walked streets I'd never seen before. I felt happy and fulfilled but didn't really know why. I touched my nose where Lucy's tear had touched me. For a few seconds, I had a part of Lucy with me.. The tear had now dissipated.

As I entered my building, I saw Tina arriving at the same time with her shopping. I never normally saw Tina on her own and I wondered whether she and Tim had split up? I watched her place her two shopping bags at the door of her flat as she located her key. Once it tuned, she pushed open the door with the toe of her right foot and entered. I took the opportunity to sneak in, curious to see what the situation was.

The furniture in the flat had all been moved around and, tellingly, in the bedroom there was a book and a bottle of wine along with a single glass at one side of the bed – and nothing at all at the other. There was no sign of Tim. At that moment, her mobile rang and it was her mum calling. Tina gave her an update and was quite upbeat about things. I felt uneasy listening in, it was one thing I wouldn't miss when things were back to normal. Sometimes you just have to let people get on with their own lives on their own, within their own circle of friends and family. I had quite a caring nature – which is possibly why my friends said I should think about being a nurse – but I found it easy to get drawn into other people's lives, especially when being invisible made it so easy.

Years before, I remembered watching a movie called Rear Window with my parents. It starred James Stewart who was confined to his apartment after breaking his leg. As a photographer and journalist, he spent all his days watching his neighbours go about their business from his window. He became addicted to their lives and he knew when they changed their daily routines. He also became intrigued by their intimate lives and became increasingly voyeuristic. But however, when he spied a lady who lived opposite in a distressed state after she got rid of a date who wanted more than just a 'drink back at hers', he felt like he'd completely overstepped the mark with his covert observations. I felt exactly the same, watching Tina. I had no right to do it and it made me disgusted with myself. However, listening in to Tina's life was not for any voyeuristic pleasure, but purely because I had been upset at how she'd been treated by Tim a few nights earlier. I genuinely wanted to make sure she was alright.

I returned to my own flat.

The first thing I did was trip over my rug and then make a cup of tea. I turned on the TV and crashed down on my large, three-seater settee and watched the news. As expected, the lead story was about the Christmas sales and how the high street was struggling, but internet sales were booming. When it came to the end of the news, they finished with an unusual item:

"Shoppers were treated to an incredible busking performance today on the South Bank where a performer's creativity took the crowd by storm. 'The Invisible Man' played by Nigel Maughan performed a series of spectacular stunts which had everyone amazed…"

A clip of me – and Lucy – in action was shown. It was obviously filmed on a mobile and was shot over the shoulders of onlookers. Even though I say it myself, it did look fantastic!

The BBC had obviously arrived on the scene too late to catch Lucy and I, but they managed to interview Nigel, who seemed a little sheepish about 'his' act: "Yes, my routines seem to go down well, but erm… it was my friend HG who came up with the idea!"

It was nice to get credit and Lucy called me within five minutes to say she "saw" us on TV – and that Michael and Rebecca were totally impressed to see her helping out that "amazing busker!"

My plan for the evening was to make sure I got in and out of JC Cosmetics in good time, to replace the phials of oil, so that when everyone returned to work on January 2nd, everything would be as before.

Behind a tub of Flora in my fridge were three phials of the special oil. I had used one completely and so shared out the remaining two, between the three bottles. I would have to take them back to work tucked down my sock, which was my preferred method of transportation. My idea was to leave for JC Cosmetics around 8pm, so it would be easy to move around without anyone seeing tiny cylindrical phials making their way through the streets of old London town. Then it would be back to bed and wait for my body to return to the glorious state it was in just a week before.

The route into JC Cosmetics was simple, and within thirty minutes I was in and out courtesy of Norman the security guru performing his evening duties and going outside to have a smoke. It hadn't mattered if anything had been captured on CCTV, they still wouldn't know who the person was who'd stolen the phials. I was free and one step nearer to the end of my seven-day experiment. It had been breathtakingly easy to return the oils and was one of the few things which had gone super-smoothly.

As I walked back, feeling quite good about things generally, I decided to order a pizza as a treat on my last night. I also decided to call my ex, Sarah and invite her round the following day for a heart-to-heart about our baby. This was a part of life I had been trying to block from my mind, but it needed sorting out quickly, for everyone's sakes.

Two hours later, I lay in bed with the lights out. Completely naked, with all my well-worn clothes draped over a chair near the door, I felt myself in a non-sexual way to make sure that every part of me was still as it should be.

Everything felt completely normal. My mind wandered as I thought about my last seven days. Far from the wonderful, carefree adventure I had imagined, it had been nothing but stress and worry, with one or two lighter moments thrown in for good measure. As I nodded off to sleep, I had no idea that even more drama was heading my way.

My alarm for the next morning was set for 9am, but it never went off. My invisibility was due to wear off at exactly 9.15. However, I was awoken at ten past nine when I heard the door to my flat open and then the latch dropped as the door was closed. Someone was inside.

The first thing to enter my mind was that I was stark naked. I felt much more vulnerable than if I had clothes on, but there was no time to do anything about it. I touched my genitals – yes, I was definitely naked. I have no idea why touching my genitals was the deciding factor, but it was. I slowly got out of bed as silently as I could. I needed to sort out this 'break-in' problem as soon as possible, as I was due to lose my invisibility in less than five minutes.

It was typical. Just when I was looking forward to normality, another stumbling block appeared. My bedroom door was slightly ajar, and I could hear someone walking around. I got a quick glimpse of someone, but I couldn't see their face. Whoever it was, they were obviously looking for something. If they were looking for Meat Loaf albums, they'd be sorely disappointed.

With little time to lose, I needed to instigate something before I became visible again, as then I'd instantly be a much easier target. Maybe it was Michael? After all he had a spare key – perhaps he was setting up a surprise 'Welcome back from Switzerland party?'

Gently, I eased open my bedroom door as drawers and cupboards were being opened in the kitchen area. I tiptoed a few paces and stood there looking directly at someone's back. I couldn't see their face yet, but I had an uncomfortable feeling that it was one of the drugs boys. How had they found me? Before I could think of how to handle the situation the intruder turned around. It was Leon. Had he sensed something? He was obviously aware of my invisibility. He was twitching like a scared, cornered rat, his eyes darting left and right. Yeah, he knew alright. The scary thing was, he was holding a large kitchen knife. And it was only two and a half minutes before I crash landed back on earth as a real person and he'd see me in the flesh.

Leon said, 'I know you is there, my man!'

I waited a few seconds and then replied: 'And I need to tell you something…'

'What?'

'Your English grammar is fucking terrible!'

Leon began moving forward, prodding out with *MY* kitchen knife. I was scared… *And* naked. We both moved backwards and forwards, like Olympic fencing competitors, Leon armed and dangerous, me unarmed, but with my 'weapon' on full show, albeit invisible at that moment.

Without looking, I crouched down and placed my arm behind me in an effort to grab something. My fingers felt something, I clasped it with my hand and brandished it, whist proclaiming, 'Let's see how you handle this!'

Unfortunately, I was holding a giant Toblerone (it's amazing what can get with Amazon Prime).

'That doesn't look very dangerous to me, man innit!' Sneered Leon.

'Well, you'd better be scared, because I've also got a Magnum!'

'Where is it then?'

'It's in the freezer, stupid… otherwise it would melt, wouldn't it?'

There was a downside to having something in my hand and it didn't matter what, because once I was holding something, my location was given away. Leon knew exactly where I was and he wasted no time and almost ran towards me, but he tripped over my annoying Rylan Clark-Neal rug. It was a gift. Thank God I hadn't thrown it out, even though I'd threatened to do so on a regular basis. I'd tripped over the thing countless times myself, but this time it quite possibly saved my life. Leon crashed to the floor, spilling the knife which summersaulted to the far side of the lounge. He grabbed my ankles and I fell on top of him.

It was just about 9.15.

As we rolled around my floor, I could feel a slight tingling in my toes and then in my fingers… I was on my way back…

Both trying to gain the upper hand, it was pretty much even-stevens and I hadn't had a single opportunity to use my fully-loaded Toblerone. We rolled one way, then the other… and then Leon's struggling came to a standstill. He looked at me, hardly believing what he was seeing.

Slowly there was colour returning to the extremities of my body. Where there had been nothing before, there was now a crystal cloud, it reminded me of the transporter beam from the original Star Trek series. It was a slow, but captivating process. But it was working - and I was gradually re-appearing. God, I looked good! Actually, even though it was obviously me, it was like I was having an out-of-body experience. It looked like I was watching someone else.

By 9.18 I was back. And back in one wonderful piece.

The mind-blowing sight of me coming back into plain view from a haze of crystal had Leon entranced. I swear he was almost hypnotized by the process. We were on our feet and he just stood there gaping at the site in front of him. Thinking slightly quicker than my adversary, I grabbed the giant novelty Toblerone - which had cost me twenty-eight quid and held it with both hands, like it was a mighty sabre, rather than a triangular prism of chocolate, honey, nougat and almonds. And I brought it down like Thor, the God of Thunder, with a satisfying crunch on top of Leon's head. He tippled forwards, hitting his head on the arm of my favourite chair. He landed face-down on the floor in a crumpled mess. The strange thing was, even though he was unconscious, he had a stupid smile on his face, like I was E.T or something.

Who would've thought that my 'holiday lie' about Switzerland would have saved my life, but it did, with the help of the arm-rest of my 'TV' chair. And the piece of metal I'd placed inside the chocolate bar to stop it from getting crushed.

After a nibble of the giant Toblerone and otherwise silent contemplation, I celebrated by running around my flat completely naked. Only the old lady in the house across the street who was drawing her curtains pictured my joy, *AND* my pride and joy, come to that – but I didn't care. I was back. And it felt good. And I got two thumbs up from the old lady.

The main thing was that I was back – and I immediately searched for the familiar. The mole just below my left breast was still there. The slight bend in my right little finger was still there. Yes, my imperfections were still there, and I looked at myself in the mirror, refreshing my own memory about my looks. Stroking my face, re-adjusting my hair, I was back, and in one piece.

Feeling euphoric, I dressed quickly in some new, fresh clothes. Heaven! I was so eager to get outside to see what it felt like as a normal person that I didn't even put any underpants on. Yes, I was a maverick and the world just had to cope with me as best it could!

As I removed Leon from my flat, the big guy from upstairs was on his way down. 'Do you want a hand with that?' he enquired.

'Yes please!' I replied. The strange thing was, the big guy never even asked why I was removing an unconscious person from my flat. I was so surprised by his disinterest, that I never offered to tell him either. The moment was beyond bizarre, but I'd got used to 'bizarre' over the past week.

Keeping Leon's mobile, I flagged down a taxi, and sent him on a long trip to Scotland. He wouldn't wake up for most of the day, as I had thoughtfully given him some sleeping tablets left behind by my ex. I was sure he would appreciate John O'Groats.

I was 'back in the room' as they say, and I was loving it.

CHAPTER FIFTY:

The Chirpy cockney

Yep, I was back alright! It was December 29th and the world was out there for me to re-discover. I messaged Sarah and arranged for her to come around to my flat that evening. First though, I was going to visit Michael and Rebecca and their hottie lodger, Lucy.

Living naturally was so easy because I didn't have to watch for people innocently clattering into me, they could see me as a solid object. I could go into any shop and buy anything that I wanted and then simply carry it to where I was going. Sitting in a café was a doddle. The simple pleasure of having a drink without having to look over my shoulder like a wanted criminal was a complete joy. Social interaction was back in my life. No matter how insignificant it seemed, I realised that we humans needed it, we needed that personal contact. And, it didn't have to be the spoken word. Eye contact was enough to understand and to be acknowledged. I felt like some chirpy cockney-geezer strolling through the streets. I had to hold myself back from saying phrases such as: "Alright there guvnor!" and "You alright there my dahlin?" What I'm trying to say is, I was so happy to be back, and back safely. I'd taken a punt on Wyngard the scientist, and he'd delivered. Bang on the dot, I was back in the real world.

When I arrived at Michael's house, he was already opening the door just as I was about to knock. I was extremely nervous because I was about to meet Lucy for the first time. Would she recognise my voice? Would she like me? Would she fancy me? I had no idea at all. It was like going on a sort of blind date and I was more than a little terrified as I stood outside carrying my huge, slightly damaged Toblerone.

'Hey Coop' you're back then? Come on in...'

'Yes, what a week I've had!

We hugged, then Rebecca appeared, and we had more hugs. The hugs were great, so I insisted on having more.

'Jesus, you've only been to Switzerland for a week!' remarked Rebecca, as I continued to hug for an unnaturally long time.

'Yeah, but when you've been for a week in Switzerland it feels like a fucking year...'

'It looks like you've had a few tumbles on those slopes,' said Michael, examining my cuts and bruises. I'd got all those from my boxing fiasco and then fights with drug dealers, but I had to play along with the holiday scrapes story.

'And how was Samantha?' asked Rebecca expectantly.

'Samantha?'

'Yeah, the girl you went with. Did anything happen between you?'

'Oh, Samantha. No, we were OK when we were on the slopes together – but it was all downhill from there…' I nodded.

'Anyway, where's Lucy?' I asked, somewhat nervously.

'Lucy's gone. Her parents have come over from Spain and she's gone to see them. That's the bad news, but the good news is that she's coming back for our New Year's Eve party – and you're invited, of course…'

'It's a fancy-dress party!' interrupted Rebecca. 'Come as an icon!'

So, it was going to be New Year's Eve before I met Lucy for what would be the first official time. That was only a couple of days away, but it seemed like a lifetime.

'Great!' I said, trying to put a brave face on things. 'Anyway, I could only get you this Toblerone from Switzerland!' It was completely bent, like a boomerang and it had been opened at one end.

'Yeah, there is a piece missing… those bastards at immigration had to test it for drugs…' Well, I had to blame someone!

Later when my ex, Sarah arrived at my flat to discuss her pregnancy and my role as the vitally important father, I decided to just come straight out with it.

'Right, where the fuck are my Meat Loaf albums?'

'Oh, did I take them by accident?'

Sarah looked a little like Rene Zellweger in Bridget Jones' Diary. Her hair was dyed blonde and she actually looked a little oriental, but she was from Walthamstow, this side of the Peking delta.

'You haven't just asked me here to discuss your albums, have you?' she asked.

'No, I have asked you here because I thought it was important that we discussed things out in the open...'

Sarah looked at me without her expression giving anything away.

'How are you feeling about things?'

'I'm fine,' she said, still showing little emotion.

After a few moments I said, 'I just wanted you to know that I'm fine with being a dad!'

'What? You're going to be a dad?' Asked Sarah, covering her mouth with both hands, and then starting to laugh.

'Of course I am!'

'Well do you mind if I ask you something?'

'No, ask away,' I said, becoming slightly confused.

'Who is the mother?'

'Well, YOU ARE!'

'It's the first I've heard of it!' replied Sarah, screwing up her face. 'To be honest, the mother is usually the first to know...'

At this point I was completely confused. Just as I was about to dig deeper, there was a knock on the door. I could hear a woman's voice...

Standing there was the big guy from upstairs, along with a woman.

'Hello,' I said, 'how can I help you?'

'This is a bit awkward,' said the woman, who was around thirty, had long black hair and was wearing what I would describe as a mish-mash of styles and colours which should never be worn together.

I invited them both in and to be honest, it was a bit of a welcome relief after discussing parenthood with Sarah. They introduced themselves as Clive and Martha.

It was Martha who spoke: 'I won't bore you with all the details, but me and Clive had a fling...' The pair looked at each other and smiled. 'Anyway, for one reason and another we didn't get in touch with each other due to a mix up...'

'I thought I'd found the girl for me...' chipped in Clive. 'And I was scared I'd never find her again as I didn't know much about her...'

'Anyway,' continued Martha, 'I obviously knew where Clive lived, but the night we came back to his, we were both a little bit drunk. So, when I found out I was pregnant, I came to deliver a note to tell him. But I put it under YOUR door by mistake...'

I was silent. Basically, I was trying to figure out what this actually meant.

'So, what does that mean?' I enquired.

'It means, said Martha, looking a bit confused by my dimness, 'that the note was meant for Clive – I'm pregnant with HIS baby. So, I'm really sorry if there was any misunderstanding.'

'Oh, I get it now... I thought I was going to be a dad' I said, and then looked to Sarah, '... and my message was to discuss your "pregnancy!"'

The whole mix-up was sorted out and it meant one thing. I wasn't going to be a dad after all – and I knew I could cancel my online order for the cot and baby car-seat!

Clive and Martha seemed very happy, and I was pleased the situation had worked out positively for them both. I hoped Clive's Lego fixation wasn't going to be a problem, as they left for a day out at Legoland!

CHAPTER FIFTY-ONE:

Fabulous Frank

December 30th.

Michael and Rebecca's New Year's Eve party couldn't come soon enough. But first, I had to visit Frank at his café. Michael drove and we were soon parked-up and within a minute's walk of Sherlocks.

It was bitterly cold, with a threat of snow, which never actually materialised. When we got to the café, we were treated to one of Frank's best-ever coffees.

I introduced myself as Cooper, HG's best friend! Frank was keen to know if I'd heard from his favourite apparition, so I gave him a creative update. Michael was totally stumped by our conversation, even though I'd already briefed him that it may sound a bit strange.

'I've got all this stuff in the back,' said Frank. 'And about £60K which HG told me to give to you.

'Funny you should mention that.' I explained, 'HG spoke to me and said that you should give me just £20K...'

'And what about the rest?'

'He said you can keep £20K to launch your own special brand of coffee and the remaining £20K should go to a little girl called Keisha who has cancer, for her and her family to go on a fabulous holiday to Disneyland…

Frank became all emotional and could only utter the words, 'That HG is a true diamond geezer! He might be dead, but he's still givin' it everything on this 'ere earth!'

£10K was handed to Michael and I felt satisfied that not only had he got his money back, but had made a healthy profit too. The other £10K was destined for Lucy as it would enable her to rent a place of her own – and generally get herself back on track. I hadn't made my million, but I didn't care.

All was going well. Frank and my dad were talking every day and getting on like a house on fire. I guess they were just two lonely guys, with a shared passion which could take them out of their daily routines.

'Did HG happen to say when I could put those clips on to social media?'

'Oh yeah', I said, forgetting about the stuff we'd filmed. 'Do it whenever you're ready!' Frank was so excited, he had to break off and phone my dad with the news.

We spent a couple of hours with Frank discussing ghosts and conspiracy theories and devoured lots of coffee and cake. It was a brilliant, fun afternoon which we all enjoyed. There was such indescribable pleasure in sharing a coffee with friends, especially when your friends could see you.

New Year's Eve.
I still had a couple of things to attend to if my plan was to succeed. Yes, my secret plan – the plan that I'd spent

hours devising whilst laid on my bed with my homemade eye-mask giving me the night-time darkness I needed.

Originally, I'd had the idea to woo the girl at work, who acted like I was invisible *all* the time... that was the first thing on my list. This was still obviously a work in progress and quite honestly it looked set to be on a desperately slow-burner.

The second thing on my list was that I would aim to accumulate one million pounds. After a series of financial blunders thanks to my ill-thought through plans, at one point both my friends and I were actually in the red. Things had picked up a little and at that moment, Michael and Rebecca were in profit, Lucy was getting 10K, Frank had a pretty penny to develop his own coffee range and Keisha was going to Disneyland. So, things weren't quite as bad as they had been after my first three days of failure.

The final part of my plan was to meet one of the genuine superstars of the entertainment industry Elton John. I knew he was a 'Sir' but didn't like to call him that as it made him sound superior somehow. He'd certainly lived up to my expectations. He was charming, witty, and pretty much a normal bloke who just happens to have an incredible talent.

As I considered how my week had gone, something was happening in Kensington which was about to set off a chain reaction which I was responsible for.

Over at the headquarters of would-be International drugs lord Jeremy Tockwith-Smith, there was the realisation that a big mistake had been made.

Seven days earlier, I had taken the bank cards of sex offender Fabian Judson and laid them in my invisibility liquid, rendering them completely see-through. Before I left the Kensington address with Lucy, I casually scattered them

311

around the place. These were invisible clues which would appear exactly seven days later.

Seven days later, they duly did appear, Tockwith-Smith put two-and two together and came up with Fabian Judson as being involved with stealing money from him. And just to be on the safe side, I'd also secretly planted some bags of their drugs in Judson's house.

Over the next few days, it was revealed that Fabian Judson had disappeared and was never seen again. I knew in my own mind that he was probably on an extended and much-deserved holiday in a bin-liner at the bottom of the Thames. As long as the women of London were safer, then it was a job well done. But the drug-dealers weren't going to get off lightly themselves.

The gang were then dropped in it by the overwhelming evidence that I made sure the authorities received, which included video footage of the gang weighing-out their drugs. This led to the arrest of Jeremy Tockwith-Smith, Leon and Joe for a variety of offences ranging from multiple murders to supplying class A drugs, extortion and blackmail.

Had my plan actually worked? For once everything seemed to have gone swimmingly. I'd fucked up numerous times in the past week, but it seemed that at last, I had finally got something right.

But then, something hit me like a lead weight. I began to panic. I had completely overlooked something. My own downfall would be imminent if I couldn't sort it out.

When Lucy and I had left the "kidnap house" in Kensington, we had made sure it was clean of our fingerprints, but I had completely forgotten to do the same with the Mercedes. It had our prints all over it. We were just one link away from being implicated in the whole thing. Lucy had links to the gang through Carl, and I was implicated through Lucy. We could so easily be drawn in and dragged down.

CHAPTER FIFTY-TWO:

Fancy dress party

Arriving early at Michael and Rebecca's for their fancy dress party, I desperately needed to talk to Lucy about the Mercedes. It was imperative that it was sorted out immediately before the police located it. I was agitated and not my normal self.

Michael was in the kitchen, cleaning the worktops when I walked in. He could barely say hello before I blurted, 'Does Lucy still have the keys to that Mercedes?'

'No, I do.'

'Fantastic. It's a long story, but could you get them for me?'

'Well it won't do you any good, I saw the police taking it away earlier when I went to the shop…'

'Oh no!' I cried, looking towards the heavens. What was I going to do? My heart was racing, and I felt a tingle of stress ripple through my entire body.

'What's the matter?' asked Michael, rinsing his cloth.

'I can't go into it now, but I desperately need to get into it… desperately… it's vital.'

'It was in a right old state when I went to find Lucy's purse…'

'What! You've been inside it?'

'Yeah, Lucy thought she'd lost her purse, so I volunteered to go and have a look for it with her. Honestly, it made me feel sick looking at all the mess, so I went and got all my cleaning stuff and went over it from top to bottom. You wouldn't find a single fingerprint in that car – it was like new…'

'What?'

'Well, you know me and my OCD. I couldn't bear to see it like that. I polished every bit of chrome, everything, I gave it complete valeting! Even Lucy was impressed. Of course, we wore gloves, and she even wiped all the door handles as we left.'

Immediately a huge weight was instantly lifted from my shoulders. I was in the clear, and so was Lucy. Everything was sorted, thanks to Michael and his OCD. I gave him the biggest hug, whilst he looked at me completely baffled by my reaction.

Rebecca came in as we hugged.

'Oh, have I interrupted a bro-mance?'she laughed.

'Yes, you have, but there's room for one more,' and I beckoned for her to join the moment. Rebecca didn't know it at the time, but she would soon have a massive weight lifted from her own shoulders too, and it would change her life.

'Don't worry Michael,' I whispered, 'I'll tell you all about it another time. Where's Lucy? Is she here yet?'

Due to the urgency of the Mercedes situation, we hadn't even discussed our outfits, which made the whole situation seem quite surreal. The majority of people who would attend the party adhered to the dress code – you were supposed to attend as someone iconic. There was wide scope and after a quick trip to the nearest fancy dress shop, I had decided to go as David Bowie. It turned out that Martha, the new and pregnant girlfriend of the big guy, Clive, who lived above me was a make-up artist, and after she'd worked her magic, I really looked the part. Michael was Donald Trump and Rebecca was Lady Gaga.

Other guests attending included Elvis (x2), Boris Johnson, Beyoncé, Rita Ora, Dizzee Rascal, Harry from One Direction, The Spice Girls, Cher and quite a few more A-listers. There was even a Louis Theroux!

As far as Lucy was concerned, I was just a friend-of-a-friend. OK, I was friends with HG, the Invisible Man, but she had no idea I was the same person. As far as she knew, I was the friend who'd been on holiday to Switzerland, Swaziland, Venice or wherever! I would reveal myself to her at some point, but not at the fancy dress party. I was too shy to go up and talk to any girl, so for now it was best not to do or say anything. But I was dying to see her sweet face again.

As I stood in the kitchen having a gin with Michael, a girl made her way to the doorway and then stopped. It was Amy Winehouse. To be more accurate, it was Lucy, dolled-up as Amy Winehouse, with a large beehive-style hair-do, wearing a black denim jacket with black jeans and boots. She looked incredible. Really incredible.

Michael stepped forward to introduce us. 'Cooper, you haven't met Lucy, have you?'

'Pleased to meet you?' I said shyly. I wish I'd had the guts to talk in a David Bowie voice, but at that moment I completely bottled it.

'Who have you come as?' she asked.

'David Bow...' Yeah, I know said Lucy laughing. It was blatantly obvious I was Ziggy Stardust.

Michael interrupted us with some news.

'Oh, Lucy I forgot to tell you, there was a delivery for you today, I was told it's important!'

'Oooh, where is it?' she asked. Michael told her it was in her bedroom.

'OK, let's go and see what it is...' She quickly headed towards the stairs, looking back for me and Michael. We all clambered the stairs like a herd of colourful elephants in our cumbersome outfits.

Lucy stopped outside her bedroom door and waited for Michael and me to catch up.

When she opened her bedroom door she stood there silently.

'What is it?' I asked, trying to look over her shoulder, with Michael trying to look over mine. I knew what it was, but I had to act as if I didn't.

Lucy was crying and she wasn't even trying to hide it.

There in front of her, were all the possessions which her grandma had given to her which had been sold by Carl. I had set Frank the task of buying as many of the objects back as he could – and fortunately he'd tracked down the pawn shop where it had all been sold as a job lot.

Michael hugged Lucy whilst she wiped her tears, trying her best not to spoil her make-up. There was a message with the items, which Lucy did her best to read aloud:

Dear Lucy, I hope you are OK. I managed to find some things which I thought you might appreciate. Most of the hard work was done by my friend Frank, who makes the world's greatest coffee! Anyway, I hope you are having a lovely evening and have met some nice people... (At this point Lucy broke off reading the message and hugged Michael and me).

...I have to go now, but I hope we can both see each other soon. Happy New Year. HG X

The note was attached to ten thousand pounds.

Taking a deep breath, I attempted to lighten things by singing in my best David Bowie voice: 'Whoever that HG is... He's a STAR, MAN waiting in the sky, he'd love to come and meet us but... "(and everyone joined in) "... but he thinks he'd blow our minds... He's a STAR, MAN..." and we continued together....' We ended with another group hug, which was excessively emotional.

CHAPTER FIFTY-THREE:

Midnight approaches

Michael, Lucy and I spent a fair amount of time together that evening, we had lots of laughs, drank quite a bit of gin and even shared the odd cocktail. Lucy was tremendous fun and I had to be careful not to be too overbearing – after all, she hardly knew me.

Inwardly, I suspected that if Lucy thought she recognised me from somewhere, that wouldn't be an issue because I was dressed as David Bowie – or Ziggy – in full attire, which hid my identity. Also, I was sure she wouldn't recognise my voice. Prior to being invisible, I think the only phrase I'd ever uttered to Lucy was, "Excuse me, have you finished with your cup?" Plus, it was a typical New Year's Eve party, the music was loud and with the constant noise of chattering too, my voice was not quite its normal self.

One of the highlights of the evening was when we had the competition for best lookalike iconic figure: The winner was cross-dressing artist Greyson Perry, I came second as David Bowie and third was a duo of Elton John and David Furnish. I felt quite sorry for the pair because they weren't even lookalikes, they were the real deal! Elton had kindly given me his personal number when we met backstage a few days before. I hadn't really expected the pair to turn up, but they did – after visiting Keisha, the little girl with cancer who loved the Lion King. Fucking hell those guys knew how to party and they never even touched a drop of alcohol – they got high on sheer exuberance!

Elton treated everyone to an impromptu, shaky rendition of "I'm Still Standing," after which he fell over, exhausted. Elton, my hero. I did get the chance to have a chat with him and reveal who I was. It was the start of what would be a great friendship.

The worst thing about New Year's Eve for me was always the "midnight kiss" thing. And all that Auld Lang Syne crap. Unexpectedly, Lucy came and sat with me at 11.45pm. I was balanced on a stool in the kitchen having a twiglet with my cocktail.

'Hi Zig!'

'Hey! Amy, how's it going?'

'Not too bad thanks. Although I think I might be a bit drunk.'

'I hate this part of New Year's Eve!' she said, echoing exactly what I was thinking.

'And me. I Usually go home well before midnight on New Year's Eve and just be on my own, like a lonely loser.'

'Fancy going for a walk?' she asked.

'That's a very good idea – even in these fucking platforms. It's so hot in here, my make-up's starting to run, and this wig is an absolute nightmare!'

Two minutes later we were walking along Aristotle Avenue, very, very slowly. My silver platform shoes were rubbing my ankles and Amy was hanging on to my arm. I think it was her beehive hair-do that was giving her balance issues. Well, that combined with a few gins. We must have looked hilarious as we teetered along together.

We could see the first droplets of snow as we passed the streetlights as they meandered their way to the ground. There I was, with the girl of my dreams, alone together on New Year's Eve, but it wasn't how I'd imagined it a week earlier. In those daydreams I wasn't dressed in a silver suit and high heels. And I wasn't wearing a wig either.

For a few moments we walked along together not saying a word. It seemed we did actually get on well together, and I figured that if Lucy didn't like me at least a little bit, she wouldn't have asked me to go for a walk with her – especially on New Year's Eve of all nights.

'So how has your week been?' I asked in my "Ziggy" voice.

'God, well, I can't even begin to explain it… how would I describe it? Well a week ago, I had a, "sort-of" boyfriend and a week later, he's now dead, I've been kidnapped, rescued, been a street entertainer, made a movie with some international drug dealers, made some great new friends, got all my grandma's things back, and seen stuff you couldn't ever imagine. Yeah, that's the sort of week I've had…'

'You're so boring!' I said, sarcastically.

'It has been the best week of my life!' she stated, jabbing her finger hard on to my arm. The force unbalanced me, and I fell over. It seemed to take me ages to tipple from the great height of my platform shoes, but when I eventually hit the ground, Lucy followed, as her arm was still entwined with mine. She landed on top of me. We were laughing uncontrollably. I was struggling like a tortoise on its back, wriggling my feet in the air.

Then, it must have been midnight, as we heard much more singing and in the far distance fireworks beginning to crackle and illuminate the night sky.

'Oh no!' it's THAT time!' I cried, checking that my nose wasn't broken as she'd almost headbutted me in the fall.

'Aaaarrgghh!' we both cried.

Lucy suddenly went silent. Was she going to be sick? She had a strange look on her face.

'What is it? What's wrong?'

'Nothing's wrong,'

'Are you sure? You've suddenly gone quiet…'

'Oh, yeah,' she said. 'it's just that I noticed you're wearing something very unusual…'

'Tell me something I don't know. This silver suit and platforms aren't my normal everyday attire…'

'I'm not talking about your outfit, you fucking space oddity…'

'What are you talking about then?'

'On your hand…You've got a very unusual ring on your finger…' She took my hand and held it just a few inches away from her eyes.

'Happy New Year!' I said, trying to deflect attention from it.

She looked at me, said 'Happy New Year HG, it's nice to meet you!' And kissed me.

CHAPTER FIFTY-FOUR:

A Perfect ending?

If this 'confession' was a movie, Lucy noticing the angel design of my ring would have made the perfect ending: She notices the design, gently runs her fingers over the raised pattern of the angel's wings and then slowly raises her beautiful face to look at mine. Freeze the frame, dramatic music and roll those credits. That would have been perfect. A tear in her eye would have been the icing on the cake and a possible Oscar nomination.

The first time I met Lucy as the invisible man, I revealed my existence after intervening as her boyfriend Carl assaulted her. It was then that Lucy noticed the unusual ring I wore, tracing the shape of it with her fingers. I vividly remember that it was as intimate as you could get with someone who you didn't know and who couldn't see you.

I witnessed Lucy at her most frightened and vulnerable - just a girl in a controlling and abusive relationship. At that moment I changed from being a shallow-ish twenty-five-year old kitchen technician into the guardian of an exposed, defenceless young woman. That was the moment my week changed from seven days of potential fun and excitement into seven days of stress and danger. If I had my week again, I would do things so differently – but it would still involve Lucy Perfect Ten Pendleton, of course.

So, there we were on New Year's Eve, on the freezing pavement together, with our first 'proper' kiss bringing in 2020.

Maybe I'd been a bit naïve thinking that Lucy wouldn't recognise me.

'Oh, my ring gave me away!' I exclaimed.'

'No, I knew you were my invisible man within two minutes of meeting you. I put the pieces together and came up with Cooper McRae! The ring was an obvious thing that I'd forgotten about'. She looked into my eyes and then looked closely at my features. Her thumbs made an effort to smudge my make-up away to get to my actual skin.

'The invisible man! You were invisible then, she said several times. 'I guess you really do deserve this kiss…' and her lips met mine for what seemed like forever. And even that still wasn't long enough for me. I really was in love and the moment was as perfect as anything I could imagine.

It seemed like that would be the end of my story – my confession – but no, it doesn't end with blisters on my ankles, smudged make-up and a pavement kiss on New Year's Eve.

CHAPTER FIFTY-FIVE: Back to work

Being back at work two days later seemed really strange and I was still readjusting to life as a normal human being. Lucy wasn't in work as she had previously booked extra holiday, so was out shopping in the West End to take advantage of the on-going sales.

When Ledley arrived at JC, he was animated and couldn't wait to tell me all about the excitement of his experience trying to save someone jumping off the top of The Shard.

'Coop, my God, I wish you'd been there. And then I got tazered by accident. And I have never, ever felt anything like that in my life!'

I couldn't stop laughing as he proceeded to do an impression of himself being tazered whilst lying on the floor. He looked like a goldfish which had jumped out of its bowl.

'Ledley, I've got you something, sort of a late Christmas present, but something just to say, Happy New Year to the best boss ever!'

'Cool!'

His eyes widened as I handed him the gift, which I'd hastily wrapped in festive paper. Ledley opened it enthusiastically and then froze in disbelief.

'A Rolex? This is a fake, right Coop?'

'Well, actually, it isn't.'

'It's not?? But, these things are expensive. Yeah, this looks totally real – even the word 'Rolex' is spelt right! But why are you giving me this – not that I don't appreciate it – but this is probably worth a lot of money!'

'Yours is an Oyster Perpetual Daytona model. It's worth £40K. If you think you could use the money more effectively, to pay for a wedding etc, then by all means sell it!'

'Are you serious? Are you a secret millionaire or something? Yeah, that's it – I always knew there was something about you, Coop…'

I laughed as Ledley tried to figure out where my secret 'wealth' had come from.

'Ledley, I am NOT a secret millionaire, but I was given this watch by someone and I just thought that you'd like it. And I'm fed-up of looking at your cheap mis-spelt copy!'

Throwing his arms around me, he said, 'Well, if you ever change your mind, you can have it back anytime and that will be totally cool with me.' That was typical of Ledley and was one of the reasons I really wanted him to have it.

'Coop, I forgot to tell you, you've been invited to attend a meeting in the boardroom at 9.30.'

'Me? What do they want to see me for?'

'I have no idea. But looking at my new Rolex, I think you should go now, because it starts in less than five minutes…'

In haste I darted out of the kitchen area, along two corridors, jumped into the lift and pushed the button for the third floor. Normally, the third floor was strictly out of bounds for people like me. The last time I had ventured into such territory, I ended up hiding in a cupboard and... you know the rest. This time, I wondered if I was going to be sacked for leaving cups and saucers lying around prior to leaving work just before Christmas. Or perhaps they were summoning people for redundancy?

When I arrived I knocked on the sturdy boardroom door, I opened it as gently as I could and popped my head inside. There was MD Samantha Penhaligan, Professor Wyngard and several other people who I was acquainted with in my out-of-work life, but who didn't work for JC Cosmetics.

The board room was a long, slim room with oak panelling and paintings of previous directors adorned the walls in gregarious frames.

My mind couldn't process the scene fast enough. What was going on? Sitting there were Nigel, the Invisible Man busker, the big lad who loved Lego from the flat above mine, Tina the jilted young girl who lived on the first floor and the sexy woman who was living with Fabian Judson – the one who'd given me a live sex show. Norman the security guard was also there.

Eight people all sitting in a row, positioned behind a single, long glass table, in front of which was a single chair which I was invited to take by Miss Penhaligan. What on earth was this?

The MD began by saying, 'Mr. McRae, you may well be wondering why you have been invited to this meeting. And who these people are who sit here...'

'Yes, it had crossed my mind,' I replied, impatiently waiting for the explanation. My eyes darted quickly along the row of people and then back to the MD. Was this some sort of practical joke?

Suddenly I felt dizzy, my peripheral vison became blurred and I could feel myself becoming light-headed, very quickly. My brain couldn't process what was going on, was this a dream of some kind? Why were all those people gathered together in the boardroom at JC Cosmetics? I half expected to wake up and be in a hospital bed or something. Yet, even though I did pass out for a few moments, when I came around, I was still in the same place, sitting before the same people. My brow had been mopped and I felt like I was in the middle of a weird, hot flush.

Samantha Penhaligan continued. 'Perhaps I should introduce to you the gentleman on my immediate left. This is Mr. Miles Patterson, head of our SOP – Secret Operation Programs. And apart from our chief scientist Professor Wyngard, all the other people here today are SOP operatives.'

SOP operatives? What the fuck? Norman the security guard, an SOP operative? For a moment I almost started to laugh in disbelief.

Miles Patterson, head of Secret Operations Programs was grey-haired, around sixty and had tiny spectacles balanced upon his impressive nose. He looked like an insurance salesman and placed in front of him was a box file.

'Cooper McRae, may I call you Cooper?' he began.

'Yes, of course,' I replied.

'Well Cooper, ever since we were made aware of Professor Wyngard's invisibility oil, we began a search for someone to take part in perhaps the most unique social experiment ever conducted. We wanted to see what a 'normal' person would do, once bestowed with the ultimate power of being invisible. When we realised that you had stumbled upon the secret – and intended to "borrow" the oils, we decided to use you as our guinea pig, so to speak… As the situation obviously had implications for national security, you were intensively monitored throughout the whole time, giving us a huge headache, I might add. However, we kept all this internally, no outside agencies were notified. This was all kept top secret within JC Cosmetics…

'Within the oils is a unique concoction of elements which means that we can trace a person. It's basically a similar method to being able to track a person's whereabouts via their mobile. Therefore, we immediately set in motion a complex surveillance operation…

'For the whole seven days, we've had over fifty operatives monitoring you and following your progress. We've tracked everything you've done and followed your movements – morning, noon and night. Our covert cameras have watched you play with your toothbrush to defeat in the boxing ring. And you really must get rid of that Rylan Clark-Neal rug, you're going to do yourself some damage if you aren't careful…'

Almost numb, I listened in total disbelief. My life had been under a microscope and my immediate thoughts were, had I let myself down in any way? Just as I had spied on people's behaviour, someone… a team had been spying on me. It made for uncomfortable listening. Sitting on my plastic chair, I squirmed as I learned more about the operation and my own failures.

'Without going in to all the fine details,' continued Patterson from SOP, 'we acknowledge that you have broken the law on a regular basis during your time of invisibility, but this has been a high-level covert procedure, and so no action will be taken in that regard... but suffice to say, we have all the information here...' and he gently patted a red box-file in front of him.

'All the people in this room – people you thought you knew – were all part of the surveillance team. Several of them were recruited hastily to ensure our monitoring was comprehensive and the data we received was accurate... there were many others involved too and every aspect of your behaviour was scrutinised intensely. A full, top secret report will be made in due course. Tina, Clive, Nigel... were all going about their normal lives – nothing you saw was set up. You entered their lives without their consent – which perhaps was predictable. No one could have known how you would have used your invisibility, but essentially, it was soon ascertained that your plan was not one that would put national security at stake. In many regards, you provided help and assistance to people in need, stopped crime and quite possibly saved lives. It is also noted that you showed a commendable kindness of spirit and generosity towards others whom you did not know.

'Several of your more risqué actions could not be stopped, but we, too were trying to come to terms with this inconceivable situation. As of now, you are not allowed to make any public statements or release any social media footage of your experiences. Should you do so, appropriate action will be taken. Do you understand?'

'Right, so I can't say anything?'

'You can discuss it with your friends, but realistically, they won't believe you.'

Patterson was right, who would listen to my story without thinking I was completely mad? No one.

'Do you have any questions so far?' asked Samantha Penhaligan

'Yes, I just have one question…'

'Okay, what would you like to ask?'

Actually, I probably had a thousand questions, but there was only one which I needed answering right there and then.

'Can you tell me… is, was… Lucy Pendleton in on all of this?'

If the answer was 'yes', then realistically, our special friendship would be over.

'Ah, Lucy Pendleton…' began Samantha. 'We discussed approaching her, but, after much deliberation, we decided not to. We consulted with a top psychologist who concluded that she wouldn't be any help as her bond and loyalty towards you would be far too strong for us to overcome. So, the answer to your question is "No" Lucy was not in on this.'

The boardroom meeting went on for an hour, but all I could think about was that Samantha Penhaligan said Lucy's bond with me was "far too strong". What a wonderful thing to hear. I just wished she had explained that further, but I was still ecstatically happy, despite finding out I was not quite as invisible as I had thought at the time.

So that was it. I had unwittingly been part of a social experiment. I'm not sure it would be quantified as a success by SOP as I wasn't aware of their criteria – maybe there wasn't any as such – but, from my own point of view, I had certainly accomplished a couple of things which had changed my life for the better.

But Tina, the girl from downstairs recruited to spy on me? Lego man? The busking invisible man and many more… the very thought of it all was too mind blowing to take in. It also probably accounted for why Professor Wyngard wasn't freaked out when I toyed with his scarf in Trafalgar Square on Christmas Day. I was being monitored. As I thought about the team assembled to monitor me, I didn't have any negative thoughts towards them at all. They were just trying to help out with something which was incomprehensible. Who wouldn't have wanted to be a part of that?

As I left JC Cosmetics, I was still employed and sworn to secrecy. My lips were completely sealed, although I was still able to discuss my experience with friends. I had never been the subject of a social experiment before and hopefully I never would be again. It had been a surreal meeting in the boardroom, and I was just grateful that Lucy Pendleton hadn't been a part of SOP or that would have been a crippling blow. A blow much bigger than the one I'd taken from the boxer Dwayne Dixon.

CHAPTER FIFTY-SIX:

Two weeks later

Lucy and I were officially a couple and we had already found a new place together in Clapham. Notice had been given for the flat on Eversholt Street, Camden and I was ecstatically happy. Things were great, in fact they were unbelievably great.

Frank and I were in touch most days and I had even popped around and shared a coffee with him and my dad at the café whilst they recounted their ghostly experiences with HG.

One Saturday morning, Frank called my mobile saying he had to see me asap. He sounded excited, so I told him to come straight round.

Lucy and I were in bed, snuggling up together like any normal couple might.

'Every morning when I wake up, the first thing I do is check that you're visible…' she said, running her fingers across my chest.

'Funnily enough, I do the same thing…' I replied.

Lucy was the girl for me. When I'd revealed I worked in the kitchens at JC, she thought it was great, as we could go to work together and then socialise together straight after. In my mind I'd convinced myself that she wouldn't be happy with my career. Perhaps it was just my own low self-esteem.

Said Lucy, 'Is there anything about me that really annoys you, so far?'

For a few moments I considered Lucy's personality and habits. 'Besides the fact that you use the same knife in the jam *AND* the butter, you're pretty perfect... but the jam thing is *REALLY* annoying!' I said, jokingly pretending to be annoyed.

'For you, I'll change...'

'Lucy, please don't ever change. I want jam in the butter...' We laughed and kissed. Our chat petered out as our kisses became more than the usual pecks...

There was a knock on the door. Frank was standing there with his hands on his hips and a car tyre against his shins.

'Have you had some car trouble?' I asked, moving out of the way to let him in.

'You could say that....' Replied Frank, still panting whilst rolling his tyre into my flat.

'Do you need me to get your tyre sorted or something?'

'No. What do you think of this?' he said, removing a folded magazine from his back pocket and thrusting it towards me. The magazine was called: Ghost Hunters Monthly, and there, staring back at me on the front cover was Frank, standing outside his café. The headline read, "Frank's Ghost Café!"

'Brilliant! Absolutely brilliant!' I laughed and went to put the kettle on as Frank took a much-needed seat at my kitchen table. The social media post he'd made of the ghost in his café had gone viral with the whole ghost-hunting community and beyond creating a frenzy of interest. And his café had never been busier.

Lucy made her way into the kitchen, dressed in one of my old Ramones T-shirts.

'Hiya Frank,' she said, whilst trying to make her hair look more presentable.

'Morning Lucy, sorry – have I woken you up?'

'No,' laughed Lucy, peering over my shoulder to see the magazine. 'Frank, that's fantastic. Congratulations.' And she proceeded to give him a hug.

'But, I haven't come about the magazine,' he said, still a little out of breath. 'It's about my tyre…'

'There's a garage just around the corner on Foxton street.' I suggested.

'On my way here I got a flat tyre – so I changed it…so I don't need a garage because I've already sorted it…'

'Frank, I know that tyres have the potential to be exciting if you work in the car industry perhaps, but I'm not feeling the excitement myself…'

'…This is the flat tyre I replaced …I want you to have it…'

'Well, I really appreciate the gesture.' I said, pulling a face whilst looking for my decaf tea bags. Frank had already confused me rambling on about his tyre, and it was about to become even more bewildering.

'I want you to keep it. It's yours.'

'What am I supposed to do with it? I haven't even got a car. This is all a bit strange, are you sure you're alright, Frank? Can I get you a Paracetamol?

'I've never felt better in all my life. I think you should examine your tyre!'

I picked it up, moved it around... I wasn't even sure what I was supposed to be looking at. For almost a minute I rotated the tyre, not seeing anything apart from what I expected... but then I saw it. I narrowed my eyes and moved as close as I could to the rubber tread.

'You see it now, don't you Coop?'

'Oh yeah, I see it...' I couldn't take my eyes off it. Suddenly all the pieces of this rubber-jigsaw came together. How could we have missed this?

'What is it?' asked Lucy, who was just putting bread into the toaster.

'Lucy, you'd better come here...' I said, without taking my eyes off the tyre. We pushed both our faces as close to the rubber as we could. Our faces brushed each other as we both stared.

There, wedged between the tread of Frank's semi-deflated rubber tyre was a diamond. A very impressive diamond.

The night I'd been diamond hunting courtesy of the President of Guinea I managed to get two diamonds before I was hit by a moped. I found one of the diamonds, but thought that the other had disappeared down a drain. In actual fact, Frank had been driving around with it stuck between the thread of his tyre ever since.

'I wonder how much it's worth?'

Frank took a deep breath and said, 'Quite a bit. I came via my friend in Hatton Garden and he told me that it's known as a pink diamond. Bids for the last one which came up for auction started at — wait for it - half-a-million pounds.'

'What did it actually sell for in the end?'

'I think,' said Frank, taking a big gulp, 'you had better sit down…'

CHAPTER FIFTY-SEVEN:

The End

As the proud new owner of a rare pink diamond, I now had more or less everything I wanted. The last pink diamond sold for a staggering £4.7 million.

With the proceeds, I'd make sure all my family and friends were looked after, and the charities helping to ensure people had clean water in Africa would also be very happy when a series of huge cheques landed on their respective doormats.

Frank revealed that with his café's new-found popularity he was on the lookout for a new, dynamic kitchen supervisor and possible business partner, so it was nice to have an exciting new opportunity to consider. I asked him what model of dishwasher he possessed? He said, 'It's a top-of-the-range Fagor Commercial model!'

I didn't need to think: 'Count me in Frank!' I replied.

*****

So, this has been my personal confession of what happened over a breathtaking seven-day period in my life.

It had been a crash-course in what goes on behind closed doors.

Had I enjoyed the experience? Well, I wouldn't exactly describe it as enjoyable. My mind was still struggling to comprehend what had really happened and the more I thought about it, the more confused I became. All that surveillance stuff was like something from James Bond and in the cold light of day, none of it seemed plausible, so I tried not to think about it.

On December 23rd, I basically had no money, no love life, and zero chance of ever meeting Elton. Now all three were ticked off and my life changed forever. From that perspective, it had been a definite success, so I'll always be grateful to Professor Wyngard for putting his immense brain to good use. He was the creator, like a modern-day Dr Frankenstein, I suppose – whilst I had been his "monster!"

However, what I would like to have known is how the experts would have evaluated my performance during this incredible social experiment?

An experiment is a procedure carried out to support, refute, or validate a hypothesis. I didn't even know what their hypothesis was. Or if they had one at all? All I know is that I didn't use the seven-day superpower to try and change the world, I used it to try and change *MY* world. And let me say that it wasn't a selfish decision, just the decision of a young man looking for love. That's all I wanted to find.

I really just want to say thanks for sticking with me and listening to my extraordinary story. The only proof I have that it happened is a new girlfriend, a diamond and Elton John's mobile number on a piece of paper in my back pocket. Oh, and a few little injuries from exploits in the boxing ring and wearing platform shoes. These are just little reminders that the last few weeks really did happen, no matter how unbelievable it all seems now. This isn't one of those corny stories where someone wakes up and it was all a dream, this all really did happen. Would I take the opportunity if it ever presented itself again? I'm not really sure. However, as Lucy would discover a week later when making us lunch, all sorts of things can get hidden away in the fridge. Behind the butter she discovered a small metal phial which just didn't fit in my usual grocery and dairy items. 'Is this a salad dressing?' she enquired?

Smiling, I said, 'No, it's not a salad dressing. I'm not sure exactly what I'd call it, but I know it lasts for exactly seven days...' Lucy shrieked with excitement as she realised what it was.

I tried to tell Ledley about my week of invisibility and he seemed to listen, sort of. Anyhow, his mind is currently elsewhere as he's getting married and so has a wedding to arrange. The girl at the top of The Shard said 'yes'. Ledley is in his element and I couldn't be happier for him. On our lunch hour we enthusiastically flick through wedding magazines together, making those important decisions.

Michael and Rebecca sat and listened to my story and hardly said a word throughout. When I'd finally finished, Michael paused for a few seconds, looked at Rebecca and said matter-of-factly, 'Well, I think I'll put the kettle on...' We all laughed and devoured too much Toblerone. Lucy looked at me and blew me a kiss. At least *we* knew.

So, this is it. In the last three weeks I've gone from being a loser in love to be the luckiest man alive. As I write this, it's 7pm and I can see Lucy sitting on the edge of *our* bed in her sexy underwear doing her hair. Three weeks ago, it was me sitting on the end of *my* bed, doing a kebab.

Tonight, is a special night. I'm taking Lucy to my favourite restaurant, Joe Allan's in Covent Garden. And I must tell you, she looks absolutely incredible.

Thanks for sticking with me. I'll write more soon...

The End

Acknowledgements

Special thanks to: Taryn Johnston at Chronos Publishing. Once again, Taryn has put me right where I was going wrong, hassled me to get things done (even though I was going as fast as I could), and handed me astute advice to make things better. Yes, she can be really annoying! Also special thanks to Samantha Eastwood for her amazing design work. (And WHAT a wedding that was!!!).

About the Author

Graham Hey lives near York, North Yorkshire and has two daughters. Likes include: Chinese takeaways (Singapore Noodles), hanging around in second-hand record shops, the late, great Johnny Moore, coffee and cake.

Connect with the author:

Graham's blog: **funny-writer.com** is updated every few days with comedy, guest blogs, pieces about my books, and general things to make you feel good!

Facebook: www.facebook.com/Letshearitfortheboy

Instagram: hey.graham

Twitter: @hey_graham

About Confessions of an Invisible Man

I remember reading an incredible book called Memoirs of an Invisible Man by H.F. Saint whilst I was on an island off Thailand when I was backpacking many years ago. I have a photograph of me somewhere, sitting on a deserted beach in my red and white striped shorts reading the book I'd bought from a second-hand book shop in Chiang Mai. The book was extraordinary – I'd never read anything like it before and it had a massive impact on me, instantly becoming my favourite read of all-time.

The concept of being invisible is one which probably everyone in the world has thought about at sometime or other, so I was determined to write a version of my own if I ever got the opportunity.

My version is a rom-com which is hopefully entertaining and funny. I didn't want to get deep into the psychological aspects of suddenly becoming invisible, I wanted the power to be bestowed on a young guy with simple aspirations. I also wanted to make it funny, if possible, and for it to revolve around Cooper's desire to get together with Lucy Pendleton. Cooper isn't based on anyone I know, but his friend Ledley is based on a great guy (and brilliant footballer) I knew at school called Alwyn Simpson. Whatever happened to him?

Originally, the main character Cooper McRae was set on revenge – aiming to kill Carl, Lucy's druggie boyfriend. Taryn at Chronos said that she didn't think Cooper was the type to go down that route – and Taryn's always right (at least I let her think that!), so I changed the slant of the story to something less serious. That's where the Elton John story came in, making it much lighter. After all, this is supposed to be a rom-com, not an out-and-out thriller.

No-one (especially me!) could write anything as grand or meaningful as H.F. Saint's mighty book – but I hope you enjoyed my effort to create an entertaining story with likeable characters. It was fun writing this fantasy-based rom-com, and in the back of my mind I wanted it to have the feel of an old Alexander Korda movie. He produced a series of classic fantasy movies back in the 1930s and 40s and I have always loved them. Check out 'The man Who Could Work Miracles'.

Someone asked me if there was going to be a series of books about Cooper McRae as The Invisible Man? Even though I quite like the idea of that, I'm not sure I'm motivated enough at the moment, as I have other books I want to write - if Chronos publishing are still able to put up with me!

If you've enjoyed reading this book, it would be great if you could review it on either Amazon or Goodreads.com If you didn't enjoy it, I'm really sorry I've let you down!

Graham

Coming Soon by Graham Hey

Love on the Ropes: One man grappling with internet dating.

Norman Dilworth's bad luck with women is transformed when he beats mystery man 'The Wishmaster' in a wrestling match and is granted a single wish. Believing it to be a joke, Norman wishes for the ultimate chat-up technique. However, his amazing new dating skills and success with women alienates the girl who really loves him. True love is on the ropes…

Read Graham Hey's debut novel: Let's Hear It For The Boy

***** The perfect summer tonic, hilarious! Uri Geller

When twenty-something James Valentine pays an unscheduled visit to a fortune teller in Whitby, he is told that he's going to meet three women that will influence his life in ways that he could never imagine!

It's the fabulously funny story of a struggling magician trying to find true love somewhere amongst the gay bars, working men's clubs and cake shops of a West Yorkshire town.

A fruit cake, an International drugs dealer and the Heimlich Manoeuvre play pivotal roles in this tale of romantic failure set during the '80s.